GEYSER LIFE

GEYSER LIFE

a novel

Edward Hardy

Bridge Works Publishing Company
Bridgehampton, New York

Library of Congress Cataloging-in-Publication Data

Hardy, Edward, 1957–

    Geyser life : a novel / Edward Hardy. — 1st ed.

      p.   cm.

    ISBN 1-882593-16-2 (hardcover : alk. paper)

    1. Brothers and sisters—United States—Fiction.   2. Fathers —

Wyoming—Fiction.   I. Title.

PS3558.AG2373G48   1996

813'.54—dc20   96-7433

                                              CIP

2 4 6 8 10 9 7 5 3 1

Book and jacket design by Eva Auchincloss

Jacket illustration by David Gothard

Printed in the United States of America

First Edition

For Tamar

Acknowledgments

For their interest and advice along the way, I would like to thank: Paul Cody, George Estreich, Jane Hardy, Ernest Hardy, Sloan Harris, Liz Holmes, Tamar Katz, and Steve Marion. Special thanks to Peg Lower and Barbara Phillips for their help in shaping the final version.

PART ONE

ONE

I woke to the sound of chainsaws. That's how Tuesday started. It was the day I found out about Grant, and the men across the street were already cutting down the wrong trees.

At 7:15 the newspaper discovered that I was among the missing, and as that was my place of employment, they decided to call. The phone rang and rang on the second-floor landing, but I stayed in bed, listening to those voices out on Lexington Street arguing in loud Italian over the rumble of idling machinery. My housemates were already at work, and in spite of myself, I continued to count the rings. When the toll reached nine, I went down and answered the phone. Across the street, out in the fog, I watched as a father and two sons stood beside a half-destroyed white oak. Their meaty arms flashed through the gray and warming air.

Maris, my boss, sounded as though he'd been awake for weeks. He asked in a practiced way why I wasn't at my desk an hour ago, particularly on a day when he was short on bodies. The morning was already getting a zooey feel to it, he told me. Maris could be a sly, cerebral comedian, one of those people whose jokes you don't get just at first, yet in reality he was the paper's metro editor, and most likely a lifer.

Back in my room I hauled my blue-striped button-down, the one with the black tie already knotted and threaded under the collar, out from the closet's dark side. I ran downstairs, trying to remember if my cordless shaver had enough zap left in it for one more twenty-seven mile Belmont-to-Lawrence commute. Out in the driveway, I did a final button-zipper check before starting my bumperless, tank-green Karmann Ghia and backing away into the gloom.

On the way up to work, everything seemed out of sync. For instance, none of my favorite incoming commuters were waiting at the

Route 16 lights. I had already missed the cute and dangerous-looking woman in the Horizon who always appeared flustered but pleased when I waved at her. The runner in the *Boston Globe* T-shirt wasn't by his normal spot in front of the U-Haul Self-Storage place. I began shaving anyway, a driving habit that Claire, my newly lost love, always thought weird. Then I buzzed up the I-93 ramp, scooting under the sign for SALEM N.H.–LAWRENCE and on past the General Foods plant with its forest of steaming pipes that two afternoons a week made the universe smell like raspberry Jell-O. My paint-flecked boom box was running off the lighter, because someone had pried the radio out of my dash again. The boom box was tuned to BCN and when I turned it on, for some reason the thing burped into Norman Greenbaum's "Spirit in the Sky." That song has always annoyed me. Even before the lyrics started, I couldn't get them out of my head. How is it that certain things can go directly to long-term memory? Within minutes, I was passing tractor-trailers far too quickly, and wishing that I were someone else.

The incoming New Hampshire commuters, the ones who have to rise with the birds, were already backed up in the southbound lanes. The fog-burning sun had forced down their minivans' visors. My father always rose with the birds. Then he'd sit, telling stories to himself in the padded chair in our half-finished, slowly brightening kitchen. This was when we lived on top of the hill in Vestal, and he'd watch as the clouds cleared across the cut in the valley, waiting for the moment when you could see through to Binghamton and then nearly to the river. Sometimes he'd be setting up breakfast when I crept down to spy. Very softly, almost through clenched teeth, with his glasses dangling by one earpiece from the corner of his mouth, he'd say, "Ray, think about that," and his voice would stream off. I was maybe in fifth grade, or younger, but the wiry, deliberate way he moved still seemed odd. Right after what happened to my mom, my father began to sleep walk. He would come into my room and mumble things that I couldn't quite make out and then leave. Which was probably why later I kept slipping downstairs to watch, as if with enough time and observation I could sort him out.

The stories my father told were about people he knew in World War II, when he was a combat engineer. Or they were about people he'd met at disasters. These were stories that I never heard otherwise. And when he must have seen me around the edge of the door or sensed that I was there, the monologues would turn silly or twist back on themselves to end with morals and aphorisms. Sometimes he would even talk to my mother, who died when we lived outside Syracuse. It scared me a bit, listening as he went on to recount my most recent bicycle injuries or my mysterious failures in math. For years I've been afraid of running into my father somewhere, of walking by as he plunked quarters into a parking meter, and not even recognizing who was there.

In the middle of the exit ramp, I switched the radio over to AM. I was trying to get the weak Lawrence station so I could pick up their 7:45 news. It was the fifth of July, and mornings after holidays are generally slow, but you could never tell. Maris always believed in that mythic 747, the one with the dead pilot, the one that would glide in to slaughter a fleet of overloaded school buses right at deadline — all part of a larger conspiracy to derail his meticulously laid-out pages. He was indeed a product of his own frightened imagination, but then worrying into the future did sort of define his job. The WILL news-casters were as breathy as ever, but there wasn't much. A fatal heart attack that had caused a van accident in Haverhill, seemed to be the highlight.

I passed the line of sleeping black and red *Chronicle-Democrat* deliv-ery trucks and caromed into the rear lot. Earlier in the century the newspaper's long, three-story brick building had in fact been an actual woolen mill. And when Maris handed out particularly bad assign-ments, he was prone say, "We're all millworkers in this building, buddy," as though he were as overburdened as the rest of us. The *Chronicle-Democrat* was the second daily paper in a destitute city that could barely support one. But the paper stayed alive because it was perched atop an empire of small, very profitable weekly papers that blanketed the more affluent suburbs. Every eight months or so we would hear rumors that the company was ready to close down the daily and ship us all out to the weeklies, but that never quite happened.

As I backed into an empty parking spot, the reflection in the first floor windows told me that my brake lights were no longer working. I flicked on the headlights and got out, only to discover that this mysterious ailment extended to my taillights as well. Add it to the list, I thought.

My vinyl-covered key card for the rear door never worked very well, and that morning it took three tries before it buzzed me in. I should have taken that as a sign. I loosened my tie and hovered for a second in the doorway, wincing at the sweet, sharp smell of fixer coming from the darkroom. I caught myself checking the parking lot for Claire's silver Honda, which I found instantly. Claire was a copy editor and we had been involved for about eight months, until very recently. For that whole time, we blindly believed that no one at work actually knew about us. We never drove in together, we met only occasionally for lunch and tried not to stare across the newsroom at each other too openly. It added something. We thought we were getting away with a secret. But everybody knew; we just didn't find out until the moment we broke up. Claire claimed two weeks of vacation as soon as things unraveled. Since then, we had both been taking odd shifts and volunteering to work alternate weekends, all to avoid being in the same room together.

At the end of the hall I tried imagining how I was going to come up with anything like a smile as I stepped from the red elevator and into the newsroom. Who was I kidding? I couldn't smile. I couldn't even push the up button, at least not without coffee.

When I walked into the vending machine cafeteria it occurred to me, as it did almost every day, that I could do with something dull for a while. I could do with something where I wasn't in the middle of everyone else's trouble. Travel agent, I thought. For this amount of money, I could do that. Four years ago, when I started working at the paper, they had me on nights. That meant covering stray meetings, regular car wrecks, fires, murders, and lots of cop stories. People telling me how scared they were to walk their dogs after sunset, that sort of stuff. Then they switched me to schools, which meant I got my nights and weekends back, but it also meant sitting through endless meetings and spending time coaxing four-foot-high children to say something more expansive than yes or no. A month ago, I was suddenly recast as a no-brain utility infielder — editor and rewrite machine in the mornings, and the metro editor's flunky past deadline. I'd apparently fallen from grace in some way that was impossible to pinpoint.

Even so, at that particular moment in the cafeteria, all I wanted from the world was a rubber donut from the vending machine and a hit of that liquid-dirt caffeine. The vending machine people always claimed that if we drank more of their bad coffee it would taste better. That way, they said, it won't be sitting in the machine for weeks on end. Sure. Their tiny paper cups were printed with poker hands. I never picked up more than a pair of sixes.

Coffee in hand, I turned and saw three composing room guys sitting elbow-up at the table nearest the door, staring into yesterday's sports section. A man with a soft pelt of bright silver hair shuffled in and started singing, "Hey-de hey-de hey-de ho." He was well over sixty, maybe a year or two younger than my father. I watched him snap open three buttons on his short-sleeved shirt and tug at a bright yellow tank top. "See that?" he said. "The B52s. Ever heard of that group? They're the greatest."

This unnerved me, and I backed into the hall thinking: It's time. Go in now. Yet I knew Claire would look up the second I walked out of the elevator. It was as though we were still miswired into the same relationship radar network. Then as the elevator door opened, I flashed to one of those late-night join-the-army ads. The kind where some nasty, paint-faced guy with free-weight biceps jettisons you out of a plane before dawn, while the voice-over says: "We do more by eight in the morning than most people do all day." At that instant, the headache — that familiar, dwarf-size pinhole of pain above the back of my neck — began marking out the day's territory.

The newsroom itself was a bright and narrow space. Huge wooden beams and silver heating vents roamed far overhead, and long archipelagoes of desks were rammed together under the tall multipaned windows. When I walked in, all the heads along the copy desk front were pulled deep into their terminals. The last place I worked everyone called them "tubes," here they were "machines." Claire didn't look up. She wore a schoolteacher's blouse and new red, metal-framed glasses, which made her proper blond bangs seem even brighter. She was smoking again. Menthols. It had been like that at the start, and I could never kiss her for long.

Koch, the news editor who weighed in like a defensive end, began proclaiming random wire service heads as they scrolled up on his screen. I landed my jacket on the chrome rack as he shouted: "Bestiality up, group sex down, survey says."

Maris kept scrubbing at something on his desk that had been left behind by the night shift.

"Is that new Coke or Classic?" I asked.

"Classic," Maris said, concentrating on the transparent brown stain. "It's stickier." My boss always had the chronic, slightly wide-eyed face of someone who had suddenly shaved their beard and switched to contacts after years of hiding behind glasses. Even straight on, watching his lips move, I couldn't always tell exactly what he wanted from me. Maris tossed the disintegrating gray towel under his desk and meditatively rolled a capped plastic Glue Stic back and forth between his palms. "I have this fear that one day I'll mistake Glue Stic for Chap Stick," he said. "Wakes me up at night. Didn't mean to get you out of bed."

"No problem." I smiled and tore open the plastic bag holding the rubber donut.

Maris watched as though my stockpile of official concern was still way short. "You know, your situation here is beginning to deteriorate. And you will remember that evil comes to those who leave life unattended." He folded his hands. "Everyone's elsewhere this morning, so you'll get a jump on inside cops. Suburban already picked up the Haverhill fatal."

"Fine." I always did inside cops. In fact, I should have just sleazed in, acted like I'd been there for hours, and started punching those speed dial digits into my phone. But all of my major discoveries are made well after the fact. I pulled the blue acetate folder with the list of police and fire numbers from the pile on my desk and dialed. Go ahead, give me trouble. Big trouble, trouble on call-waiting. I've got the caffeine. I can control it.

The police stations on my list were all small and up in New Hampshire or out in the Massachusetts shrubs. Rory Adair, the police reporter, drove each morning into Lawrence, Methuen, and Haverhill to scan their police logs. This was known as outside cops. Most of the police dispatchers I talked to already knew my voice, and their departments generally hated the paper for one deeply embedded reason or another. There could have been bodies throughout some of these towns, two or three propped up in the squad rooms, and they'd say, "All's quiet." That morning though, they were booking everyone they could find with difficult-to-spell names. Real high consonant-to-vowel ratios. At 8:40 I was through the thickest parts and asking Austin Glazier, the city hall reporter, where Zoar was. A drunk driver picked up in Amesbury lived there, and I'd never heard of it.

"It's a suburb of your mind," Austin said, grinning through his red mustache.

I was about to call Amesbury back when Rory suddenly came on the phone. She was calling in from the Methuen police station and had been transferred to me because Maris's line was busy.

"Who's he talking to?" Rory asked. "There's a triple fatal here. Anybody get it? Three kids in a van? Went through an iron gate in a cemetery and hit a bunch of tombstones? I also hear there's a murder in Lawrence, near the line, which is how the Methuen cops found out. Something with a buck knife? You know anything about that?"

"Nope," I said. Rory gave me the Methuen kids' names, and I'd started wondering if we had the right high school yearbooks for head shots when I remembered that this was a suburban desk problem. Actually, it was the Methuen reporter's problem.

When my phone rang again, a faint, harsh voice said: "If I sound like a distraught woman that's because I am. Give me Representative Bouchette's number." She coughed twice and started to shout. "I am a lower Tower Hill resident and every day here school lets out. These children on the street they bother me. They shrink down very small. To about an inch. No more. Then they get their tiny space ships and buzz my head. Buzz my head. It's worse when they burrow into my sweater and start shouting obscenities. Things like 'NIPPLE' and 'HOUSE,' which is exactly the same thing that happened when I got arrested for shoplifting."

I flipped through the Rolodex for Bouchette's number. "That's not right," I said.

"You don't think I'm off on something?"

"Oh no, not at all." I gave her the number.

"Well, I think it's a message from God, that you, *you* should slow down." Then she hung up.

The cursor on my computer screen blinked back, green and

anxious, as Maris asked for the fire log. "I've got phone loonies," I said. He gave me his best so-what look.

Rory called in a minute later with the murder notes, and I told her that she had to write it up because there was nobody else left to do it.

"Dandy," she said, as she began describing the buck knife. "Like a really long fishing blade," Rory said, but her voice got smaller and then disappeared. A second later Rory came back to say, "Holy shit," and the line went dead. All across the room people looked into their receivers, as if they could actually see the problem.

At 9:10 Rory bounced into the newsroom and the phones went back on. The first edition had to be downstairs in twenty minutes. "Nice phone job," she said, her long graying hair alive with static.

"Can you do both?" I asked. "Cops and the murder?"

"There's also this guy trying to beat two kids up with an auto-graphed Ted Williams bat, because they hit his house with rocks," she said. "Then the kids climbed back into his yard, took the bat, smacked him a few, and ran off. It's a Louisville Slugger."

"Might not fit," I said. "Is this guy in the hospital? Has he got a condition?" Rory shrugged, as if to say how could she have had the time to find that out? "Put the story in the log and I'll break it out for a couple of inches." I wrote a big C on a nearby legal pad, just so I wouldn't forget the critical calls. These were hospital updates on accident victims, or victims in general, that we had to check on to see if they were still alive. Everyone called it Dial-o-Death.

At 9:40, the big-pay editors decided to turn the baseball bat incident into a full-scale story. They were going to use it for the second edition's page one because, as Doris Flick, our executive editor, who lately had been spotted walking around chewing an unlit cigar, explained: "It shows the entire range of human emotions. The entire range."

Something unintelligible came over the police scanner and Doreen Sticker at the copy desk shouted: "Did they say something about a body?"

Rory frowned at me and crossed her legs. "Nope. Somebody said, 'Buddy. I'll get back to you about that, *buddy.*'"

Claire roamed the room, handing out stories from a cut-up photo-copy of the first edition's front page. She asked, "Can you read?" at each machine, meaning we should search for typos. She stuck a tiny wire story about CIA death threats in the cracks of my keyboard.

A new, chopped, and out of breath voice rose from the scanner. "Man down in river," it said.

"Anybody hear *that?*" Doreen Sticker asked. "Scanner says there's a floater."

Maris pointed to my phone and picked up the red receiver on his desk to raise a photographer over the two-way radio. I called the Lawrence cops, who explained that the guy was in the Merrimack, near Casey Bridge, but on the move.

"Take a radio," Maris said, and for a second I didn't understand. Then it became clear that he meant that I should go.

Rory watched cautiously. I knew she was afraid that I'd slip out of it for some reason and in the end this would turn out to be more work for her. "I had the bad smell beat last week," she reminded me. "Remember? The old dead guy on the third floor? You want my Vicks?" She put her dented walkie-talkie on my desk and pulled a tiny, deep blue jar from her pocketbook. A little in your nose works against the smell.

All during the drive up into Lawrence, I kept thinking that I could do without seeing another body. As I crossed Casey Bridge, the Merrimack was forest colored and dimpled, almost benign looking, but I continued to peer downstream, looking for that blue and red emergency-light flicker. I bumped over old potholes along Canal Street, and passed the backsides of the rolling brick mills. I could never drive for long beneath those great rows of silent, identical windows without getting a bit creeped out, especially at night. Something about those mills always seemed out of proportion with the rest of the world. I would imagine the people who once worked inside, stuck in the noise, year after year, shift after shift, and wonder what in the world I had to feel sad about.

I crossed the Merrimack again, this time rattling over the steel-grate Duck Bridge, and spotted a trio of police cars, plus a fire truck and an ambulance, all a-glitter on the Everett Mills bank. They were about a thousand yards away, in the parking lot behind a converted mill that housed a computer company. Maris had sent Casler, one of the photographers, out to shoot this. I parked behind his mud-flecked Delta 88 and ran toward the sparkling lights.

"Hey," Casler said. "This is one high-speed guy." He nodded toward the river.

The body was coming toward us headlong. It was waxy gray and bruise colored, and starting to spin, feet first, out into the current. Most of a navy work shirt clung to the man's large shoulders. A T-shirt underneath said "Rideout's" in red script. The man wore dark work pants. He had curly black hair and a square, surprised face.

A firefighter in yellow boots, her hair tied up in a ponytail, dropped a lit cigarette as she reached out over a rotting piece of wood with the boat hook. I had maybe twenty-five minutes left to get anything into the final edition, so I radioed Maris, who told me to pick up what I could and call it in. The firefighter with the boat hook missed again. After a third flat splash, the body began to spin away into deeper water, submarining through a glistening ripple.

"Get a rope and cast for him," a rough voice behind me suggested. The grind of the pumper's engine climbed a notch.

"They can still drive on some," Casler said, rubbing his blond stubble. "It's all grass farther down. Good thing this guy wasn't up on the other side of the dam. Turtles'll eat you there."

"Naw," I said.

"Really," Casler said. "I've seen it."

We walked along the scrubby bank, stepping over bottles and ancient packing straps, as we followed the slowly rolling pumper. The engine stopped and a spry-looking firefighter took a yellow nylon rope attached to a four-pronged hook from a compartment above the rear wheel well. The ambulance moved ahead of us.

"Floater's still moving," I said, radioing it in to Maris.

"Well, keep *chasing* him," Maris shouted. Casler smirked and loped ahead to shoot back at the scene.

The hook caught the man's shirt and gently lifted his arm from the river. He rolled over on his back as two firefighters strained to pull him in. The body bag was already unzipped. The floater was maybe forty. He had the same blocky build as my brother, Grant. There was no wallet.

"Jesus," a short, neat cop next to me said. "This guy's been swimming for quite some time."

It was only as I drove back to the paper, after I'd called in the story from a pay phone, when I realized that I was singing to the radio, that I began to think about it again. I wondered a lot then if my reactions were still what they should have been. If I was working too hard to block away the parts of it that got to me. Keep a close focus, I thought. Keep all of this in the present tense. Move that next item off your plate. It is an irrational world, but none of this applies to you. Yet how long could someone go on that way? The floater had a white and green plastic pen holder in his front shirt pocket, but he'd lost his shoes.

The newsroom was nearly empty by the time I got back, as most everyone had gone to lunch. The few people who remained were languidly reading the first edition and eating Tootsie Pops. Claire looked up when the elevator doors opened, and we locked eyes. Her bangs shook as she stood to check her mailbox. I slouched into my chair and it skidded back a foot or two on impact. The air smelled like microwave popcorn.

"Nate's depressed," my pal Beth Salino said from the next desk over. Beth covered courts. She had quick eyes and told the truth whenever it was around. She waved her pita pocket in front of my face. "Let's broadcast it. Nate's depressed."

"Am not," I said, though that was mostly wrong. Missing people unnerved me.

"Hey, on days off they drag my body behind trucks, breaking up cement," Austin Glazier turned to say. "And he's so glum."

I sat up, realizing as I flipped a few envelopes across my desk that I'd forgotten to eat. I really didn't have much set up for the afternoon, only opening the mail and confirming a list of gardening events for a summer supplement. Second-line tasks. Then as I stared at it, the phone rang.

"Mr. Scales?" The voice was male and hesitant, almost skittish.

"Right. What can I do for you?"

"You are the younger brother of Grant Scales?" Hearing the name jarred me. I hadn't actually seen Grant in years and years.

"Who's calling?" I asked, but it came out with too much edge.

"Robert Lathers. Your brother's attorney. I'm calling from Bing-hamton, well actually Johnson City." He paused, as though he were looking for something on his desk. "We, strange as it sounds, did not realize until recently, that you, and your sister Sarah, whom I have not yet contacted, could be located. We understood, or assumed, because Grant never mentioned family, that he was an only child. Yet in dealing with this estate —"

I stared at my reflection in the black terminal screen, as the voice on the other end of the line grew louder and rounder. I wasn't really thinking, it was more like staring into a hollow space.

"You have been notified," the voice said, as if it were a fact.

"Of what?"

He pulled in on the next breath. "I'm sorry then, but your brother passed away. Twelve days ago."

I touched the screen. I sat back and suddenly noticed the keyboard clatter in the air. When the voice said "estate," I'd thought for a second that it was talking about my father. Then I felt Grant's name on my tongue. Yet it was strange, because at that instant it seemed only as if he had been displaced, not that anything had been lost. There wasn't that sudden missing-wall feeling, the way it was with my mom.

"At first we were afraid your brother had died intestate," Lathers explained. "And from the papers, well from this search in fact, it is apparent that you were not close." The phone on the next desk over rang twice and stopped. "I realize that this might not be the best time, with the work day and all," he said. "I can call again or you can take my home and office numbers. Please call collect at your earliest convenience. Are you in contact with your sister?"

I worked my red ballpoint slowly into the soft white cardboard cover of a nearby notebook. "She's sort of moved near here," I said. "I mean Boston."

"Good." Lathers sounded relieved. "I've left a message with your uncle's service in St. Louis, but as yet I have no way to contact your father. This, I trust, you will discuss."

"What happened?"

"An apparent heart attack."

I copied down the numbers and hung up. I looked around the newsroom, but everyone kept on typing and answering phones. I stared at the calendar on my desk. It was barely July and then — Grant was right before me, spread-eagled across the hood of the Mustang that Sarah used to drive in high school. He was hanging on to the front cowling, pressing his grinning, oafish face into the windshield. He had just dropped from the garage rafters as I pulled out. I'd had my license a week. He'd had his for thirteen years.

I almost laughed. This is entirely wrong, I thought. Entirely. Yet you had to know Grant.

The scanner made a noise that I couldn't quite understand. I stood up. A woman's voice came back and made it sound as though there'd been a robbery, somewhere downtown. "At the corner of Essex and Amesbury," she said. "A BayBank branch. It's confirmed."

No one in the newsroom seemed to be paying attention, so I decided to go. And right then I was thinking, today I'll make extra mileage. My brother was dead, and I was counting on twenty-six cents a mile.

Two

I knew how it was supposed to be. You were supposed to be numbed by grief. You were supposed to be submerged in your own reflexive, memory-induced bubble. So overwhelmed that nothing could get through. But I roared south on I-93 with the windows down and Lou Reed cranked. I was hyperaware and logging in every imaginable nugget of information. How the heavy-cream tan of a plastic dachshund jogging its swivel head in the back of a Buick Electra was the same color as those Bit-O-Honey candy bars. How all the way to Route 128, the only tractor-trailers going north were either white or silver. Every unassembled detail.

At home, I decked the white vinyl Santa Claus punching bag on the front porch, changed into real clothes, and opened a beer in the kitchen. But I couldn't settle anywhere. Back on the porch, I flipped the empty lime-green kiddie pool — flotsam from an April beach party — over the railing before working my shoulders into the hammock's warm cotton web. I hung there, watching the leaves wilt on the newly fallen white oak across the street, all the while trying to will myself to some less irrational place.

I had to call Sarah. I knew that. My sister had started working four nights a week at this slick bar in Cambridge, near Harvard Square. The owner dangled antique boat parts from the ceiling and called it Rowing International. It was still before five, so she was probably home and getting ready to go in. Even so, that drew me no closer to the phone, which sat just past the screen door on a maple fern stand.

None of this should be a surprise, I thought. None of it. It was freaky, but heart attacks ran in my father's family. My grandfather and his brother, my father's youngest brother, Uncle Peg, whose actual name was Philip Alexander. One of those might have been a stroke but still, I was running around with a history of bad hearts and unreliable veins.

That line of reasoning calmed me down for five, maybe six minutes, until another guilt tide rolled in and I felt bad all over again, even though it was Grant. How should this work? I wondered. Anger, denial, and some other stage. But something was clearly, even categorically, wrong with my reactions. I'm called at work, told that my older brother, the substitute parent, the rule-making manipulator, has died, and I check myself right out to cover your standard-order bank robbery. A masked-male-upper-twenties-no-weapon-shown-no-one-hurt-undetermined-amount-of-cash-taken kind of robbery. I came back, typed up my notes like an obedient mule, and drove home, as though it were a regular day.

Grant didn't even bother to let us know. He could have planned ahead. We could have been found sooner. Simple in-case-of-emergency stuff. I bet we didn't even make his address book. That would be normal. That would be typical. It was probably pure chance alone that this lawyer tracked me down.

I landed my beer on the porch floor as two girls on shiny white bikes rode past the box elder hedge. One girl held her hand over her head and it looked like a periscope cutting through a sea of shrubbery.

What's left to mourn? I thought. That we all can't sit around at Christmas dinner and trade embarrassing moments? Talk in our own peculiar code? Not that we ever really did. The last time I actually saw Grant was six years ago, after my junior year at Syracuse. He got in touch to say that he was selling the house in Vestal, the one that Dad gave him, and moving to Owego, which was ten miles west and on the other side of the river. If there was stuff around that I still wanted, Grant said I'd better hustle on down. I got there and my brother was all brisk and strange, like some process server. I had to put my bike frames and the lacrosse goal in my friend Mark Costello's barn, which wasn't a problem, since his parents had almost sort of adopted me for a while. I don't know. It was a weird, sad, and tiring afternoon.

At that point, my father still had an apartment in Binghamton, but he hadn't retired and still traveled all the time. We had dinner, but Dad has always defended Grant far beyond the call of anything. Mostly my father talked at me about where he'd been recently, that time I think it was Minnesota, and about a '36 Cord with front-wheel drive and headlights that disappeared into the fenders. He'd bought the car cheap and was planning to restore it, assuming he could locate enough parts. It was pretty much like always.

And Grant, he was always far easier to deal with at a distance. We used to talk occasionally on the phone, or he would talk and I would listen, but I'd never seen his place in Owego. It was difficult even imagining my brother's personality unchained in a house of its own. This was the Grant-of-legend, the guy who in junior high won the Soap Box Derby and turned down the trip to Akron. Life Scout, all-American kid with a star cluster, the adolescent entrepreneur who kept his savings bonds in numerical order. The guy who would later be packing our lunches and making peanut butter sandwiches for Sarah and me to take to school. Two Oreos each, no more, and there could be no crumbs in the lunch box when you returned. Once, somewhere in there, while I waited in the back seat of our giant deep blue station wagon, it dawned on me that Grant would always be older and because of that, he would never have to forgive.

The lawyer's phone numbers were upstairs, crumpled in my shirt pocket on the back of a While-You-Were-Out slip. Before I dealt with Sarah, I had to call back and find out what else there was to hear. The house my housemates and I rented was a faded, stucco, 1920s version of a mansion, complete with a servants' stairway in the back. And as I climbed those stairs, a new, knotted ridge of nervousness kept resurfacing. I hadn't handled any of this at all well. I knew that, even as my mouth kept rehearsing the phrase, "Robert Lathers, please."

By the time I made it to the third floor I was exhausted again, so I flattened out on the daybed in the den-size landing off my bedroom, directly in front of the TV. Our set was one of those huge black and white console jobs that you don't have to feel guilty about because it isn't color anyway. When I clicked it on, the Cajun Chef was humming and spreading mint jelly on a baking sheet of gray chicken thighs. But when I woke up, there was Mr. Rogers, moving serenely through his well-controlled television house. I rubbed my eyes, as it appeared that Mr. Rogers's major problem for the afternoon was a dead guppy in the aquarium. He didn't think the guppy was quite gone, so he netted it and placed the fish in a clear container. It floated there, ventral side up, listing like a troubled U-boat. "Shaking the dish will sometimes revive a fish," Mr. Rogers explained. Then he tried salt, sprinkling in enough to raise the blood pressure of plastic. I waited for the evolutionary miracle, but when they cut in for the close up, Mr. Rogers spooned out the guppy and said: "Sometimes it's sad when things die. We'll take this out to the back yard to bury it."

I crawled over, turned down the sound, and flattened Lathers' number on the dusty gold carpet. I reeled the phone in from under the daybed by its silver cord, and dialed. A girl's bright voice asked, "Is this Scotty?" before I could even say hello. I told her no, that I was looking for Robert Lathers and was he her father?

"Daddy, it's not him," she shouted, her voice dropping as she turned away.

Lathers picked up in a burst of clatter and thanked me for reaching him at home. No one I've called from work has ever done that.

"Well, maybe you've had some time to adjust," he said. "Again, I offer my condolences on what I know must come as a shock."

"What else did you have to tell me?" I asked.

"Have you been in touch with your sister?"

"Not yet."

"What terms are you on?"

"We're OK, more or less." I walked the phone into my room. Grant would assume that we couldn't get along. He would prefer it that way.

"I shouldn't be so obscure," Lathers said. "You see, it is very likely that you two will be listed as primary beneficiaries. I'd prefer for us, all of us, to meet later this week, if possible."

I watched the ceiling. Beneficiary. That's a laugh, I thought. Grant wouldn't leave us a thing, and even if he did it would certainly come along with a net full of conditions. My brother was Mr. Rule. Always trying to bring order to the irrational universe. The sort of person who used to spray paint lines on the gravel in our driveway to mark out parking spaces. Someone who tried, for a while at least, to run the house on military time. Dinner at 17:45. My sixth-grade friends thought this was cool. "Yeah, but there are hitches," I said. "Like liens on everything, right?"

"Unknown," Lathers replied. "Actually I doubt it. Your brother was in many ways quite a straight arrow. At any rate, I would like to see you both."

"To hear the will?"

"In part."

My dwindling vacation days spun up like calendar pages flickering by in an old movie. Go out of town, I thought, and that's when things at work turn precarious. That's when they start jerking you around. Stuff like switching you to obits forever. I told Lathers I'd talk to Sarah and call him in the morning.

I lied about Sarah. We're not close at all. We're more like different planets with totally unbreathable atmospheres. We get along for about forty-five minutes, then our microthin coatings start to wear. Sarah left for college in Wisconsin when I was in eighth grade, and after art school she began spiraling out in a hundred different directions. She's been a paralegal in Chicago, a raft guide in Maine, and for a while she was doing medical illustration, which she was good at, but she booted as soon as it got boring. Sarah plans all the time, but at the last minute she'll dump everything for a new idea. It's as if thinking about something long enough is the same as actually doing it. She moves to a new city every two years, falls in love with the chronically unattainable, and is now probably on about her millionth relationship. My sister remains overwhelmed by what to do with herself, but even so, I'm not exactly sure why we don't get along. Maybe it's her unfair exuberance. This unfounded sense that she can simply *do* anything, as though it were inherently obvious.

Ever since Sarah moved up from D.C. for a marketing job that in the end didn't materialize, she's had these ideas. First, she was set on being a copywriter, and to that end she started doing freelance car-part ads while building a portfolio on spec for a slot at an agency. I could never see why that seemed so enticing. Ad people get canned all the time. But maybe that was the draw, spending her life on one more thing that couldn't quite work out. My sister's other idea was that we should actually *be* a family. Which was fairly ridiculous. We existed in name only, and barely that.

It was weird when Sarah first called, after she moved here. Her voice had that brassy long-distance twist, but she was only six miles away, in Somerville. Because our schedules are so wacked out, we tend to play a lot of phone tag and let our machines do the talking. And my sister can devour a message tape. It's an invitation to deliver a monologue. Once when I called and asked why she decided to move to Boston, Sarah called back and told my machine that it was more like launching darts at the map or shopping for fruit. Wherever she ended up had to be someplace you could get out of fast, a city with good museums and within range of an ocean. Which to me sounded like D.C. I don't know. Sarah's always away on some ledge, dancing the fine crescent of catastrophe. Working us out would take years of therapy.

When I finally did get around to dialing, I got Sarah's machine, which was at least better than getting her zoned-out roommate, Monica, a woman I could barely talk to. Sarah's voice came on after the sound of whooping helicopter blades sucking air. "You've reached this number. Leave the usual info." It's always different, sometimes they're Louis Jordan songs: "Ain't nobody here but us chickens . . ."

"This is your brother," I said. "Calling on Tuesday." I came perilously close to blurting out the actual reason I'd phoned, but the way I'd been handling it, as if the news were someone's petrified lunch I'd found at the back wall of the refrigerator, kept me quiet. "We have to meet," I said. "Tonight. Tuesday. It would be best if I saw you. This is Nate, Sarah's brother."

I hung up, realizing that I'd sounded weirdly clipped and had also said the day twice, like some fake, repetitive spy.

Sarah called back while I was out running, and one of my housemates took the message. She wasn't working, so I should come over whenever I felt like it. And though I never really did feel like it, by 8:30 I'd started the drive over to Somerville. All the way there, I kept rephrasing and rehearsing new and different ways to give the news.

My sister's apartment was the crimped third floor of a gray ship of a house, just off Davis Square. When I was there last, they had *Scientific American*'s over all the registers, to fence out the cigar smoke from the physicist who lived on the second floor. As I stood on the porch, only seconds before hitting the bell, I remembered it was also Sarah's birthday.

"Hey look," my sister said without quite smiling. "It's the big family reunion." That struck me as funny, but I couldn't react. "I'd offer you a beer," Sarah said, "if you'd brought any."

-21-

"If I'd brought one I would have drunk it already."

"Ah." She stepped back into the room and arranged herself on the wide arm of an overstuffed chair. "So — where's my present?" Sarah wore purple running shorts and a thin, black, inside-out sweatshirt. She looked somehow shorter than I'd remembered. She clicked on an Art of Noise tape with her left foot and the room chugged and gurgled in a washing machine kind of way. From certain directions my sister has a very striking face, at other times she looks perfectly ordinary. Sharp angles and deep eyes framed by black feathery bangs, but she's always been too skinny. "Isn't that why you called?" she asked. "Or did you forget?"

"Forget what?"

"You did." Sarah smiled and relaxed. "My birthday. The one belonging to your sister. Your thirty-one-year-old sister."

That was where I should have made the announcement. Calmly and rationally, I should have said, "Yes, I forgot, but today I got a phone call at work." I should have used that very sentence, blunt, necessary, proper, and safe as it was. Like I'd obviously been too preoccupied to remember a birthday. I hate making people's lives miserable, especially when you have to watch. As soon as the words are away, you know there's going to be a reaction and someone will have to do the emotional mop-up.

"It's not that I forgot," I said. "It's only that I didn't remember. There is a difference. Happy birthday."

"A subtle difference indeed," Sarah said. I didn't realize that she was teasing. Her glance circled the room, as if she had something new to show me but couldn't find it. "Well, I guess you're forgiven," she said. "Thirty wasn't bad exactly. I got used to it, because I spent the year before running around going, I'm almost thirty, I'm almost thirty. Then I was. It didn't feel like such a big deal. You don't want to hear this. You've got plenty of time."

I had to use the bathroom. On the edge of the sink, Sarah had a potted African violet, a sixty-nine-cent bottle of antiwrinkle cream, and two kinds of deodorant — Sure and Secret. It looked like a little diorama. I came out saying, "You know you've got an orange sitting in your drink-cup holder?"

"Oh," she said. "Is that where?"

I sat in a shaky dining room chair and blathered on about my wonderful day, or parts of it. Sarah interrupted once, to find out how big the guppy was. "I don't know," I said. "Guppy size."

"Oh." She smiled again, this time with more distance. Sarah got up and began walking the edge of the throw rugs, as if they'd formed a sudden and intriguing tightrope. Her hair looked different, I thought. It had always been longer in back, but right then it seemed kind of alive. She stared at her feet and interrupted my recap of the floater story.

"Nothing else?" she asked. "There's no other reason? That was a pretty definite message."

"Not especially," I said.

"Good." She clicked off the tape, put on the thin gold earring she'd been fiddling with and charged into the bedroom. "I'll find pants — then we're doing something. Your car."

My sister's idea of doing something always involves driving. It's been like that since high school, and on that particular evening she wanted to cruise for neon sights. This meant that we had to go north, along Route 1 where everything was huge, glossy, late-1950s optimistic, a tiny bit run down, and decked out in neon. There's minigolf with a seven-foot dinosaur. A life-size schooner replica living out its life sentence as a steak house. Beside that, a seventy-foot-tall leaning Tower of Pizza. In thirty years the area will be a historic district.

We headed up into the heart of it, as my sister began explaining advertising tricks. Fast-food places, she said, pick yellow and red for signs because those colors make you salivate. Expensive cars sell better in jeweled hues — gold, silver, and garnet. From there on, my sister stared quietly, as if she'd run through the conversation tape and couldn't locate how she happened to be riding along in her little brother's battered car. She tugged her left ear. "Or we could do something stupid like close the Exotic Pineapple."

My arms already had that drooping, paralyzed feel to them. It felt like I was driving around with something heavy in the trunk. I must have frowned, even though the Exotic Pineapple was just ahead on the right.

"What's that supposed to mean?" Sarah frowned back. "Have *you* been there?"

I shook my head. "Bars are bars," I said. "People get drunk, they fall over."

"Well — I'm curious. Isn't that supposed to be your job? Being curious for money? Besides — I've never been to a strip joint. Who else am I gonna go with? It *is* my birthday."

"This'll cost, like, forty bucks."

"Look, it's Mr. Economy and he's whining."

I could sense a quick insult about to pounce, so I turned in. At the edge of the parking lot I heard the pop of thin bottles shattering. A fistful of guys in torn practice jerseys were lolling around a jacked up Blazer and crushing silver cans against various parts of their bodies. I paid the seven-dollar cover for both of us as the gray-haired bouncer examined our licenses. "You two together?"

"Yeah," Sarah said. "People mistake us for brother and sister all the time."

He handed her both wallets and watched while the big-necked guys swarmed in behind us. Sarah pushed open the blue, padded inner door as an amplified voice shouted, "Tanya!" A naked woman in heels began dancing with a feather boa to Dire Straits.

"Wow." Sarah's fingers slid across her lips. "They really use those."

The air smelled like scouring powder. Only five of the maybe seventy tables were filled, and those were up close, next to a brass rail that surrounded the stage like a moat. We sat one row back, as guys to the right of us kept licking the backs of dollar bills and sticking them to the railing.

Sarah tapped the plastic tabletop with her nails and flicked away an empty Marlboro pack. "Just like the V.F.W.," she said. It was: a room of hijacked Mediterranean dinette sets. My father would never belong to the V.F.W. He said that being a veteran was one thing he certainly didn't need to be reminded about. When I was a Cub Scout, he'd even balk at taking me there for pack meetings.

My sister paid for four Lite beers, two for each of us. I hate Lite beer. "That is all you could drink here anyway," she said, giving back my wallet. "We have to preserve the aesthetic. Anyway, it's happy birthday to me."

The five guys from outside suddenly moved around our table like a well-muscled stream. They clustered loudly at the chairs directly in front of us.

"Shit," Sarah said. "This happens at movies too."

"Whoa, pull up on those air brakes, fella." A blond steroid fugitive in a Raiders half-shirt thumped someone, who looked like his brother, in the chest. The rest of them spread out, flopping into seats an arm's length from one another.

Sarah squinted, as though she were trying to fit this scene into some larger mosaic. I couldn't focus. My stomach hurt. I remember her saying it was no wonder women obsess about their bodies, but everything else seemed skewed. Tanya's glittering fuchsia high heels squeaked across the black polished floor. On a basketball court you'd get that same noise, exactly. Long gloves floated down into the patchy, ankle-high, dry-ice smoke. Every time Tanya came close, I kept seeing her as a young mom in extra makeup doing aerobics. Then Grant began coming back at me, in quick little images, yet his face kept getting mixed up with the floater's. People die and never realize the wake they leave streaming behind, I thought. What if they had to go around notifying everyone? What if they had to deliver the news? They'd never do it.

The sound system whined into the Stones' "Start Me Up," as the Raiders guy plucked at his mesh shirt and shouted along in a monotone.

Sarah tapped the rim of her bottle. "These are warm," she said. "Let's send em' back."

"No," I said.

"Come on. If we don't drink these beers, what's this place going to do? Fold? We're not cynical enough."

I grabbed her wrist and softly shook it. As I did I remembered that this was something my mother used to do to get our attention. "There's another reason I had to talk to you tonight," I shouted.

A look of alarm fluttered into my sister's eyes.

"I don't know why I didn't say it before, but I got a phone call at work from Binghamton. This guy Lathers, Grant's lawyer, about his estate. He's dead."

"Who — the lawyer?"

"No, Grant."

Sarah's eyebrows made a pinched V. She pulled back and looked away to the stage. The song was almost over. She glanced at the space between us, as though she needed to check to see if the words I'd shouted were still hanging there and readable.

My sister shook her head, but not in an entirely sad way. "For real?"

I picked up my beer and nodded.

Sarah frowned at the brass rail. The men in front were up and stamping around. My sister leaned back and looked slightly dazed. Then she sputtered. She planted the bottle on the table, and laughed.

"You're kidding," she said. "When?"

"A week and a half ago."

"You're not kidding?"

I shook my head and Sarah laughed harder.

The music stopped, but for some reason no one applauded. Tanya held out her arms. "Don't everybody talk at once," she said. It was a mini-intermission.

The Raiders guy, who'd been taking everything quite seriously in what I imagined was a kind of drunk and playful way, turned and let one branch of an arm dangle at his side. "Hey, you tourists," he said. "Quit laughing." He waved a thick finger in my direction. "Cool your jets. There's nothing to laugh at here."

"Oh, a barbarian," Sarah said.

"What?" He moved in, leaning over the table. "What the fuck's wrong with you?"

My sister looked up and lost it again, I think when she saw the purple veins coming out around his neck. "This is truly great," she said.

"You tell your woman here if she doesn't like it to get the fuck out. This is the wrong night for her, anyway."

And here was my mistake. I stood up. I was three or four feet away and thinking in slightly dumb and heroic terms, when something made me start explaining. "You," I pointed, "have got it *all wrong*. This is *my* sister and she's laughing because I just told her that our brother had a heart attack. And he's *dead*."

The Raiders guy stared as though I'd been let in on a day-pass from some parallel universe. "You're too much, buddy. Too fucking much," he said. "Tell her to stop. I don't want the two of you sitting anywhere near me. No, no and no."

My sister stayed pinned to her chair. The Raiders guy took a second step toward me and pushed against the table with his thigh. Sarah got up and left, weaving through the maze of red plastic chairs, but snickering and carrying her second, untouched beer by the neck. The Raiders guy shoved the table again and it screeched like a docking ship, which attracted the management's attention. His friends looked bored, as if some version of this happened every night.

I followed Sarah out, as two bouncers walked right around us. Just before the padded inner door slammed shut, I looked back and saw the Raiders guy readjusting our table and patting the top, as if he'd finally settled a fine antique planter into an intricate corner.

"No shit." Sarah said. She burst out the front door. The air had stayed sticky. It was waiting to rain. A moth fluttered into my forehead. I batted it away and my foot sent an empty schnapps bottle spinning. "A-mazing," my sister said, beating me to the car. "Did they have a funeral?"

"Not really, but everything's done." I unlocked both doors and sat in the driver's seat with my left foot still touching the glittering, glass strewn blacktop. I told Sarah about the estate and how we had to go to Binghamton.

"Huh." She balled up my tan sportcoat from work and rooted through the back for tapes.

"What are you putting in?" I was already driving in a small circle, shooting the headlights off the corrugated aluminum wall of the furniture store next door.

"Dead." She sputtered, again.

"Why is this so funny?"

"You don't think so?"

"It just felt —"

"I know — preposterous. When are we going? We have to go." My sister was quiet for a minute, as if she'd taken a deep breath and had decided to test herself to see how long she could hold it. "The weird thing was — for a second I thought you were going to tell me Dad had surfaced or something."

"How would you have handled that?" I asked. We were driving

south on Route 1, toward the Tobin Bridge. You could take that road all the way to Florida.

"I wouldn't," she said.

"This lawyer said he had no way to contact him. I mean Dad."

Sarah bit her lip. "But the will lists us?"

I nodded. A red haze of taillights had collected itself several thousand yards ahead.

"That is strange. So — are we immoral or what? For laughing?"

Getting closer, I saw gray and blue state police cruisers parked on both sides in the median, perpendicular to the road. Their headlights angled into the buggy night like flying buttress supports. I looked behind us and saw that we couldn't turn around. Another cruiser waited in the northbound lane. "This is a roadblock," I said, "and I don't have any taillights."

My sister pulled her beer up from the floor. "No shit," she said slowly. She took a sip.

Five or six troopers lined each side of the road, some in slick fluorescent orange vests, others with clipboards. Ahead on the right, half a dozen cars were getting tickets. One guy in tight black jeans and a cobalt-striped shirt stood uncertainly, his arms out like he'd been playing airplane. A gigantic trooper motioned him around with a finger. We crawled to a stop. I reached behind the seat and pulled out my jacket. "There should be a camera in the glove compartment," I said. "There's a flash with batteries in the door pocket."

Pulling out of line, I rolled up and parked behind the nearest cruiser. I took an already-filled notebook, half glued together with ancient spilled coffee, from between the seat and the parking brake. I felt my pockets for pens.

"I get it," Sarah said, hooking up the flash, holding it to her ear for the high whine before letting off a silver burst. "We're supposed to be reporters. You know there's no way anyone on the planet is going to believe this. You could just take the ticket."

I unfolded my wallet as I got out, being careful to expose my state police press pass. I found the nearest trooper. "Nathan Scales," I said. "*Chronicle-Democrat*, from Lawrence. How's this going? Anybody from our area involved? Are you Andover barracks or Topsfield?" I kept glancing around, as if I'd just made it, only a little late.

"Speak to the captain," he said, eyeing us unkindly.

I waved and only remembered to shout, "Thanks," once we were walking along the shoulder. The captain was a short man with big sideburns and a Napoleon kind of grin. "About time we're getting some proper publicity," he said after examining both sides of my press pass.

"You?" He pointed at Sarah.

"Only a stringer. I'm more like a summer intern, really. It's pretty good for —"

"Well? What do you need?"

I asked the normal numbers questions. Sarah took head shots.

"You still got film in that?" the captain asked. The flash had stopped.

"Oh," Sarah said, looking at the front of the camera. "This is new color stuff. Real fast and you can still push the hell out of it."

I thanked him, rechecked the spelling of his name, and we wandered around for another five minutes, watching the troopers stare into cars and ask fat guys wearing suits how their evenings had been while they checked for glazed eyeballs. When everyone seemed to be ignoring us sufficiently, we strolled back to the car and drove down the shoulder on the wrong side of the orange cones, dipping into the median and nodding at the troopers. No one stopped us.

"That was unreal," Sarah said. "You had your big reporter handshake out and everything. I never remember you being this resourceful."

"It's a front," I said. "Sometimes I can do it at work."

"Well," she said, "Now what? Weren't we always doing something?"

THREE

How am I? I'm great. Simply fine. Here's why. I'd been toiling away all afternoon behind the bar at Rowing International when these three fat-trolls-from-purgatory appeared. Plump man number one waved a thick finger at me and announced that they were there to drink "nipples." A fun new drink his brother-in-law had thought up. Great. A genius idea. This drink, however, turned out to be one of those pour problems, where you have to get the layers exactly right. So — I told them we were out of cream, or they could have the rancid stuff. Therefore, no nipples.

Next, they wanted peanuts. They insisted. These were guys whose lives probably revolved around peanuts. Then the blond one in the salmon shirt (clearly a color invented so guys would not have to wear pink) began to moan. "But the *Sheraton* has peanuts," he went on. Next, he let me in on a dirty little secret. He and his brothers owned two *or* three trucking companies. So while I might be cute, what kind of a bartender would I be if I couldn't give them nipples or peanuts?

"A happy one," I said, and drifted firmly to the TV end of the bar. You see, this is my life, or most of it. Sunshine and light every day. So, when the trolls started banging the pretzel bowl on the bar — as if, as if I were about to trot into the Square and pick something up for them — that's when I said: "*Go* to the Sheraton. *Have* nuts. *Be* happy. What's the point of being on the planet if you can't fulfill at least a few of your desires? Am I right?"

"There goes your extraordinary tip," said the salmon guy. "Besides, if you keep talking like that, you'll always be lonely."

Right then, and lucky for them, Julie, the other bartender, answered the bar phone and said that Nate, my remaining brother, waited on the other end of the blinking light. I picked up and Nate was still at work. I made a mistake, right away, by giving my brother still more of a difficult time because he forgot my birthday. Nate was in no mood to be jocular. He sounded truly paranoid about his car and wanted to take mine on Thursday, when we went to Binghamton. My car. My car is a Tonka toy, I explained. Things fly off. Whenever I come back from anywhere, somebody has to put it all back together. Plus, I told him, my clutch was feeble and my insurance wasn't exactly current.

Dauntless, Nate kept pleading. Please, please, he said, in that sad and worried voice that once upon a time used to get him extra cookies. It isn't far, only six something hours. We'd surely get arrested if we took his car. I could see the look, the droopy gray eyes and all. It was too bad about his taillights but —

"No," I said. "Believe me. We'll never *return* if we take my car."

Nate began explaining that he was having another regrettable day at work. He was in big trouble over something to do with a bank robbery. As disclosures went, I suppose, this was a big opening for us. One small step down the road to sibling rediscovery. Most people do get a little weird when their cars don't work, but should I really go and sacrifice my clutch?

Nate kept pitching, but I put the phone down and found a fresh cherry Chap Stick in my front pocket. This brightened the picture a little. So — I decided, why not? I'd consider it, I told him.

I hung up and went back to slicing limes. I was smiling, because I was thinking, this could turn out to be an interesting trip. Then that idea quickly turned to a kind of dread as I imagined watching Nate do his best Eeyore imitation for hours on end, against a backdrop of rolling scenery.

My little brother is such a difficult one to figure. When he came over Tuesday night, all sad and jumpy like a puppy lost in a parking lot, I couldn't decide what to do with him. I guessed there had to be some kind of a problem because he said "Nope," and licked his lips when I asked if he had anything to tell me. Nate always licks his lips after telling a lie.

Then — two hours later — he finally got around to explaining that Grant had died. Which, when I heard it, strangely cracked me up. It wasn't as though I didn't believe it, what I mean is — Grant should have died a long time ago. Is that harsh? I'm sorry, but it happens. The trouble is, I'm not one of those people who can get overly sentimental at a moment like that. Besides, Grant was *my* oldest brother. I can be as harsh as I like. This is what I think: I think Grant spaced himself right out of the picture. He got too ridiculous to live and it caught up with him.

Nate and Grant, of course, always did have a fairly complex and destructive relationship. When Nate was little, especially — and that always left me in the middle. Like the time after we moved to Vestal and Nate burned off his bangs with a lighter. He was trying to set a telephone pole on fire. It didn't work, and after hiding in the woods for a few hours, he finally told me about it, because he wouldn't dare tell Grant or Dad. So — since we did have this big drawer full of clippers and barber's scissors that Mom had used on us when we were little — I gave Nate a buzz cut, and no one was the wiser. I was always sticking up for Nate. I mean, if we ever counted it out, he would still owe. It's not that he's such a kid now, just so kidlike. He still can't tell anyone bad news. It wouldn't have surprised me a bit if Nate had suggested playing a few hours of miniature golf before he got up the courage to tell me about Grant. Truly.

Nate seemed a little more normal after our lovely time at the Exotic Pineapple. But I should have suspected, from the start, that something huge was behind his sudden visit. Like when I opened my apartment door and found him wearing that bedraggled-looking button-down. Once upon a time, no one could get Nate near anything that had ever been on a hanger. On Sunday mornings, Grant used to chase him around with a tiny short-sleeve shirt and a clip-on tie. This was in the pathetic period, when our father decided that we were going to go to church. We were supposed to get a Protestant foundation. But he spent the morning outside in the car, with his feet up on the dashboard, chewing a cigar and reading Ross Macdonald. What did he think we were getting by being in the building? If you're Catholic, at least there's some ceremony, a little pageant. After about twenty minutes of chasing Nate, Grant would give up and leave the shirt and tie outside little brother's door. When Nate thought no one was watching, he would sneak out and try them on. You can't tell him to do anything — still.

Meanwhile, back at work. When the trolls finally left, I calmed down a touch and began explaining the story to Julie, who can sometimes be a wee bit snippy. She's a mixed-media person at the Museum School, so we occasionally bicker about art. Anyway, by the time I reached the roadblock part, Julie was staring at me with these gigantic, dumbfounded eyes. "He takes you to a strip bar to tell you your brother's dead? That's ridiculous. You poor thing. What kind of jaded creephead is he?"

"But going to the strip bar was my idea," I said.

"It doesn't matter." Julie only has one brother, who she won't admit to worshiping. My family, at least to her, always appears exotic in this minidrama kind of way. But as I tried to explain, it shouldn't have been a surprise that Nate couldn't tell me about Grant. We're WASPs. We can't tell anyone anything. It's secrets all the way down. I never did get a chance to say that hearing the news at a strip bar did make it all seem even more ridiculous. With those implants bouncing across the stage, and the morons below hanging their tongues out. I suspect Grant would have liked it.

I let Julie go on some, but she kept traveling that same jag. The one about how my little brother is a horrible person. I finally interrupted and said I had to get a couple of nights off, to make this trip to Binghamton. So — could she sub for me?

"You're going with *him*?" Julie said. "I don't care if he is your brother, someone that callous would strand you at a rest stop. In a minute. You should never go anywhere with a brother like that."

That did seem a tad hasty. I tried to point out that Grant would have felt right at home at the Exotic Pineapple. But I realized — again — how amazingly hard it is explaining parts of my family to people who haven't actually been there. Isn't that true enough of most things?

Later, as I loaded the blender with bananas, Julie came up and apologized for being so hard on baby brother. Which was sweet. She did a subtle dip with her shoulder and said that things with Nate would probably be fine once we worked out our cross-aggression.

"Cross-aggression?" I asked.

"Yeah, you get cross at him and he gets cross at you. Cross." She looked over in a semisuperior way, which nearly set me off, again. I smiled and made the blender whine. I'd decided to make myself a little healthy. Perhaps work on a new personality. I offered Julie some.

"It's brown," she said.

"It's bananas."

Julie winced and carried off the tumbler. She placed it on the bar and started watching TV.

When the phone rang and I picked up and just said, "Hello," like I was home, instead of saying the name of the bar. That frightened me — a bit. But when this familiar voice on the other end said, "Sarah?" for a second I thought it was Kelly, a friend from Madison who lives in Medford with her year-old son and husband. Almost every time we try to get together it falls through. "This is Phyllis," the voice said. "From Anderson, Slay and Styles?"

"Oh — of course."

"Mark Maycomber's assistant?"

"Sure," I said, meaning to sound professional.

"Well, Mark would like to reschedule." Reschedule what? I thought. Until I remembered. "Instead of tomorrow, how would the Thursday after next be?" Phyllis asked. "At two?"

Without checking my book, I said that would be fine. Maycomber is a guy I met right there in the bar, oddly enough, who has turned out to be my best contact, so far, in this new and vaunted copywriting career. He's an exec for an advertising agency in the Hancock Tower. He's tall and witty and has a very dry sense of humor. The amazing thing was, we started talking and within forty-five minutes he had offered to take me on as a special project. He liked my spark, he said. I was dubious at first. You know, meeting someone like that in a bar. I kept thinking, is this the way the world really works? It seemed so — unofficial. But it turned out to be real, and not at all sleazy. Every two weeks or so I'd bring copy and layouts for products that never could exist up to Maycomber's office. He'd examine these and say, Hmmmm, while I squirmed in the nearby leather chair. He'd toss out a suggestion or two, ask what I was working on next, and Phyllis would make another appointment. It was all rather mysterious. He liked my eye, he said. I was improving, too, but not to the point where they'd risk me on some pro bono account — which would be the next step.

I hung up and thought, oh God, now I've got to invent all this new stuff. I was supposed to be thinking of a new phrase that would get people to switch from oil heat to natural gas. It was my current pretend project. But, that wavelet of career anxiety lasted all of about three seconds. What could I expect, with everything else I had to worry about? Grant and driving to Binghamton, for starters.

See — I really couldn't imagine Grant leaving anything to us. But I could imagine that Nate and I would drive to Binghamton all right. We'd have some small hysterics, a minor revelation or two. Nate would explain what it is about me he can't approve of. Though I really don't care. I don't, even if he is all the visible family I have left. Anyway, we'd arrive, hear the will, and discover that this was all some annoying Grant joke. We'd bond over that, the past would fall away, we'd start anew as brother and sister and live happily ever after. You know, Grant would get this ridiculous look when he was scheming, or even thinking. He'd cock his head and stare blankly into the upper right-hand corner of the world. If he could have moved his ears, he'd have been a dog.

What I couldn't explain to Julie, or anyone for that matter, was how it felt in the instant when I suspected that Nate was going to say it was Dad who'd died. Or that he'd found him. Or that Dad had found us. I couldn't explain it, because every time I tried to imagine one of those situations, I'd freeze up. Does my father even know about Grant? I wondered. But my father and I have so many years of unresolved and probably mutual disgust between us. Even though I don't really know if that's true, which is part of the problem. I'm certain he's disappointed because I can't seem to stick to things. But please — tell me about drifting.

Yes, of course, our life was entirely different before my mother died. How could it not be? My father was different too. Like when I was tiny and we lived in Syracuse and I couldn't sleep on a very hot night. He would say, "Ride time," and we'd drive in the station wagon, just the two of us, with the windows down in the warm and dark air, until I fell asleep on the foam pad in the way-back. He used to sing me to sleep with Big Ten fight songs. I never understood why, but he said he could always remember the words.

After we moved to Vestal, this changed. Nate and I were older and my father became elusive. Even when he was around, working on his cars or something, we had to almost act up to capture his attention. Or that's how I remember it. It seemed as though we were never important enough to make time for — even if no one ever said that. Besides, Grant was always in the way, being Grant.

Ever since I moved to Boston, I keep having these pangs — simple, repeated cravings, just to see my father. They pop up at the oddest moments. Like on the T or when I'm buying groceries. As if there were this huge and unnatural thing I'd left undone. The idea of it, of finding out about him, keeps sneaking through and clouding up everything else in my life. I keep thinking, if I could only sort this one thing out, everything else would be manageable. In the perfect world — I suppose that might be true.

A minute later, some off-kilter little twinge forced me to call Nate back and say: "Fine, we'll take my car. Only you'll pay half if the clutch goes." My brother didn't respond right off. I could even hear his brain calculating the cost of airline tickets, which were too much for either of us — I'd already checked.

"OK," he said. "But I want to be driving by seven."

"Impossible."

"Eight?"

It sounded like my little brother was eating something. Which made me wonder if he still chewed pencils. In elementary school, Nate could gnaw a Ticonderoga number two down to the metal end. I wanted to tell him to lighten up. But telephones were ringing away in the background on his end. So — I lied and tried to sound agreeable. "Great," I said. "Fine. We can handle that."

FOUR

Sarah pulled up in front of my house at 10:34 Thursday morning, bright and early for our impending six-and-a-half hour drive. I, however, had been awake and ready to roll for about the past three and a half hours. Basically, I got up early to worry. I worried about my taillights. I worried about Sarah's clutch. I worried about how in the world I was going to survive two and a half days of close contact with my sister. Then, I moved on to why I kept screwing things up at work. I had to literally beg to get these days off for the trip, mainly because I'd botched the bank robbery story — the one I went out on right after I heard about Grant.

After a robbery, they always lock up the bank. You can't walk right in and talk to people. You have to watch the doors and wait for the detectives or the FBI guys to emerge, and then catch them before they hop into their cars. Well, I watched the wrong door. I never found the detectives, and the other paper got the good part of the story, which was that the bandit escaped on a moped. I didn't think mopeds still existed. The next day, I endured a scolding from Doris Flick, one that quickly degenerated into a review of my many shortcomings, at least until I told her that my brother was dead. Personal tragedy always shuts her up for a minute or two. That got me Thursday and Friday off, but I had to agree to work Saturday night and take the police beat. Even so, I felt phony all afternoon. How could I have used Grant as an excuse? But what could I do?

I heard Sarah's car closing in as I paced a long, narrow line in the front hall carpet. My sister had this ancient orange Subaru that always sounded like it was ready to drop a few pipes. I snatched my stuff and the sleeping bag — since it wasn't exactly clear where we were going to stay — and ran out to the front porch, forgetting to recheck whether or not I'd locked the back door. Sarah drummed on the steering wheel to some neo-surf guitar band on her tape deck that throbbed out into the street. When I pushed up the rusting back hatch she shouted, "Hello, mon ami."

"You never make sense," I said. I walked around and reached in the open window, unlocking the passenger side door. I turned down the volume and saw that my sister had push pins stuck into the padded blue edge of her dashboard. For some reason, that annoyed me. She was wearing a gray sweatshirt with "Maryland Badminton" printed in gothic red and black letters across the front. The tan car caddy behind the parking brake held an unopened bottle of red nail polish and a crumpled parking ticket. A green mitten covered the gearshift knob.

Sarah adjusted the bandanna she'd been using as a headband. "Ha!" she said, as her left hand vanished into a box of granola-raisin cereal. The box was crammed into the space between the seat and the driver's side door, like a feed bag. "Want some?" she asked.

"That stuff hurts my mouth."

She gave me a look, as though she'd planned on using these first little interactions to predict the tone of our upcoming time together. "I can't stand these dried raisins," she said. "They fit like caps — right over your molars. Here." She picked out three and dropped them into my palm.

I threw the raisins out the window. "What's with the sweatshirt?" I asked. "You never went to Maryland or played anything."

"God, you're happy." Sarah banged my thigh with her fist.

"God, you're late."

"Oh, come now," she said. "What else have we got to do today?" She tugged at her sleeve. "This is outlet stuff. It's great. Customers get to make conversation about my badminton career and I get to lie."

I frowned while Sarah plopped the cereal box in my lap. Her clutch squealed like a faraway cat as she rammed us into reverse.

We were out on the Mass Pike for maybe twenty minutes when I fell into a deep sleep. I suppose that shouldn't have been a surprise, what with all the stress. When I opened my eyes, it was hours later. I was still in Sarah's car, but we were parked beside something called the Out West Diner.

"So — you're awake." Sarah looked at me sideways. It took me a while to stop squinting. I didn't really believe it when she said we were already outside Albany, on Route 20. But all the cars did have New York plates.

My neck hurt and my right arm was still asleep. I began shaking it around as Sarah eyed me cautiously. At that point, I'd been having entirely out-of-hand dreams on an almost nightly basis. Really wacky stuff, and that last one fit right in. I'd been flying above some dense, old-growth forest, strapped into the wing seat of an ancient jet, and watching the rubber seal on the emergency window flap in and out. My father, Grant, and Sarah were across the aisle in the same row. They were smiling and throwing honey-roasted peanuts out the window, but I kept wondering who would be sucked out next. Soon the plane lurched low over Binghamton, and someone started shooting into the fuselage — all these dull metallic thuds, like hail on a car roof. We crashed slowly, and next Grant and I were driving a rented metallic-blue car, dodging stumps as we worked through a blackened and burned-over valley. It was a great charred space, a place that had once been a park or a national forest, and we were looking for my father. I kept reaching for the door or trying to roll down the windows while Grant lectured. He was waving his arms and shouting because I'd made a series of "false moves." I couldn't get my hands to work.

I didn't want to dream about my dead brother. I didn't want to be out on that morbid errand. I didn't care about the will, I only wanted it to all be over. I wanted that entire episode deeply embedded in the past tense. Clean up the sad verdict and get out.

"Come on," my sister said. "I have an overwhelming desire for blueberry pancakes."

We sat in the first booth by the window, at a table covered with wood-colored formica. They brought us coffee almost instantly, and I ordered a big omelet. But when the waitress went away, my sister drew her elbows in close, as though a board meeting had just convened. "We really should have a lot in common," she said, but in a kind of deadpan way.

"Maybe," I said, "if we actually started talking."

"We are talking," she said. "This is like a conversation. Go ahead. You start."

"What about?" I tested a spoonful of coffee.

"Our brother," Sarah said. "We can't go into this without the proper mind-set." She slid off one silver hoop earring and rubbed it between her fingers like a charm.

"Yeah we can." I said. "This'll be surgical. We'll go in, discover what there is to know, and escape."

My sister gave me a gray look, as though I were missing most of the point of everything. Then she nodded, as if, yes, I could go on holding that quaint little notion for the time being. "Stuff is going to happen with this lawyer," Sarah said. "I don't know what — but I can't believe this is on the up and up." She sampled her coffee and poured in about thirty seconds worth of sugar. "I don't like his name."

"You don't like his *name?*"

"Yeah. Lathers sounds like — bad bubble bath."

I began gazing out at the lazy traffic sliding along Route 20. How could anybody take her seriously? I wondered.

"You've got your sad dog face out again," Sarah said.

"I'm overtired," I said. "And you're doing a pretty good imitation of a paranoid beneficiary."

My sister stared at me, her green eyes narrowing in, as though she couldn't believe we were sitting at the same table, much less related. For a second, it did feel as though we were complete strangers. I do not know this woman at all, I thought.

"Being paranoid doesn't mean they're not after you," my sister said. An odd smile squirted across her face. "We have to be pumped. Psyched. This is the chance you get once in — I don't know — forever. To take things back. Or put them in place. To make amends."

"Who are we getting back at?" I asked. "Grant's dead."

Sarah waved this off. "Maybe it all fits — in some way that I haven't figured out — but this was Grant. We shouldn't be caught up in any needless sentimental muck."

"He was a jerk of a brother and now he's a dead jerk of a brother," I said. "Can't we just leave it at that?" It sounded hard, even as I watched the words fly away. All week I'd been waiting for something to build and bloom, like an infection of grief. I was waiting to feel really rotten, so I could only remember the good about Grant, but it wouldn't happen.

"Nope," Sarah said. "He made it hard for himself." She did one of her secure head shakes, the kind that instantly brought back tree fort arguments from behind the house in Pompey, when we lived near Syracuse. "We're not wrong to feel this way," Sarah said. "People die and you're supposed to feel sorry. I'd be deluding myself if I started to feel that. I'm not giving Grant the satisfaction. Give me the worst time. The worst Grant time."

"No," I said.

"Come on. This is what I mean by the proper mind-set."

"Like he knows we're doing this?" I accidentally made a fist. "If he could know, he'd love it. He'd be thrilled to death, knowing we're sitting here ready to review his greatest hits."

"Relish it," Sarah said. "Grant would relish this."

"Probably start to drool."

"Nevertheless," she said, "our brother used to measure his beard clippings to see if his beard grew faster in winter or summer. He told me. Did you know I kept a calendar, and marked off every day he made me cry — all through eighth grade?"

"I'm not doing this," I said.

"Look — so you're feeling lousy because you don't feel worse," Sarah said. "This isn't like Mom. This is entirely different. This is therapeutic. Grant was the spiritual descendant of John Wayne and the emotional equivalent of a VCR."

My sister sat back and the food arrived, as if on cue. I took my own sweet time opening the gold packet of grape jelly that came with my toast.

"I still have arguments in my head with him," Sarah said. "You want to hear the latest? You should."

"Nope."

"You know," she said, "all you have to do to get along with me is tell me I'm right."

I rearranged my toast around the edges of the omelet. When I cut into it, I discovered far too many peppers and not enough onions.

"He used to break things off your bike and tell you I did it, just to see what would happen," Sarah said. "Like some irrational little experiment."

"This is so trivial."

"He let your milk snake go. The one you found in the gravel pit. He could be like that — with animals."

"This is not how it works," I said. "Trivial stuff is not supposed to go on and on and on. It's supposed to be trivial and then disappear. You know, another new —"

Sarah hummed, as though I would some day get over that little idea as well. A white pickup stopped at the traffic light beyond the window.

"Did you know that I once rolled a pickup?" she asked.

"No." And it surprised me, because my sister has historically been this kind of amazing driver. Even in high school, she'd do donuts and jumps. Occasionally she'd bribe me to help push the Mustang out of the driveway, so no one would hear us leave late at night. I was in junior high and we'd drive for hours, go to Dairy Queen, and finally push the car back across the crackling gravel to the edge of the garage. Sarah only had a learner's permit. She wasn't allowed to drive after dusk. "You really rolled a truck?" I asked. "Why are you telling me this when we're going on a trip?"

"It was Art's. I picked him up and we were driving to Greek Peak for this freestyle competition. I was feeling lucky and going about forty — to blow snow off the hood. Then we flipped once in a ditch and landed right side up. The truck didn't even get a big dent. But before this, Grant was talking to Dad and saying, 'As long as Sarah keeps driving that way she's going to have a serious accident.' So actually — it was his fault. If Grant hadn't said that, it would never have happened." She smiled.

"Where did you learn to do logic?" I asked. Who could possibly care about this stuff now? I wondered. I started eating my omelet before it had a chance to get any colder.

Grant was in his early twenties and had just graduated from RPI when he got some engineering job and moved home. We were in Vestal by then, and I remember thinking that his arrival did seem a little strange. I was seven, and for as long as I could remember, my brother had only been around on holidays. Then when he showed up, it was like, Who are you? Before that he'd always seemed like some distant but annoying adult, an uncle maybe. My father had changed jobs at that point, and was traveling a good deal of the time. I guess he believed that having Grant there would be better than the parade of babysitters and nannys we'd been running through since Mom died.

Grant went right after the discipline stuff. I don't know, maybe that's where the minor-god complex started, from working too hard to fill the vacuum, trying to take over a few vacant roles. Aloof, mysterious, and all-knowing Grant must wield power for the ultimate good. He placed a homemade electronic lock on the television and took it off for only two hours a day. He timed showers. We had to alphabetize things, even magazines. You had to ask for a ride the day before you needed it. After about six months some rules went away and others appeared, but Grant did all this with a certain annoying gusto. Big trouble and other idle threats, forever after.

"Grant's just helping out," my father would say. And when my father was home, things did return to subnormal. But he could have paid more attention. So what if things were rough for him? He must have seen, even slightly, what was happening. Then to decide not to deal with it. To slide off and focus on the next disaster? I know it's years later, but if he didn't care then, why should we care now?

"You home?" Sarah waved her last forkful of pancake around, as though she were hoping to hypnotize me. "Nice apartment — but nobody lives there."

"Are your records alphabetized?" I asked.

She shook her head. "Good," she said, "you're remembering."

There was also a stretch where Grant made us read the paper before dinner and then quizzed us during "Fact Time." You could earn triple points for science answers. I knew, somewhere out on the fringe, that we were having a weird childhood, but it didn't always feel horrible at the time.

"How'd we grow up?" I asked.

"I don't think we did," Sarah said.

As we closed in on Binghamton, Sarah's car kept overheating. Then it started slowing down and losing power. It was nearly dark by the time we made it over to Owego. Little bits of neon buzzed to life as we crawled past the giant Civil War monument in the center of town. It was strange, just being on those roads again. I kept getting an odd feeling as we passed the Binghamton exits on Route 17, even though there wasn't anyone living around there that I still knew. The Costellos, for instance, had moved to California, years ago. But it didn't matter, I kept glimpsing ghost cars from my past. Once, for a second, it even felt like I was riding shotgun again, in Frank Santori's Dart Swinger, with my lacrosse buddies from high school. We'd spend night after night, bombing away to nowhere.

"Where are we staying?" I asked.

"Grant's house," Sarah said.

"No we're not. We should find a motel, or go wake up Mrs. Deschamps." She was our closest neighbor when we lived in Vestal. A widow who lived with her sister and who once tamed an injured bluejay and let me feed it cat food from their deck. "You don't even know where Grant's house is," I pointed out.

"Yeah I do. I was there. Besides, Mrs. Deschamps lives in Sarasota."

"When were you there?"

"Couple of years ago. I was on the way back from Chicago. Before I went to Maine? I had a feeling Grant knew what Dad was up to — so I stopped in. The whole thing was very unpleasant. We just yelled. I felt like clobbering him. But for the first forty-five minutes, he was all smooth. Like, 'Oh it's so great to see you.'"

"We don't even have keys," I said.

"So." My sister smiled. "We'll break in," she said, as if that was going to be the fun part.

At the end of East Main, Sarah turned, and the road looped past an open field until we were driving in the shadow of a long, wooded ridge. Orange streetlights flickered to life as we passed beneath them. After a few minutes, Sarah said: "Come on. It's like I'm blocked. Owego isn't that big."

She turned on the headlights as we came up to a side street that we'd missed the first time through. The beams caught the word "SCALES" in silver letters on a small sign halfway down the road. We drove closer and saw a pair of stunned ceramic deer in the middle of the broad lawn. "Hey ho," Sarah said.

My brother's house seemed smaller than I'd expected. It was pale blue, two stories high, and had a fieldstone foundation. The outside glistened, as though it had been recently painted. Stone pillars held up the side porch, while the curving driveway formed a pond of lawn before the front door.

Sarah downshifted and turned in. The clutch pedal made a sad groan and I watched her leg extend until her heel hit the fire wall. "Shit," she said. The car stalled and rolled to a stop on the grass. Sarah reached down to wiggle the pedal with her hand. The clutch cable had broken. "My car's cooked."

The headlights were still on and gnats darted through the beams. Bullfrogs and all kinds of bugs were screeching somewhere in the near distance. The air was warm and draped and smelled like cut grass, and I noticed a huge silver and black Ford van parked under the carport, right in front of the narrow stucco garage. The van was caked with mud and salt, but on the rear wheel cover, in chrome script, you could make out the words "Rudy's Van World."

I opened my door and a fluorescent light went on at the back of the house. Its frosted glow spilled evenly across the lawn. "Someone's in there," I announced.

"Come on," Sarah said. "Look at that van. Those deer. Who else could live here?"

"The Dobermans."

"Arf. Arf." My sister smirked; I remembered exactly how that look could annoy me.

"He might have friends," I said. "Maybe someone's already renting the place." I stood on the grass and started to lock my side of the car.

"Dear — what are they going to do? Steal this car? We should be so lucky." Sarah plucked a lavender flashlight from the glove compartment, slammed her door, and walked toward the front steps. I waited in the ankle-high grass, feeling dumb and blindsided. It was uncanny — like so many years ago, when Sarah began acting like the voice of authority and I was the young and cautious one, scared of too many everyday things. Helicopters, traffic, large short-haired dogs, and bad news.

She frowned back at me in the fading light. "You weren't like this the other night — with the troopers. Then, you were magnificent."

I could have waited longer, but I followed her across the lawn.

Sarah pulled at the aluminum screen door, but it wouldn't open. She pushed the doorbell before I had a chance to tell her not to. The chimes made a dull, clipped sound.

Beyond the hedge, a car cruised by, leaving the first six notes from "Born To Be Wild," sprawling through the air. Fireflies made slow half loops beside Sarah's dead car. She winked the flashlight in my face.

"Want to try the back?" Sarah suggested. "The bulkhead?"

"He's always had a bulkhead," I said.

Behind the house we found a VW Rabbit, a cord of firewood under plastic, a canoe on blocks, and a small, brown aluminum barn. It was the kind of building you'd buy by accident one afternoon at the mall. The bulkhead was painted silver, but it had started to rust.

"I bet this is barricaded from the other direction," I said. "I bet he's got attack dogs waiting down there. Drooling, unfed, attack dogs."

"Come now." My sister tossed me the light and pulled the bulkhead door up about two inches, before the latch tugged back.

I'd started to feel bad for the way I'd been acting through all of this. We were already there, we couldn't do anything else, so I should at least help out, I thought. "We could pry it," I suggested, looking around as if I expected someone to magically slap the perfect tool into my open palm. I started walking toward the stucco garage. It was dark and locked, but there was an old white car inside. It looked like the 1936 Cord, the one my father restored. But I thought he'd sold it. I noticed that the plastic on the firewood was anchored with a short length of lead pipe. I walked back to the bulkhead, holding the pipe like a wand. Three tugs later, the bulkhead's top hinge broke off. When the other hinge flipped away, we folded back the door. It made a tremendous clanking sound.

My sister pressed a theatrical finger to her lips.

Grant had removed the steps from beneath the door, and Sarah had to jump down into the cellar. Her running shoes made a hard slap, as the flashlight beam skittered up across the joists. "Careful," she whispered. "It's been remodeled." She waved to include the whole house. "He did it in a really dumb way, too. The cellar stairs come up in the living room."

The basement smelled faintly of varnish, and rows of power tools hung from sheets of glossy pegboard. There were stacks of precisely labeled cigar boxes on the workbench, each one holding a different constellation of tiny electrical parts. It was the perfectly ordered universe.

I nicked my head on a hot water pipe and watched the ceiling, waiting for the footsteps I knew I'd surely hear. Sarah found the stairs and motioned me on. The door at the top was open.

Grant's cellar stairs were wide and carpeted with artificial turf. I was still concerned about that fluorescent light, and I had this odd sense, almost a taste in my mouth, telling me that Grant was going to be there. He would be sitting in his motorized recliner, leaning back with a ridiculous cigar in his hand. He would have known all along that it was us in the driveway. He would have enjoyed the wait, the suspense, while we broke into his stupid home.

Sarah turned out the flashlight and crawled up. I was behind her on the stairs, with my left hand pressed into the prickly, fake carpet. She stepped up, far enough so that from the living room, you would have seen the top of her head through the open door. I watched her click on the flashlight and cut the beam from left to right.

"Jesus," my sister said, as she crashed back into my shoulder. Her elbow rammed my nose. I knew it was going to bleed. "Jesus fucking Christ," she said.

I landed on my left knee, and a pinpoint of deep pain rolled up into my thigh. I pulled Sarah's arm out straight because she wouldn't let go of the flashlight. I stood and aimed the light up through the door. Three drops of blood hit my right wrist.

A dozen honey-colored eyes stared back. Each set seemed attached to a large dark form. Some of the shadows were table-size, while others were as big as blackboards. Sarah's fingers let go and the light made a cracking noise as it bounced down the stairs.

I was sure we'd interrupted something, a seance or a birthday. I expected a voice to croak, "Surprise," before we were blinded by strobes. I sank to my knees and held my nose. It wouldn't stop bleeding. Then, with the streetlight's aid, I began to focus on a set of antlers, outlined against the front window.

Sarah crawled down to get the flashlight and whacked it against her palm. On the fourth try, it brightened. She climbed up and pointed the beam into the living room. Then she made a noise like a deflating inner tube. "Look at this. He's turned into a goddamn taxidermist."

I stood up, and a fully mounted, twelve-point buck stared back at me from the far corner, beneath the clock. Its head was up and its left hoof hung in the air. The thing seemed ready to leap.

"That jerk." Sarah scattered the light across the overstuffed leather furniture. There were elk heads on the other walls. A full-sized doe gazed disinterestedly out the picture window, apparently contemplating the neighbor's yard. A snowy owl hovered over the mantle beside a pair of bobcats. Two raccoons were up on their hind legs by the window, all set to bossa nova.

"I can't believe this," Sarah said. "Taxidermy is disgusting. And it's been going on in our own family?" She turned off the flashlight and handed it to me. Neither of us thought about the fluorescent light in back, until we both remembered it at once. "If someone's here," Sarah said flatly, "they're more worried about us than we are about them."

"I'm not turning on the lights," I said. "Technically speaking, we're breaking and entering."

My sister began making police scanner noises into her cupped palm. "One-niner four, see the man with a report of stuffed animals."

I pointed the flashlight at her as she put her hands by her ears and wiggled her fingers. They looked like antlers. "Oh calm down," Sarah said. "Besides, you're bleeding."

I took my sleeping bag and spent the rest of the night in Sarah's car. It wasn't too bad, with the seats folded down. I don't know why the inside of that house creeped me out so thoroughly. There was too much crowding in. Plus those animals. The fluorescent light turned out to be on a timer.

When I went back inside the next morning, Sarah was still asleep. She had her purple mummy bag pulled across the couch. She woke up with a start, after I sat in Grant's green velvet electric recliner and by accident stepped on the floor switch. When the chair started up it sounded like an outboard motor. I almost spilled the bowl of dry Raisin Bran I'd been picking through.

"Stop it." Sarah's hand seemed stuck in her hair. She sat up, still wearing the black V-neck shirt from last night. I silenced the chair with my heel. "What are you eating?" she asked.

"Stale cereal."

She held her eyelids down with two fingers and rocked back against the cushions.

I waved at the wildlife. "None of this was here when you saw him last?"

"He doesn't do it," she told me. "There are tags at the base of the deer. Some company in Quebec. He must have bought these."

"I already called the lawyer," I said. "He'll see us at eleven. Half an hour."

"Take my car and we can get there by two," Sarah said.

"We could take the van."

My sister sat up slowly. "Look at this," she said, holding her hand out as if presenting me to an imaginary audience. "He is — almost with the program."

"There are cartons of Raisin Bran in the basement," I said. I'd been poking around. The house wasn't half as bad in the light. "He was buying in bulk. You remember when Mom did that for a while?"

"How could you be so freaky last night, and now you're sitting around eating his cereal?" Sarah asked.

I didn't have an answer. It hadn't even occurred to me.

"You should hear his answering machine," she said. "It's incredibly strange. I didn't listen to any calls — yet." She crossed her arms. "Our brother definitely was the kind of personality you could think about for a long, long time."

I went into the yellow wallpapered kitchen to look for the van keys. Everything was exactly positioned. The utensils all had perfect, shiny red handles and just enough space between them. The drawer in every kitchen that's full of string, lost screws, rubber bands, and birthday candle nubs was nearly empty. Only four rolls of electrical tape and a Ziplock bag of twist ties. In a cupboard over the sink, I found a small forest of vitamin bottles, plus kelp pills and wheat germ. The next cupboard door I opened jingled. There were hooks inside and the door was lined with keys. The one marked "BULKHEAD DOOR" hung by a thread of candy-striped telephone wire. I found three sets of Volkswagen keys, some keys for a Dodge, but nothing with Ford emblems. "Let's go, Grant," I said, without thinking.

When I turned around, I saw some health club literature taped up on the refrigerator door. Next to that, a red, white, and blue bull's-eye was held in place by a magnetic Hide-A-Key box. Inside I found two keys. A small patch of adhesive tape on the square one said "EXTRA VAN" in Grant's perfect black ballpoint.

I was sitting on the couch, tossing the van keys up and down and making faces at the animals, when Sarah returned from the bathroom. "Got 'em," I said.

My sister nodded and slipped into her running shoes. She seemed tense. "How hot is it out?"

"The same," I said.

"We've got to comb this place before we leave," she said. "No matter what. Can you promise? There's stuff here about Dad."

FIVE

Back at the very beginning, I always wanted a van. A big one, of course. Nate could never believe this, which I choose to take as yet another Y-chromosome perception problem. It is fairly seventies, I'll admit. I could probably do without an airbrushed, bare-breasted mermaid on the side — but hey, these are details. Besides, the minivans today all look like little lunar rovers. They've lost the aesthetic. They have.

Those were my thoughts as I warmed up Grant's van before our lawyer encounter. I swiveled the command chair around, flicking all the switches. As soon as I had everything I could reach — the tiny fans, the compass, the map light — going full blast, I started searching for the radio stations of my youth. I was interrupted when a tiny orange light beside the speedometer came on. It was there to announce that our main gas tank was nearly empty. Whoops. I flicked a toggle, and presto — on to the auxiliary. How simple.

The air positively thrummed. Nate looked over with a glare. He thought I was wasting time. Please. Of course, this trip didn't start off with the greatest glow for me either. It's small, I know, but the night before we left, my avocado committed suicide. It jumped right off the sill — no note — and sprayed vermiculite onto my sheets. I had to push my feet through the dirt all night, which gave me dusty toes and some very untidy dreams. Lots of digging.

My brother was brooding in a way I couldn't figure out. I knew all of this was affecting him differently, but how far should a person take a thing? I mean, Grant — what did we really lose? It made me feel a little bad to think it, but still, it was almost a relief. That's what I resolved last night, as I sat in Grant's leather love seat, staring back at all the dead animal faces on his walls. My other brother, the dead taxidermist. I couldn't get around that. How did he feel living in a room full of hunting trophies?

Of course, it was all pretty complicated. I knew that, even if I'd decided to block out the magnitude. I'd decided to concentrate on the here and now. That seemed safest. So I did an inventory of the room and felt only a faint flicker of self-pity. Some of Grant's furniture had once been in our big old house in Pompey. The blue step stool in the kitchen with the bubbled plastic seat. It made a searing sound and smelled horrible when Mom melted the seat with a pot of oatmeal. The oak end tables were from Vestal. My father picked those out. Where was he? Why wasn't he here doing this with us? Why wasn't he here to deal with this? We didn't have a clue. It was all too ridiculous to believe.

I knew that if I sat there much longer I'd get misty-eyed, which rarely happens to me. So — with Nate camping out in my dead car, I started to browse. First, I discovered a big splash of letters on the hall floor, beneath the mail slot. They'd piled up like driftwood on Grandmother Ruth's lilac rug. Three electrical engineering journals, *Omni*, *Playboy*, computer magazines, pay-up requests from NYSEG and NYNEX, plus two Visa statements — each with no balance due and stunning credit limits. I left an official-looking letter addressed to Mrs. Grant Scales unopened. The return address was for some medical school's pathology department.

Grant's answering machine was in the downstairs study. Its tiny green message light flashed patiently for me. So — I pressed it. Nobody was there; only some long-distance hang ups. If I were dead, who would be calling me? I wondered. Grant had two outgoing messages. The first began with a door slam. "Grant here. Leave it and I'll call back."

Grant here. Oh please, I thought. As if he were stationed on the front lines. As if. It did get me a little, though, hearing his deep voice. A vague growl. I know people who've called up a machine after someone has died, just to tape the voice. My brother's second message went: "OK, who's bothering me now?" That snapped me back. Enough of this room, I thought.

The Princess phone in the living room rested on its own little Doric pedestal. The dial tone worked, so I called Julie at the bar. She wasn't the best person to talk to and she was working, but she was also the only one I'd taken the time to explain any of this to. I thought some of it, at least, might astound her.

"Where are you?" Julie said, finally.

"Binghamton. I mean Owego. Nearby. We're calling on Grant's bill. How do you like that? Want to hear things?"

"Ugh," she said. "And yes."

I dipped into the awful saga, and something in Julie's breathing, maybe a little too tired, distracted, whatever, told me she still thought that whole big pieces of this were pure invention. I found that annoying. Like I'd finally become a little too strange for even her to understand. It frightened me, but what could I do?

"It *sounds* like long distance," Julie said. "Do you know who was here looking you up like a private detective? Doug."

"Oh." Doug is a problem. No, it's more that Doug and I are a problem. Or I have a problem with Doug. It's all very complicated. You see, this is someone I met through my friend Katie. Doug is sweet, charming, occasionally quite funny, and a bit dreamy. He also invented a bicycle lock a bunch of years ago that makes pots of money. Anyway — we have a pattern. At first we started seeing each other, then I began to get uneasy, sometimes because of some little thing about the future that Doug would suddenly say. "Well, someday we won't have to do that," he'd say. I can't remember the specifics, but I got the feeling that plans had been made for us, for way into the long term. It stopped being fun, and then we weren't seeing each other. That went on for a while, and we both missed the way things had been before. So next, we were living in this kind of Twilight Zone where we'd sleep together once in a while and then be vague about our plans for the next week. You see, Doug is a person who keeps being interested in me long after he should. I can get annoyed by that. But on other days, I wonder if I should just give in. On bad days, that's what I decide. I decide that I should be designing the future with Doug. I should just say, Here it is. I should start cocooning with a vengeance. But I feel sad every time I think that way, as if I'm old, and almost left behind, which I know is silly. It's not as though there isn't a connection. There is. I know that. It's very different with Doug, but that's also hard to explain. Secure maybe? I don't know. But for two months, he was all I could think of. It got exhausting. Soon enough though — and I never admit this to anyone — I always begin imagining little Dougettes scampering underfoot, and that scares the wits out of me.

The phone went clink, and I knew that Julie had rested it between the giant Kahlúa bottles in front of the mirror. Roy Orbison kept singing "Only the Lonely." If Doug weren't so persistent, I thought. If Doug didn't have that gleam in his eye. If he weren't the pursuing type.

I glanced at the deer heads on the walls and thought about how Grant hated indecisiveness, and now Nate ends up paralyzed by it all the time. They fit that way, like lath.

"Still there?" Julie asked.

"Yeah."

"Don't let it tug on your sleeve," she said. "I mean your big brother. You know, when a sibling dies. It has to make you think you're next. You are the oldest now, right?"

"That's not a bit perverse," I said.

"No?"

Grant's van stalled twice before I could coax it down the long driveway. This is an enormous machine, I thought. Bountiful even. It felt like I'd been picked through some strange lottery to pilot a giant tanker. Really. The best part was being up so fantastically high. Like getting a take on a better personality. Inside the van, past the second set of captain's chairs, there was a wardrobe, and at the back, an ugly, plaid couch that converted to a double bed. The outside was still covered with dried mud. It reminded me of clay or peanut butter, mixed with salt. We were just turning into the road when I noticed that the registration and inspection stickers on the windshield had lapsed in February.

"Oh damn," Nate sighed, as soon as I pointed this out. He ran a finger across the glass and sounded so much like our father — it startled me.

The van stalled again, but I kept quiet and glanced out my window. A man by the shrubs next door was spying on us from behind his blue-mirrored sunglasses. He was shirtless, clad in black boots and combat fatigues. The guy also had a pair of ear protectors clamped over his close-cropped hair, and he gripped a screaming Weed Whacker. I waved and drove away. But I kept an eye on him in the mirror and watched as his shoulders jerked sideways a little. It looked like his body was saying to his head: "Those people shouldn't be in *that* van."

By then Nate had burrowed through the glove compartment. He finally dredged up a red folder with the registration and insurance cards. "Everything's out of date," he said. "We're committing a felony. You know that."

"Oh my, big trouble." I smiled. "Come on — this is nothing. He was our brother. You've got far too much middle-class, property-value, law-and-order baggage weighing you down, kiddo."

"Baggage," Nate said.

But I had a quick vision. I suddenly saw us rolling up to this lawyer's office in a gleaming, shiny van, as opposed to the muddy thing we were traveling in. That van was probably going to go to someone else anyway, I reasoned. Why not drive it around sparkling while we could? I explained this to Nate. "Mr. Lawyer can wait," I proposed.

My brother, by then, had walked to the back of the van with both arms out. He seemed to be trying to balance between two opposing and powerful futures. He crouched and opened a few cabinet doors. I knew he couldn't see where we were going. So — a minute later I scooted into a little strip mall.

"Look," Nate shouted. "Grant has three cans of Bud, an open half pint of apricot brandy, two splits of champagne, and a box of Grape Nuts, all in here. Everything's secured with miles of Velcro." He brought the cereal box up front and spun in the captain's chair. "I don't think this van actually belongs to our brother."

"Oh?" I held out my hand. "Who else would stick everything down with Velcro? There's truth in symptoms."

Nate filled my palm with cereal and went on sorting out the lumpy chunks. He didn't seem to notice that we were rolling through a parking lot.

Our car wash was called Scrububble Your Buggy. It was stashed away in its own little corner of the strip mall. A red and blue cartoon car with oversize headlights for eyes winked down at us. I could scare up only four of the five quarters we needed, and Nate announced that washing the van was a "very bad" idea. Oddly enough, though, he did hand over the last quarter. I positioned us in the bay and got out. The coins rattled in my palm like dice.

"If it's still covered with salt, no one will see we're out of date," Nate complained. He had to lean out the window to do this.

"It looks like it's been dipped," I said. "Have you forgotten? It's July. Like this, we're going to attract attention." It's strange, my brother always has the germ of an idea, but he never thinks a thing all the way through. I'm the one who's left to plan everything out. Whether or not I carry through — that's another question. "I'll leave the license plates and the windshield dirty. Will that do?"

My brother got out and leaned against the vacuum canisters like a haughty model. Meanwhile, I made all the appropriate selections. Spotless or rinse? Soap brush or nozzle? The wand hissed. We had three minutes and twenty-two seconds — according to the clock. Then the police pulled up.

Nate frowned and his mouth popped open. The policeman drove halfway into the bay. I guess to prevent our escape. He turned on the lights. Red and blue flashes whipped through the fog. I couldn't stop with the wand or I'd lose the quarters.

Our cop had on a white short-sleeve shirt, but his head seemed far too small for his chest. Nate stepped through the mist to greet him. I couldn't hear what they were saying, but I did see my brother hand over his Massachusetts driver's license. The cop glanced at both sides, pointed at the license plates and then at me.

Oh no, Buster. Not me — I had to scurry to keep that wand engaged. Nate continued talking. I heard him call the cop "sir" at least once. I am habitually bad with cops.

Nate began gesturing frantically back toward Owego. It was funny, sort of. But then their chat was interrupted by a squawk from the police car's radio. A woman's voice chanted some numbers through the speaker in the cruiser's grille, and — like magic — the cop hopped back into his little car and drove away. When he turned on the siren, my quarters ran out.

Afterward, my brother was almost beaming — practically giggly. He looked like he was getting a kick out of this, though he'd never be able to admit it. The neighbor with the Weed Whacker had decided that we were stealing the van, Nate reported. So all puffed up with civic responsibility, the guy had called the police. The cop matched Nate's last name from his driver's license to the name he'd heard over the radio and seemed almost satisfied. Nate had just told him that

Grant was dead when they were interrupted. "I left a little shake in my voice," he said.

"Very good," I told him. "Have you ever considered acting?"

I was almost perky as we arrived in Johnson City. You know, another hare-brained adventure, another disaster narrowly averted, all that. The lawyer's office was way up in a new smoked-glass and brick building near some mall. I spent an extra minute in the parking lot trying to find the perfect pull-through space. Those always do feel like such a bargain.

The elevator opened up on a tiny waiting room where the receptionist sat behind a slit in a window. Nate rolled his shoulders like an athlete remembering how to loosen up. Then he announced us. The auburn-haired woman behind the Plexiglas smiled back. "Sure," she said. "Robert is waiting."

I felt jittery as she led us past the long walls of casebooks. All those thick histories of confrontations, I thought, as we finally reached Robert Lathers's open office door. He kept looking out the window until the receptionist tapped the door frame. Then he whirled, as if he'd forgotten something, and moved toward us a bit too quickly. I liked his suit. It was crisp and charcoal-colored. Even if he didn't wear it well.

"Finally. Finally," he said. "Sarah Alice?" He reached for my hand and I thought, my, you are a little unctuous. Besides, people who use my middle name always annoy me. It's my mother's. Every time I hear it I want to curtsy. I smiled pleasantly.

"Nathan." The lawyer pumped my brother's hand and moved behind the desk. We jumped our chairs up by the arms. His desk was clean, aside from one letter and three stick-on notes arranged so that the space in the middle formed a right triangle. I decided our Mr. Lathers might have a Post-it problem.

"I'm glad to see you both," he said. "Shouldn't we just start?"

We all nodded.

"I was indeed saddened, after seeing the notice in the paper that Grant had passed on," Lathers said. "And I feared that there might not have been a will. I knew your brother had revoked an earlier one, and I was not looking forward to the complications of a death intestate. But a former colleague of your brother's at work remembered hearing Grant mention that he did indeed have a will, which we eventually found in a safety deposit box."

Nate looked uncomfortable. He couldn't seem to get settled.

"Finding you two, that was another matter," Lathers explained. "A neighbor in Owego has been keeping an eye on the property and taking care of the lawns, and with his help, as well as with the investigators' assistance, I was able to locate an old address book. The neighbor, in fact, actually found your brother. I was a friend of Grant's, you see, not terribly close, but we fished some. Well, once. Your brother was a difficult person to know."

The lawyer began playing with a red pencil. I kept wishing he would stop.

"I eventually handled some arrangements for him," Lathers said. "The house and so forth. But the document before us was prepared by another attorney. It supersedes one written two years earlier, in which Grant left everything to your father. Part of my surprise came from being appointed executor."

He caressed the letter with his pinky. I shivered a little, from the air conditioning, I guessed. The here and now, I thought. Concentrate on that.

"It is strange," Lathers said, "that in the time I knew him, Grant never mentioned you two."

That, suddenly, made me tired. Yes, this was all a mess, a barbed and lousy mess. So — get on with it. I began looking at Lathers's walls. New York Law, class of 1970. A "Daddy" drawing with lavender crayon flowers mounted behind glass. I heard his voice say that Grant had donated his body to science.

When I looked back, Lathers had unfolded the letter and was holding it up like a show-and-tell project. He began to read aloud. "Duly recorded, witnessed. Signed on May 12, 1986, here in the City of Binghamton, County of Broome. My last will and testament, Grant Wilson Scales."

He began listing the items that were included in the estate — real property, insurance policies — but I couldn't pay attention. Instead, I had such a curious sensation. I seemed to be floating, but in a hazy and unpleasant way. I tried to ignore it. I tried to concentrate on the room around me. I tried to hold on to the idea that Grant had set this all up. I had a feeling that the joke was about to become clear.

"To be divided jointly among said surviving people, Sarah Alice Scales, Nathan Raymond Scales, in equal shares."

My brother took this without a flinch.

I felt it instantly, the wave of anxiety spreading across my skin from a dark spot somewhere inside. My fingers tingled. My heart paused longer than necessary. The picture before me began to flutter, only around the edges. I watched my shoes. For a tiny second, I imagined the prescription on my dresser at home. The blue, octagonal pills which I decided not to bring. Not unlike the way I'd decided to misplace the therapist's name — a woman who deals in panic as a disorder. All this before the pain. It's a feeling like you've been running too hard, and the bottom of your world has finally slipped open.

Grant tells no one we exist and yet leaves us everything.

I heard the words "months before distribution" while I stood up. I seemed to be towering over the room, watching while Nate slowly unfolded his list of prepared questions. The ones he thought up last night in the car. Someone said there were no federal death taxes for estates under $600,000. "We must complete an inventory. We must—"

I left. My fingers slipped across the spines of the red and gold law books in the hall. Everything moved so slowly. A black leather couch appeared at the end of the hall.

Why did he have to give us things? Why? So we would remember? So from now on we couldn't make a move without thinking of him? Or was this the joke? Was it that he wanted us to do battle? Did he expect that?

I pushed my back into the couch. It helped with the fluttering. Then I remembered that Grant had never mentioned my father. Why did he change the will? Was my father dead and was Grant the only one who knew? How could we *not* know? What absurd people we were to live this way, I thought.

I stared at the tiny Norfolk pine in the corner and decided it needed to be repotted. Something was very, very wrong.

SIX

By the time Sarah and I left the lawyer's office, the sun had whacked through the haze, and the fresh heat beyond the air conditioning made me squint. Everything felt untouchable and once removed, as though we'd been mired too long in some stranger-than-life home movie. There seemed to be no clear plan, so I took the keys and assumed that we were returning to the house, which yesterday Sarah started calling Grant's Tomb. My sister stayed slumped in the other captain's chair nearly the whole way back.

"What happened in the office?" I asked, after a while.

"Nothing," she said. "Or, it was like this little episode. One that hasn't come up in — ages. I don't want to talk about it," she told me. "Maybe it was that I hadn't eaten for a while."

Sarah put her hand over her eyes. I kept noticing the blue and white *Binghamton Press and Sun Bulletin* paper boxes at the end of each driveway, and I thought, if I didn't have the job I did, that wouldn't happen.

"Hey, you were almost nice," my sister said wearily. "With us it's always weird. I'm older, but you're responsible. I never know who's supposed to act like what. We do everything backwards."

The sturdy wooden sign set in the field on my right said: "Welcome to Historic Owego. Founded 1787."

"So." Sarah yawned. "If Grant's donated himself to science, does that mean we have to do something with what's left over? With Grant the cadaver?"

I checked the rearview mirror. I didn't know, or want to know. "That's probably in the portfolio," I suggested. "Like under C for corpse."

Sarah glanced at the packet on the floor of the van, but she didn't smile.

As we left, Lathers handed me a fat, pinkish cardboard portfolio stuffed with Grant's papers. "The house keys are in a white envelope," he explained. "The rest you'll get through in good time. Let me know before you leave the area." I thought, as he said this, that he sounded a little too cheerful, all things considered.

"When you went out of the office," I said, "Lathers told me that when they found Grant the alarm on his watch was going off. He'd been lying on the floor, beeping, for a whole day. It's kind of creepy to think about."

Sarah looked out the window. "The really wicked thing," she said, "is that because of this, we're going to have to deal with Grant forever. I hate that." She peered down Grant's former street with a hard stare. "What's the total?" she wanted to know. "I missed the total. How much is all this pathetic stuff he gave us worth?"

"You can't exactly tell," I explained. "Once they take taxes and legal fees, and since it depends on if we sell the house."

"If?" Sarah cocked her knee against the dashboard.

"The life insurance is about $189,000," I said. "Plus the canoe, the stuffed animals, the property. I guess there's money market stuff, a bunch of computer stocks, the van. That alone is like twelve thousand, even used." I couldn't make the figures add up or stick together. I didn't want to, because then there'd be a number, and that would be one more thing I'd have to be grateful about, forever.

"The van's mine," Sarah announced. "I'll give you a bobcat for it."

I had to maneuver around my sister's broken car before I could turn into the driveway. The Subaru waited at the edge of the lawn like an uninvited stray. As I turned off the engine I kept staring through the white glare of the windshield at my brother's absurd pseudo-gingerbread house, knowing all along that it was still full of unexplained Grantisms. Somehow, that stung. After years of trying to forget all of this, all the Grant stuff, he floats away and presto, we're left marooned in the middle of it. At least that's the way it felt.

"We should drive back now," I announced. "This afternoon. We're both working tomorrow night, this van's carrying 109,000 miles already. It could explode, or anything, before we got back. We'll grab the stuff, burger, and bolt."

Sarah stopped examining the tree line above the gable. "We just got here," she said. "Besides — 'burger' is not a verb." She reached over and plucked the keys from the ignition, then she took the white envelope with the house keys out of Grant's portfolio. "Anyway," she said, "there's so much stuff to go through." She got out, tore apart the envelope, and dropped little bits of it across the lawn. My sister was all the way to the front steps before I decided to follow along. She was still trying to outfox the front door lock when I came up behind her. I kept thinking about the legions of Fuller Brush men and Girl Scouts who'd probably waited for an opening on that very spot. My sister eventually beat the lock, and disappeared into the cool, stale air of Grant's study.

I wandered through the remaining rooms. That whole house made me ornery. Even simply sitting in the driveway and looking at it had given me a headache, like the kind you get from spending all day trying to speak a foreign language. Eventually I took my place in the recliner and scrutinized Grant's surroundings. I examined the functional venetian blinds, the leather couch, and as I did, I could hear my brother booming in with scrolls of instant rationalizations. Telling me how well leather wears. Why there were cases of paper towels in the basement. Why there was a stupid battery-powered biofeedback machine and a doctor's-office scale in the upstairs bathroom.

It was too much. I closed my eyes and tried to white out my mind, while Sarah went on playing detective in the study. If I'd known how to meditate, that would have been a good thing. After a while I started to drift and I realized that lately, whenever I'd mentioned our father, Sarah's face would pick up the same determined look, as though she could will herself to see satellites. But determined to do what? I wondered. Find him? Sure, if we're psychic enough. I had no idea where he might be. A year after I came out to collect my stuff from the house in Vestal — right before Grant bought the Owego place — I had to call my brother about something. I think I owed him money. At the time, Grant said Dad had moved to Philadelphia some six months before, because he had a new sales territory. Grant said he didn't have the phone number. That surprised me, though I've never known how much of Grant to believe. My first reaction was, well, if my father doesn't bother to keep up, even to tell us that he's moved, why should I care? Why should I bother? It was lazy, I knew that, but it also seemed to relieve me of a kind of responsibility. Yet while I sat in my brother's chair, it seemed entirely possible that Grant had been lying. It seemed likely that he was only trying to juggle us around in some grand and petty manipulation. If Grant had told my father where we were, wouldn't my father have tried to get in touch?

But my sister — lately my sister has developed this idea of family as an overriding archetype. All of a sudden, too. It's something like a myth, or worse. We have it, we're connected by biology, therefore we should actually be a family, in the Norman Rockwellian sense. Her thinking, I knew, went like this: Grant, the obstructionist, was beyond the frame, so we should put the other pieces back in place. Pound them in until they fit. Big deal for biology, I thought; there simply weren't enough pieces.

The root of everything, as I've always known, involves my mom. That's not a mystery, it's only one more unlivable idea that I get to carry around every day. How could you ever really think about it? The whole thing slips away whenever I try.

My mother was very sick and then she was shot. It was a freak death, a dumb death, and it happened a week before Thanksgiving, in 1969. At the time we lived in Pompey, near Syracuse. It still is a field-pocked, almost rural kind of neighborhood, with shingled, walnut-stained ranch houses set down in lawns that otherwise would have been fields. The bullets were 30.06 slugs, and there were two. Either somebody from up on the hill behind the house decided that my mother, who was walking in the low brush past our property line, was a deer, or both shots were strays, fired off at a great distance, and one happened to hit her. From the way the first slug drilled into the back of the house, that's what the state police concluded.

The things I want to remember about my mom now come back only in fragments, but a lot of that particular day I can pull up at will. It's freaky. I was in third grade, and at school we were practicing a play that involved lobsters. In the early afternoon they called me down to the main office and said that my father would pick me up, though no one told me why. I had to wait for hours, sitting in a small green chair, swinging my legs and staring at the pale orange walls that were covered with cutouts of fat gobblers. Kids would peek in on their way outside and stare. The buses all left, and Mrs. Gibbons, the secretary with heavy arms, hovered over me. She knew about our "family situation" from the times I'd been late or out because my mom was sick. And that's what I thought, that my mom only had to go back to the hospital.

My mother laughed and smoked Lucky Strikes and developed lung cancer. It sounds simple, condensed like that, but when this all happened she'd just found out, and they didn't know how long she might have. I remember, even before she'd started going to the hospital, the times when she'd chase me with a Ping-Pong ball gun. I'd hide in the bushes and she would have to stop, bend over, and straighten up slowly, coughing and holding out her blue sweater by the wooden buttons, as if that might allow her to breathe. "I'm OK," she'd say. "I'm OK."

When our station wagon arrived with the headlights on, I saw Sarah, puffy-eyed and crying, in the front seat. I remember her turning around to unlock the back door. My father said he'd wanted to tell us together but it couldn't wait. Then he told me, and said that we couldn't go home. We were going to stay at the neighbors, and he'd brought some of our clothes in brown paper shopping bags.

It happened on the first day of doe season, after a light snow. I remember kicking through the fluff that morning as I waited for the bus. The snow picked up off the lawns and blew away like feathers as I stamped the ground. Canada geese flew south all morning. My mother had been walking fifty yards from the back porch, through some bushes that eventually gave way to maples and, after that, a few diseased elms. She wore a shearling coat and blue knitted mittens. The first slug hit the back corner of our house and stayed hidden in the shingles until they cut it out later. The second hit her as she turned to face the woods, tracing back the path of the original sound. My father came home late in the morning to eat lunch, and he found her. She'd been outside for an hour or more. A slug can travel five miles before it's entirely spent. I didn't know these details then.

But I understood, I knew that this was the worst. It was the bottom. And only sometimes now do I still feel cheated. Only sometimes does it feel as though a whole set of opinions that I'd like to have are missing. But when I drive, especially around that part of the country, late in the fall, when the woods are that same bare-leafed gray, my stomach can still knot up.

I've never known what my father really thought about all this. Though how could you ever reconcile it? For years afterward, he would be doing something, washing his hands or working on a car he'd decided to restore, when he would just stand and stare, until one of us came by to distract him. He once told me that it didn't always feel as though she was gone, only that she was somewhere over in the next room.

I was out of Grant's chair and pacing by then. I was even half thinking about going for a long walk. But that neighbor, who'd nearly had us arrested earlier, was still at it with the Weed Wacker. He'd probably want to frisk me or something.

When I glanced into the study, I saw blue file folders with bills and brochures for nursing homes spread across Grant's maroon carpet. Sarah had taken her running shoes off. They were on top of a green vinyl checkbook that was half crammed into a big padded mailer. She was stretched across the nubbly leather couch and held a large red photo album across her chest like a pillow. She didn't notice me. She kept looking out the window, at a blond girl one yard over, who was setting up a trampoline. I'd seen those pictures in the photo album before — white-bordered black and white snapshots of my parents at their wedding in Connecticut, a trip to the New York World's Fair, Grant as a baby taking a bath and feeling his way through a Chinese dinner.

I nearly interrupted. I nearly said something sharp about getting back to Boston, but Sarah seemed so far away that I stopped. I shouldn't, I thought. I need to be patient. It is amazing, really, that she can be the way she is, going all the time, considering how we've grown up. It's like you could look back on all this and say what a shitty childhood, and that alone would be a more than valid excuse for everything else that never worked out.

In the kitchen, I clicked open a few more unexplored cupboards. On the lower level, beside the sink, I found an unopened case of Genesee Cream Ale. I took one of the warm green and gold cans and emptied it into a heavy tumbler, remembering as I did that Grant's obit was probably out in the living room, hidden in that triangular mound of newspapers by the front door. Something about my brother's obit waiting there, with no one even bothering to look for it, bothered me.

I knelt by the pile and started tossing the compact bundles, each one rubber-banded shut, over my shoulder to the center of the rug. I was looking for the next to last week in June. On my first guess, June 22, I discovered that the paper's only true obits were paid advertisements. I was sure there wouldn't be one of those.

The tiny death notices, which they probably ran for free, I finally located on the "Fast Facts" page, in with the deed transfers and births. On my next try I found it: "Grant Scales, 42, of Owego, formerly of Vestal, died Tuesday." My brother was in boldface, nestled between a discount shoe ad and a savings bank promotion. The jump head for the news story underneath said: "Major Questions Remain."

And that I softly repeated, as though somebody could hear.

SEVEN

Grant here. And I'm dead. You think you're surprised. All this and you're surprised? Think about me: I'm boxed.

That's right. Think about me — for a change. Imagine my distress at watching all this spiral out without being able to utter a lone syllable in my own defense. Imagine my discomfort, watching those two blunder about, making it sound as though I never did a single thing for anyone on the planet. There's only so much a body can put up with. They don't like my phone message. They don't like my crime-deterring wildlife collection. They don't like my electric lounger. They don't like my choice of beer under the sink. Please.

After all I've done and handed over — they're not even outwardly affected. They laugh. But they're wrong about everything in general and me in particular. You want an opinion? One unit is a cautious wimp, prone to mistakes and overcalculation, while the other is a jumpy flake, someone who will never get on track and finish a damn thing. And these are only a few of the items currently pissing me off.

In fact, why the hell not, let's get down to the real version and talk about my story. It's as valid as theirs. Maybe more so. You decide. Yeah, yeah, I suppose you're more worried about how I got here — the big event. Sure you are. Everyone is. You wouldn't be there if you couldn't wonder.

Point of fact number one: I had a coronary occlusion — not a heart attack. There is a difference. My circuits misfired. No symptoms. No warning. I shorted out at forty-two. It runs in the family and now — I'm your living proof.

But you'd like more. I know. Everybody wants more. OK, I'd come home from softball, from a practice game, and there I was in that big soft recliner. I was feeling pretty good, as I'd had a few decent cuts, a few good pokes at bat. The motor was on, massaging my back, and I was watching *Entertainment Tonight,* happy as dirt, at least until the entertainment actually started. It felt like some giant old bastard dancing on my chest with cleats. Tap, step, and boom.

I knew what it was. I knew who was knocking. I stood up, but the dancing bastard knocked me back. Knocked me down to the floor. I can't remember the hurt, which is a good thing, but I do remember deciding that I'd better find that damn Princess phone pretty quick and punch in a few emergency digits.

Even so, I couldn't move. In a second or two, touching those buttons felt like such a tiny, distant, and hard-to-comprehend course of action. The voice telling me to do it sounded like it was coming from a short-wave radio, and it kept slipping out over the ocean. There was something inevitable about it. I was thinking, you know, you don't have to worry about all those damn snag-headed details any more, that pyramid of stuff you face every day, it's — immaterial. At the same time, I'm looking down at that guy there on the floor, like it was a movie. Poor guy, I thought, he isn't going to make it to the phone. And you know what? He didn't.

Then the final split, and that's damn hard to describe. My body on one plane and the rest of me, the whatever of it all, hurtling out in perhaps a thousand directions at once. I was heading toward something entirely different.

But I don't want to go into all that. I can't, really, except to suggest that the first part is pretty close to what everyone says, only with a few variations. There's the tunnel of light, the beckoning relatives, the blah blah blah. I had a big chorus singing a Stones song, like "You Can't Always Get What You Want" but with different words. It's true, hearing is the last to go. We've got guides and stuff, we review the circumstances, then you see the movie. Hell, I'm having an OK enough time — all things considered.

Anyway. I'm sure *you* still have concerns. Major questions unresolved? You probably want stories. Most likely you want answers. Neat knots of knowledge. The building blocks of personal history. But remember, if I do tell fables, they'll be correct. I'm the one you should come to for answers.

Like this — point of fact number two: I did not jump Little Nate from the garage rafters as he backed out of the driveway his very first time. He'd definitely driven before. Several times even. Really, what can you do about other people's memories? They're always coming up with the convenient picture. Use what fits and forget the rest. But you know what really frosted my ass? Nate comparing me to that dead guppy. Maybe he didn't mean it exactly, but you certainly could read into it.

So where does this get us? It gets us to the beginning. And you can't understand a bit of this without first listening to what I have to say. In fact, right now I could use one of those little snapshot books, the kind with the tooled leather cover and sticky plastic pages of photos. I'd open it up slowly and we'd have some lightly orchestrated flashback music, a little soft focus. But rules are rules. We always had rules in Our Family. And what were the consequences otherwise? Growing up in anarchy?

Let us begin with Ray. Let us begin with my father, Raymond Scales. What should you know about him? That's much better than ranting on about me. My father grew up in Vermont, near St. Johnsbury, working for his father, who sold cars. That was where he learned to fix engines. That was where he learned to talk. That was where he learned to charm friends on a dime. OK, but jump back one space more. James Scales was my grandfather, who happened to be an alcoholic. He'd pass out at the dinner table and my grandmother would let it go. She called them "sleeping fits." He was a quiet, gentle drunk, and he died in 1948, one year after I arrived. From what I know, he spent his life trying to bend the rules and help people out at the same time. He was always giving handouts. My grandmother, who was from Halifax, said that during the Depression she discovered a chalk mark on the side of their porch. It was there to tell people drifting through that their house was a good place to stop. During Prohibition, my grandfather became a pretty famous minor league bootlegger. People couldn't afford to buy cars so, to make money, he would drive into Quebec and bring truckloads of Canadian Club, or something like that, back across the dirt roads. He always took my father along, every time, because it wouldn't look quite so suspicious with a ten-year-old in the cab. Ray knew what was up. And Ray developed a taste for adventure.

Interesting, you say, but how did we end up living outside of

Syracuse? It was after the war, and my father went to Syracuse University on the GI Bill. They had me while he was still taking classes. So, instead of becoming an architect, he settled down to be a draftsman. Maybe that seemed safe, after what he'd seen overseas, but he regretted it. Ray also knew construction and building, from his time in the army, and during his draftsman days he'd pick up spare change working for a company that did property assessments. It set him up for later on.

Years passed. I grew up, went to school, then college, and there I was in my junior year at RPI, a week before Thanksgiving, when The Incident descended upon us. I mean, we knew she had cancer, and in a way that can give you some space, a time to get set for what was coming, if not exactly for what came. I couldn't believe any part of it when they called to tell me. Nate and Sarah were wandering around dazed, and I was there thinking: This is it, the family emergency, forget school. But it was also 1969, and I thought I couldn't quit without getting drafted.

My mother's funeral was on a Tuesday, in Connecticut, where her parents lived, and they carried it out amid hail and lightning. We went through that day like we were wearing blindfolds. Then we were back in Syracuse, in our living room, and Ray announced that he'd be gone for a few days. Gone? I was late for school already, but I stayed, and the next Wednesday, at dinner, my father came into the kitchen. His wool coat was soaked, and he spread himself out on the blue stool. He'd been in Binghamton with his brother Stan, sorting everything out. So what did those two come up with? Sell everything and start over. Stan had a partnership in an insurance company, and he'd offered my father a job. Ray and Stan had even gone around looking at houses. Next, he let Stan talk him into buying this not-quite-finished split-level up on a muddy hill in Vestal, just west of Binghamton. Anyway, my father sat in our kitchen in Pompey and said he couldn't be around the place anymore. We had to move. We had to run away.

I was probably the only one who could have done anything about it. Maybe. But could you blame the guy? At any rate, I had to get back to school. By then, school was a kind of puritanical mission on my part. I knew my GPA down to six digits. I returned to Troy, got deeply into

Boolean algebra, punched up trillions of computer cards, and became hooked on the power of the machine.

That whole move annoyed me no end. Why pack everything up and tear it all out? It made no sense whatsoever. Even though it was only a couple of hours away, I didn't go down to visit until the summer. But I did go. I got a job at IBM, in Endicott, right in the neighborhood. And finding that job, so close to home, proved to be my undoing. Say I'd gone to California — but no, not me, not Mr. Altruism.

I thought I still had to worry about the draft, until a family-hardship exemption came through. My father, to his everlasting credit, thought this was wonderful. All wars are evil, he'd say, but some more than others. He'd had enough to know. He'd started World War II in an army statistics group. He was sent to England and then switched to an engineering unit that was already in France. Ray went in as a replacement and got out one night when a Jeep he was riding in flipped. He ended up with some broken ribs, a broken leg, a punctured lung, and a long ride home. My father came back happy as a clam at being alive. And afterward he was marked, energized and saddened in that peculiar way where nothing ever after would quite match up. His luck at being alive, he told me, only began to wear off decades later — about the time things started happening to my mom.

But we're way out of order here. Let us get back on track. So, as soon as Ray moved everyone to Vestal, he went to work peddling peace of mind — life insurance — for about eighteen months, until he had a falling-out with Stan. I never knew what that was about. I don't know if they did either. It happens in my father's family. Those two split, and Ray switched companies, starting over as an insurance adjuster. Suddenly he was traveling all the time. Three, sometimes four nights a week, investigating claims and writing out checks at the scene. He adjusted for wildfires, flash floods, lightning, hail, and every other act of God. The guy thrived on it, to the point where he became a disaster coordinator. He tracked disaster up and down the East Coast, and then all over. He became an expert at determining total loss.

I came home that first summer and ended up playing part-time uncle. Grant, take care of it. And like the major dummy I was, I did. Long term, it took a deal to get me into the role full-time. I still had a year of school to account for, and my father paid that off and all my loans. But the real deal came into effect only later on. For hanging back, he gave me the house in Vestal. It was equity, and like a dummy, I went for it. Who knows why? And those two are reaping the ultimate benefit of my generous endowment — though none of that has yet made it into their dense skulls. Even at this vast distance I remain influential.

A year later, I've graduated. I'm living at the house and continuing on in my job for the big business machine company. I'm just a low-life transfer designer. At work I'm looking things up in books, driving home, buying groceries, and secretly scanning the parents' magazines in the checkout line. Grim indeed.

You see, the dream goes something like this: You hook up with someone wonderful and start that pretty little nuclear family. You start clean. A blank sheet of paper. You don't have to sort out every tangled idea in your siblings' lives. If I'd been given absolute authority, that might have been one thing. But Ray would come home with those big smack-happy entrances of his in the middle of the week. Fireworks would go off. Look, he's bringing sparklers! The giver of key chains, state decals, and cap pistols. It's always best being a dad at a distance. Meanwhile, in real life, I'd be spending all week play-acting as Zeus, the evil enforcer. I felt the responsible cords of family life tightening down every damn day.

Do you think I wanted things to go in this direction? Do you think I intended to run that kludge of a household? You know, the worst job in engineering — ever — is knowingly designing a kludge, which when I came up, meant fixing something quick and dirty in the wake of an earlier screwup. But that's what I did, for years.

Here's something more to think about. You know, people in general can't imagine a world without them in it. I could. I could see it. But talk about funerals though, what kills you is the casket. Two thousand for a medium-price oak container and a cheap vault. Plus, $54 for the flower car, a c-note for the hearse, $95 for the registry, and those are just the basics. Get shipped out on a plane, and you'll cost more as cargo than you would as a breathing passenger. Screw that. I had myself donated.

I suppose all this has made me a bit of a fatalist. So now — I'm a dead fatalist, possibly the best kind. And those two don't like my phone message. Well, don't answer the damn phone if you don't know who it's going to be.

So, any questions?

EIGHT

The strangest thing happened Friday night. I was in the pilot seat, heading Grant's van back to old Boston while Nate slept. We were riding the Mass Pike and it wasn't even close to dark when I crept up on a line of maybe twenty-five cars. They were all in the right lane with their lights on, and nobody wanted to pass. It was very curious — until I figured it out. My brother and I were following a funeral.

That shook me up — a little, but I didn't let it show. The trouble was, and I should have suspected it, I had always imagined that some long day in the future Grant would come around. I had this idea that we'd all be old retired people and he would finally wake up and apologize. Or else we just wouldn't care any more. I had even almost planned on having a chance to resolve some of this with him, so it could finally float away. But now that was impossible and that fact irritated me no end. It also made me deeply anxious. Why hadn't I fixed some of this up before? I wondered. Why hadn't I simply tied everyone in my silly family down and told them how to behave?

After I dropped Nate off and got home to Somerville, I spilled everything I'd carted back out across my bed. Except I was very careful to leave the portfolio with Grant's papers off by itself in the corner, in my director's chair. A few of the things on the bed were small: an almond-colored box from the Philippines, full of my mother's baubly earrings, a wrist strand of fake pearls. I also brought back the red photo album and half a dozen trays of slides. When Nate wasn't looking, I even stole all the Etta James and Aretha Franklin tapes from Grant's collection.

I put on Etta and flipped through some photo pages, until I got stuck at one of my father and me at a racecourse. I had no idea who would have taken it, but I was in junior high and we were at Watkins Glen, standing near the pit area. I remembered that my father had wanted to take Nate instead. But my brother had the chicken pox, so Dad had to talk me into going. "I don't get it," he said, when I didn't seem interested. "We're a car family. This is what we do." That was true, we had gone to all kinds of races — jalopies on dirt tracks, demolition derbies, auto thrill shows, anything — for years and years. "None of your friends will see you," my father said. "No one will know." I finally decided to go along, I think, when he implied that there would be lots of fashionable-looking Europeans in the stands. I do remember wandering around behind him and being amazed at all the things he knew or appeared to know. He's always seemed competent in ways that I have a hard time imagining. First, there are all those facts — little bits of knowledge that seem unconnected — and then I find out he actually does know how to do all sorts of things, like rewiring the kitchen lights or making snowshoes. It sort of drove me crazy, even then. But going to that race was one of the last things we did together. Sometime after that, I think my father sort of gave up because he couldn't figure out what to do with me — but there were still times when we got along. I flipped through more pages and watched his dark eyebrows turn bushier with time. I would recognize him. I would.

When the phone rang at 12:45, I knew it was Doug. Almost all the messages on the machine had been from Doug. He was, I gathered, in the midst of a definition crisis. As in, he hoped to define exactly where we were — in terms of us. I didn't.

Doug asked to meet somewhere so we could discuss things. He'd already picked Saturday, because he was going to be out of town for most of the next week. Fine, fine, I said. But Doug kept saying how sorry he was about my brother's death. I guess Julie had mentioned it when he showed up at the bar, and that was unsettling. Sympathy in general I find unsettling. What was there for Doug to be sorry about?

"Don't," I said. "What I mean is — it's OK. But I did just get back, and things here are a little stringy."

When Doug asked about my car — since he already knew it wasn't much good for long trips — I told him I'd left it in Grant's driveway. I said I was throwing it out. Which was true. Doug hummed. Then for our meeting he suggested a "neutral" spot, like the aquarium, which was downtown near the tourist mess of Faneuil Hall and seemed inconvenient for both of us. Why? Were we ducking surveillance?

Were we worried about being bugged? Doug said no. He even laughed. He only wanted to be doing something while we "talked." I hate summit meetings.

So — I agreed and hung up and sat there cross-legged, turning the glistening picture pages, until I got to a color shot my father took of Nate and me in Vestal. We're in the driveway, theoretically washing cars, but it looks much more like a water fight. The picture is far too bright, as if the sun that day had been extra strong. But we both appear to be incredibly happy. Was it only for that moment? I wondered. Is that how we got through this? One little moment after another?

Soon Grant's portfolio began giving me the beady eye from the director's chair across the room. Heavy as it was, I spilled the contents out across the floor: the documents, the brown mailer, the credit cards, the AAA card, the newspaper with his obituary. The pieces spread across the carpet.

Several seconds after I'd sat down on the floor and started digging through the stuff I'd only slammed together as we were leaving, I found the checks — all seven of them. They were sky blue and cancelled, and made out to Willow Meadows at Sandy Run Inc. A residential complex in Crestwood, Missouri. The first was for $6,000 and the last, dated eight months later, was for $4,000. Grant had signed every one. I also found a contract for Willow Meadows in my father's name, but with Grant's signature. Both parties had agreed to pay a nonrefundable $25,000 entrance fee. The checks stopped with a cryptic letter from Uncle Stan, written a couple of weeks before Grant died. It was a copy of an agreement between Grant and Stan where Grant would hand over a chunk of Dad's assets for "future care." The amount was to be named later. This looked like Grant was signing off and turning the whole mess over to Stan.

My stomach got fluttery. Residential complex sounded suspiciously like a nursing home. Why would that be necessary? What horrible thing didn't I know?

I stood up and walked around the apartment. Then I went back to look at the checks another time. From the brochure I dug out of the pile, it looked like this nursing home had a custodial care wing, a residential wing, and a beauty parlor. Grant had even clipped a schedule of activities to the back: St. Louis Cardinals games, shopping adventures, bowling. There was an article from some money magazine, explaining that Medicaid only pays if you're destitute, so most people turn their assets over to the kids before it's time to go in. I started to shiver. This *was* what I'd suspected, back when I began going through all this stuff in Grant's den. But it was far worse to actually see it.

Grant had always known where our father was, I thought. Always. He had simply refused to give us the information. It was so petty and mean that I was more dumbfounded than anything. Why would my father have put up with this? What could be so wrong that he would have agreed to it? Did he agree to it? Did he turn all of his money over to Grant? Is that what we've inherited? It seemed impossible.

But he is somewhere, I thought. He is.

I was restless — all night. I kept pretending to sleep, but the sharp feather ends of my so-called down pillows would slip through and poke me in the cheek. At 3:30 I sat up and actually thought about calling that Willow-whatever place. I imagined asking for Raymond Scales. I wondered what my voice would sound like when I said his name. But I didn't call, because I could feel that blind halo of rage building up again. What was Grant thinking?

I needed a long and quiet bath, I decided. I found some Chardonnay in the refrigerator that had only been uncorked for a day or two and lay back in the tub as the water covered my knees. When I was little, sliding all the way under used to be one of my favorite things. My hair would float straight out. My ears filled up and the world became this safe and muffled place.

Would my mother have seen the way out of this? I wondered. What would she have done? Would she approve of the way my life has gone so far? Would she approve of all the parts? See, this is the problem — I can believe anything I'd like about what my mother might think, and it will never matter in the least. It is a very sad freedom.

Within seconds I stupidly picked up a junky women's magazine — one of hundreds my roommate Monica carts home. Exercise to reduce stress, or politically correct electrolysis? I settled on an article on palmistry — and, while squinting at the damp inner curl of my left hand, realized that I have no lifeline.

Saturday showed up eventually — luckily for me. I did finally get to sleep, but along the way I had to face one more adventuresome nightmare. It began as another claustrophobic baby dream. I was sitting by myself in a 1950s kind of restaurant, but in the next booth over, this baby kept staring at me. Then the baby appeared in my arms. She was milky and clean-smelling with tiny, perfect fingernails. We danced about the restaurant, though no one seemed to notice. I laid her down on a green tablecloth and she dissolved. Then I was back in my apartment, only Monica and I had gerbils. Monica couldn't be found. I had to go away for weeks and weeks, and the horrendous part was, I knew there would be thousands of annoyed and hungry gerbils waiting when I got back. It would be impossible to find them all homes.

I woke up at 9:30 and sprang into action. I showered and put on shorts and an ancient T-shirt from the summer I'd spent in Maine working as a rafting guide. I tried to find something appropriate to eat, but there was only this mysterious-tasting Hawaiian coffee of Monica's left in the refrigerator, and the smallest bit of two-percent. It barely lightened the cup at all. Then I put on an old Pretenders tape, real loud, to wipe that gerbil dream out of my head.

When the phone rang, it was my friend Kelly. "I'm changing the plan," Kelly said.

"What plan is that?" I asked, happy to hear her voice, but a little puzzled. Kelly laughed. It turned out that we had decided to have coffee that morning, at a place near Powder House Square — and I had forgotten all about it. I couldn't remember this at all. "I am losing my mind," I said. Kelly told me to stop by her house in an hour and we would walk over to the café with baby Max.

An hour. I really did try to accomplish something in that tiny usable sliver of the day. I thought about pulling out the notebook I'd been using for my copywriting attempts. I knew I should have been playing imaginary word games and spending that hour on my pretend project. How *could* I persuade people to switch from oil to natural gas? If natural gas happened to be a car — what would it be? If it were a man — what would it wear? Would it water ski? Would it be a herbivore? I should have scrawled through many legal pads until I found the one phrase that could not be improved upon.

In real life, I sat before my open window, sipping Monica's strange-tasting coffee while I watched Fred guard his territory across the street. Fred was this hefty orange tiger cat who lived with a family three houses away. Across the street they'd constructed a poster with an arrow pointing to the spot on the porch where Fred sat. The sign said: "This is not our cat."

Not our cat. We once owned the largest cat I've ever seen. Stupid had simply appeared on the back steps in Pompey one Saturday morning and I'd carried him in. Stupid the magnificent — half angora, largely walrus. Almost as big as my little brother. He would even allow Susan Ferolli and me to dress him in doll blouses. When Grant was home on weekends he would feed Stupid beer, or tap the electric can opener just to see him jump. Stupid disappeared when I was eleven. He bailed out right before everything happened with Mom and we moved away. Almost like he knew.

Who was I kidding? It was hopeless. I would never come up with a reason for anyone to switch from oil to natural gas. Why was I even trying this? All I could think of was that my father seemed to be in a nursing home. That, and how would I get Nate to go with me? I couldn't go to St. Louis alone. There was no one else.

You see, Nate didn't know about the papers I found in Grant's den. On the drive back, I didn't dare let him in on what I suspected. I didn't know what he'd do. This was what I feared: that I'd explain it all and instead of jumping into the fray — Nate would disappear. He would slink back to his world-of-work and let the opportunity float by. He'd be too busy. He'd have the impossible schedule conflict. But we had to find out. So — if I couldn't tell him, I reasoned, I would have to take him.

Kelly's house was only about ten blocks away. As I walked over, it seemed prophetic that she would call that morning. We were room-mates back when I lived in Madison, and we'd stayed in touch ever after. When I decided to move to Boston, Kelly was one of the reasons. Kelly and Pete would be people, other than Nate, that I already knew.

But they had also just had a baby, Max, and it had been so hard getting together that Kelly and I would snicker about it on the phone.

Kelly and Pete lived in the top of a white duplex and rented out the bottom half. When I got there, Kelly was at the dining room table with the paper all spread out in front of her. We hugged. We're almost the same size, but she has light, extremely short hair.

"Change of plans," Kelly said. "Max fell asleep and I don't want to wake him, since he was up almost all night. Can we just be here?"

"Of course," I said. Kelly made more coffee, and tea for me, while I microwaved some pecan rolls until the frosting dribbled away. It felt nice to see her. More so than I'd expected.

"Pete's welding," Kelly said and laughed at the idea. "He's decided to take this heavy metal art class, where in ten weeks they teach you how to make some large piece of sculpture." Welding did seem a little out of character for Pete, who was always kind of bookish. During the day he researched environmental problems for some consulting firm. "He won't tell me what he's making," she said, "but he did say that it might go well on the roof. Oh, you know, I saw what's-his-name."

"Which what's-his-name?" I asked. "There are so many."

"That guy when we saw you two together."

"Oh, Doug." And right then I decided, for the moment, to let Kelly believe that Doug was the biggest worry of my life. But wouldn't it be simple, I thought, if Doug *was* the biggest worry of my life? The idea of a world that calm seemed amusing.

"He's the one," Kelly said. "Doug's such a nice ordinary name. There were lots of Dougs when I was in elementary school, but none after. Isn't that odd?" She rubbed her foot. "I saw him when I drove by and he was putting a big brown box on top of his car. Do you want honey in your tea?"

"Sure," I said. But the honey in the plastic squeeze-bear had crystallized, so Kelly put him in the microwave to melt. "Things with Doug are — confused," I said. "He wants to go way, way ahead with us. I mean way ahead."

Kelly rolled a jingly cloth ball across the kitchen table at me. "This far ahead?"

I nodded and she hummed meditatively. I could tell she was holding back and deciding not to tell me again how great life with Max was. "He seemed sweet," Kelly said, "that time we ran into you two. Didn't you say it was good for you two to be together? I thought things were working out."

"He is," I said. "They were. Or maybe — are. I don't know. It was such a relief to finally be with someone where I didn't have to think up everything all the time. We were going to a lot of clubs for a while. You know — feeling spry." I shook Max's squishy blue rattle at my friend. "I don't know. It's like I'm getting to feel that I can't do everything, so I have to narrow it down to one thing at a time — for a while," I said. "I just don't want things to go way out in the future with him and get all settled. Which is what he wants. It makes me nervous. This is weird," I said, "but you know what would be really good right now? Chocolate pudding."

"There's an idea." Kelly jumped up and started opening cupboards until we found everything we needed. I had just poured the milk when there was a big thud inside the microwave. I opened the door and saw that the honey bear had exploded. He was all torn apart in a sort of spectacular way and honey dripped down the microwave's walls.

"Poor bear," Kelly said. "I forgot to undo his top. Just close the door. We'll let Pete find this. How's your brother?"

"Nate?" I shut the door on the blown-up bear, as everything I'd been obsessing about — my father in a nursing home, Grant, how to convince Nate to go west — popped back to the surface with annoying speed. As much as I wanted to, I just couldn't tell Kelly. It felt bad, but I wasn't ready to talk about it. Or maybe I hadn't figured everything out enough to answer questions. "Nate's the same," I said. "You know — moody. He's still at that paper in Lawrence and not happy. But he's so dogged. He'll keep going at it until somebody drags him away."

"The copywriting?" Kelly asked. "That guy downtown who didn't turn out to be sleazy? Are you still doing that?"

"Kind of. But it's going to take forever before I make any money. I keep thinking I should just give in. You know, go back and do design. Play with shapes. Do more illustration. Invent a portfolio. Then, that always feels like every day I'm leaving a whole part of my mind home lying in bed. Which got me thinking about the advertising. Except it is so silly."

"Some days I can't even imagine going back to work," Kelly said. "I'd rather stay here and play with Max. But I will have to go back. Are you happy?"

I looked at her, because it seemed like such a strange thing to ask. An unfamiliar set of words. A question I never had time for. "I don't know," I said. "Is happy sometimes OK?"

"I'd be so much happier if I slept more," Kelly said. "I could sleep forever, times six."

"Are you sure you want to leave all that honey in there?" I asked. Kelly nodded. "See, it's like this," I said, "but weird too. I think I'm finally tired of running all over the place. Like city to city. I am so tired of that bar. You know, how you end up hanging out with people you don't really like all that much, but you do it anyway because they're the ones you're hanging out with? It's like that."

"Was it better when you started?"

"For a while it was fun. You know — another thing I hadn't done before. I did sort of talk my way into it."

At that moment Max woke up, and Kelly disappeared to change him. She brought him out while I finished the pudding. I stayed there talking and playing with Max for the whole morning. I hadn't realized how much I missed spending time with Kelly, and that scared me a little. Then I felt very lucky that we could just sit around making instant pudding. When I told her about having to meet Doug later, to talk things out, she wanted to know why I hadn't said something before. Which made me feel bad — again — for not letting her in on everything else. When I left, Kelly told me she thought Doug might be the kind of guy who would wait — until things were ready. "You could always be elusive," she suggested, "that might work a while longer." I wasn't so sure. Being elusive takes up so much energy. Besides, how fair would that be, I wondered, to either of us?

As I walked home, I stopped at a crosswalk and it just came over me. "I can't do everything at once," I said. An old woman on the corner turned to stare. "I can't," I said. I need to tell Doug no, I decided. It was sad, because there was a connection. Really, there was. But I need to do it, I thought — before he comes to his senses and sees the sham of a person I am.

When I got home there were three messages on the machine. I flopped down on the couch to listen. It felt like I was already at the end of a long day. The first was from Julie, seeing if I was in town (or not) and whether I would be coming into work that afternoon (or not). A good question, I thought. The second was from some camera store, telling Monica that her prints had been done for five weeks and if she didn't make a move soon they were going to pitch them. The last was Doug — checking to see if we were still on. If we weren't, I was supposed to call him back.

I looked at my watch. In three hours I would be behind the bar again. I stared at the ceiling and checked my watch once more. If I didn't move quickly, I saw, I would be late for Doug, and that didn't seem wise. I started running around the apartment, collecting things for later. It felt *almost* like packing. I stashed three fresh packs of gum and a new orange lip balm in my leather bag. Then I erased the messages and locked up.

I strolled briskly to the Porter Square T stop, happy to walk, to use that third fragment of exercise to reduce a little more stress. In the plaza outside the Red Line station, I stopped at a bookstore and surprised myself by buying a road atlas. I had suddenly decided that I needed to see the layout of Missouri. I needed to study it. On the "St. Louis and Vicinity" page I spotted Crestwood. It was way out in the suburbs.

The T station smelled like popcorn. As I waited for the train, I pulled out my new atlas, glanced at the cover, and rolled it closed. How stupid could I be? Like Doug wouldn't ask why I'd brought an atlas to the aquarium? Why *did* I buy this? I crammed the thing back into my bag. I should be looking closely at the posters here, I thought. I should use this time to discern what's wrong and right with these ads. The breeze from the tunnel pushed out ahead of the train. I saw the light. I took two steps forward and barely recognized the motion.

At Government Center, I had to squint because the sky had turned a sharp robin's-egg blue. I walked toward Faneuil Hall, deciding on the way to tourist-gawk a little. At Congress Street a girl hung from the window of a Revere school bus. She pointed to the statue in front of me and shouted: "Hey look! It's Sam Adams! Hey everybody, get all excited!" Three people with cameras turned to reexamine the statue. This was far too much cynicism, even for a child, I thought.

Outside the aquarium, Doug lounged against the railing, watching the harbor seals flip and dive in their little pool. It seemed a shame to disturb him, especially with what I had to say. He wore black Converse high-tops, black jeans, and a purple short-sleeve shirt with abstract gray turtles on it — one that I'd found for him. Not a good sign.

I tapped Doug's shoulder. He pressed a finger to his lips.

"Oh, so we *are* spies," I said, but it came out too sharp. I was tired.

"Watch these guys go." Doug waved at the seals, as if he and the seals had a shared trick they were about to perform. They looked like sleek dogs. "These three are running a complex pattern," Doug said. "They do four laps, then one will crawl out across that plastic ledge. Next, it jumps back into the water and they all spin."

"Of course it's complex," I said. "The poor things are nuts. They've got a kiddie pool for a universe. You'd be nuts too." I didn't mean to flare up. I didn't — really.

Doug glanced uncertainly at the admission booth. "Want to go in?" he asked.

"It's really only fun when you're stoned."

"Yeah, you're right." He nodded, slowly. Maybe with a little regret.

"Can we just walk around?" I asked.

Doug shrugged and we began to circle the pier's outer deck. He seemed lost.

"So — what are we talking about?" I queried.

"Right." Doug stopped by the railing and stood up straight, as if he were ready to read something aloud. It was practically cute. "I'm thinking about you way too much," he announced. "Not only some of the time, it's all the time. It's even affecting my driving. I sit at stoplights now, thinking, about you. People honk. I miss exits. I almost get into traffic fights with cab drivers. This is dangerous, and I don't know if we're *ever* going anywhere. Especially with this I'll-see-you-when-I-see-you stuff. We should be, be connecting."

"Connecting?" I saw Legos.

"Are we at a stage or not? I can't tell."

"Oh," I said wearily. "Like, are we at the going-steady stage again? I hate the whole idea of stages. You know that. It's like some law of science or something. How if there's one stage after another, then there's always got to be the inevitable downfall."

"But I meant like making progress," Doug said. "Or have we already fallen down?"

"Down and out?" I asked.

"Just down."

"No — we keep going back and forth," I said.

Doug glanced over quickly. "Maybe this is dumb," he said, "but coming out and talking directly seemed to be the only choice. We used to be good together."

"At what?" I said.

"Come on, at, breakfast. We did good breakfast." He drummed against the railing. "You know, at being. We were good at being." Doug looked woeful. "Man, this sounds so horrible out loud."

"No it doesn't," I said.

"Yeah it does. It's like these things should never be pronounced. Maybe we could get little semaphore flags. Could we do this in Morse code?"

"That would take *so* long," I said. "Look, I don't have a commitment problem, I have a timing problem. I mean, we have a timing problem. Or there is a timing problem around here somewhere." This sounded like a serious but potentially fixable problem. I knew that. But I wasn't even sure I meant to be hopeful.

"Timing?" Doug said. "Like you're on another time scale? Maybe a geological time scale?"

"Stop," I said. "I've got all this family junk to sort out. I have to, because it's getting in the way and messing up everything else. Right now — this isn't what I want."

Doug stayed silent. For a long time. I thought, this is what it must be like at the SPCA, taking puppies and kittens to the lethal injection room.

"If we have to meet and negotiate, maybe that's a sign this isn't the right thing," I said. "Maybe I'm not right. I mean, I feel bad for saying it but — basically you're too nice." That one just fell out of my mouth. "I can't take this being put ahead of everything else."

"People negotiate every day," Doug announced. "I could be nasty. I can *do* hardball — "

"No, don't change or anything. Come on. Let's get away from all these fish." I took his elbow.

We strolled back across Atlantic, under the expressway, without speaking. In front of an Irish bar near the Customs Tower, I told Doug that it was my turn to buy him a Harp. Besides, I had to call in for work. I was going to be late.

It was only after we sat down and began eating tiny pretzels that things began to feel like normal. Almost the way I wanted them to be, as if our little meeting had never happened. Doug started telling me about his niece, who was six and learning to swear. "She kept going around saying 'flook, flook,' so yesterday I took her aside and told her that if she was going to say it she had to say it right, and it rhymed with duck."

This made me laugh. Suddenly it all felt very comfortable, like we were two old married people, and I thought, maybe I have just made a tremendous mistake. Luckily, they turned on the TV and a sports show appeared where guys were fishing. I asked Doug how they got away with putting fishing on TV — anyway.

"The thing I keep thinking," Doug said, "is they ought to have a channel that's just real-time video of one person's life. You could click on and see what that person was doing, at any moment. Like, look, he's watching TV. It'd be boring, but reassuring at the same time. You could check it out and go, well, I'm having a better day than that guy."

"That might sell," I said. "Really."

Doug gave me a rueful smile. "I guess this was all moderately dumb." He glanced over his shoulder, back toward the aquarium.

"Oh no — I've done dumber," I said.

"Yeah, like what?"

"When I was thirteen I put a bumblebee in my mouth."

"There you go," Doug said. "I once broke my leg watching TV. Had my knee over the arm of the chair and my leg fell asleep. I jumped up to change channels, and when I hit the floor it broke. I was twelve."

"Wouldn't have happened if you'd had a remote," I said.

"Did you know I had a job in college one summer where I was mosquito bait? It was this study, back in the days when I wanted to be a biologist. That was pretty dumb. Whether or not someone gets bit turns out to be a question of body temperature and skin color."

A minute later, when Doug asked how my weekend went, I decided that since he probably wasn't going to run away or anything, I might as well tell him. Doug the big ear. How could I give up someone with a big ear? He looked a little stunned by the time I got to the end of the saga. "You're right," Doug said. "That's far too much family stuff. How did you let those particular people into your family anyway?" He smiled.

"I don't know. They just showed up."

"Well," Doug said, "at least you've got a new van."

"At least."

"Here's what I heard. That in each life, everybody gets the same amount of trouble, only it's spread out differently. You could be home free, after this."

I laughed. Sad and funny will almost always make me laugh. Then everything picked up that dreary we're-just-old-friends feeling. I scooted a matchbook around on the slippery bar and told Doug that I was probably going to lose my job if he couldn't give me a ride back to Cambridge, right away. "I have to go," I said. I have to go. I have to go.

NINE

I was beyond tired, that whole week, after Sarah and I came back from Binghamton. I'd get home after work and stand in the bathroom, watching that washed-out looking guy, the one with tremendous purple bags holding up both eyes, wave back from the mirror.

Thursday was particularly bad. At work the night before, some mystery reporter out surfing the paper's computer system found the newsroom salary list and put a copy in everybody's mailbox. That morning, we all discovered that there was no scale at all. People with zip experience were getting paid piles more than some who'd been toiling away for years. Then, after lunch, my buddy Rory Adair, who covered cops, came out of a meeting with the bosses and quit. Everyone suspected that Rory had found the salary list, but since she actually quit, it meant the big guys were getting ready to turn on the Mixmaster in the newsroom and rearrange our jobs once again. It's a thing they just love to do.

At 10:30 Thursday night, I was upstairs, drowsily watching *Plan 9 from Outer Space*, once again, when the phone rang. I had a feeling it would be Maris and it was. "More bad news," he said. "In all the confusion we forgot to assign someone to do outside cops tomorrow. And pal, you're it." He hung up and I stared into the phone. Doing cops was not that big a deal. But for some reason I didn't want to do it that morning. I did not want to be out there first thing Friday morning, even if I couldn't say why.

Anyway, at 5:23 A.M. I found myself slicing north on I-93 with my stomach in knots. Nothing new there. When I reached the Dunkin' Donuts drive-through in Lawrence, I started drumming on the dashboard. Beth Salino taps her dashboard seven times each morning when she comes to work, so for that day, she won't have to go cover a fatal. Beth's talked to too many distraught families already, she says. Simply being in the presence of grief that can't be resolved adds up. It's akin to being exposed to radiation.

I swung by the paper to pick up a radio and traveled nearly the entire cop trail, but not one unnerving thing happened. At a little past eight, the sky had a new and burnished look as I parked in front of the Lawrence police station. The duty officer buzzed me in, and I quietly started copying entries from the last twenty-four hours out of their cloth-covered logbook. Stolen car stereos, tools lifted from construction sites, lockouts, bar fights, and domestics.

When the white phone on the console behind me twirred, a compact desk officer answered and, repeating what she'd just been told, said: "Eighteen Willow Street, house fire." I copied down the address as two more calls came in for the same fire. "The fire department hasn't lost a foundation yet," a bald cop behind me announced.

I churned through the remaining log pages, scanning for anything typed in red, and called the city desk from the pay phone in the hall. They'd already picked up the fire from the scanner and told me that a photographer was on the way.

Outside on the steps, I turned to watch as a column of tan smoke, one rooftop wide, climbed hundreds of feet into the sky before softly spreading north. I pulled out and found myself following the assistant chief's lime-green car as it headed across the river, in the direction of the tan plume. When I got to the neighborhood, police cruisers had already blocked off all the streets around the fire. I parked and jogged toward the flickering taillights of a ladder truck as a growing somersault of chalky gray smoke expanded into the street.

The burning building was a green triple-decker. Black smoke fringed with flames rolled through the roof and out under the eaves. Gray, bulging, canvas hoses with brass fittings had been stretched over one another in the street. The deputy chief in his muddy-white greatcoat circled the scene, carrying a walkie-talkie, as water the color of dirty milk rushed down the front stairs. The fire continued to climb through the core of the house and flames sputtered from the chimney. Two firefighters in the basket of a cherry picker pulled at the second-floor windows with grappling hooks, trying to get into the walls. Clusters of spectators watched from driveways or the safety of their fenced-in lawns. Except for the grind of the fire engines, the occasional sound of breaking glass, and the soft rush of flames, it was strangely quiet.

Three ambulances waited out in the street, but the EMTs had walked up to the building. They eyed the firefighters as they emerged from the front door, with the regulators ringing on their smudged and empty oxygen tanks. A man and woman with green blankets across their shoulders stood by the nearest ambulance, staring rigidly and speaking softly in Spanish.

Casler, the photographer, saw me and ambled over. "No one's here from the other paper," he said, and smiled. "There's a dead baby inside. Second floor."

"OK," I said. I was suddenly tired. I didn't care that I was the only reporter there. I didn't want to know about a dead baby. I didn't want to know anything. It was as though a shroud had been pulled over my head. I walked away, to the side of the house, stepping gingerly over the hoses in the driveway. I wondered how long it would be before one of those came loose from the pressure and snapped back.

A fat police sergeant with red hair and a boyish face stood by the back porch. He seemed to recognize me and offered a slow smile, as though he were queuing up a remark he'd been looking forward to delivering. "You do know," he said, "that we think you guys are all maggots."

"Yeah." I nodded. "I know." Only then did he show me the page in his pocket-size notebook with the names of the people who lived in the burning apartments.

A hose out in the street broke free and a white geyser of water whipped around like an angry worm. People yelled, and then an EMT kicked the uncoupled end into a storm sewer. I walked back to the front of the building and watched as a smoking blue comforter floated out from the third-floor window. It bounced once in a murky puddle. A piece of burning insulation, no larger than a paperback, fluttered down behind it and glanced off the deputy chief's white helmet. He swatted it away with a gloved hand.

I found some kids, still in pajamas, on the steps of the house next door. Their eyes glistened as they told me that they lived in the third-floor apartment. The baby's bedroom was right below theirs, they said.

The child's parents were standing out front, with blankets over their shoulders.

"Those people on the second floor had about ten TVs, all hooked together," the girl explained. "One of them exploded." In a too-grown-up voice she told me that this was the fourth place they'd been burned out of in two years. "Have the firemen brought out the baby?" she asked. I shook my head.

A minute later I caught O'Nan, the deputy fire chief, who said they had no idea yet how the fire started. The fire chaplain in his greatcoat walked in and out of the house across the street, looking for the family from the second floor. The coroner's sleet-gray van bounced across the taut hoses and backed into the burning building's driveway. The young driver got out, snapping a white surgical glove onto his left hand.

The two kids from the steps scampered through the puddles when they saw their mother come running down the street. She wore a blue uniform with "Inez" embroidered on the pocket. Her face quivered as she cried, and she jumped once in the air. Her kids grabbed her and held on. As she fainted, the EMTs ran over and lifted her to the steps where the kids had been sitting. People in the street shifted to get a better view.

The van driver brought an ambulance stretcher to the back stairs of the burning house. A small green bottle of oxygen waited in the middle of the stretcher. Four firefighters went upstairs all at once to get the baby. They brought the body down in a wet and sooty sheet, probably the one from the crib. Beside the front of the house a man, who might have been the baby's grandfather, tried to keep the mother from looking. He put a hand over her eyes, but she pried his fingers away. When they wheeled the stretcher past me, I noticed that the sheet had been wrapped in a blanket with a silky green fringe. It didn't look like there could have been a baby inside. It really didn't make that much of an impression.

I watched as the man from the funeral home and two EMTs skimmed the stretcher across the hoses and into the van. The mother screamed and the father held on to a paint-chipped porch post, sagging and crying, as a television cameraman moved closer. This is obscene, I thought. I am an obscene spectator.

As the firefighters punched more holes into the walls with their axes, looking for hot spots, I asked a guy in a Hawaiian shirt, who was standing outside his house, if I could use his phone. "No problem," he said. He led me inside and I sat on his yellow-carpeted stairs, looking at Hummel figures in lit glass cases, as I called the paper and began reading off my notes to Beth Salino. My shirt held that dead, sweet stench of building smoke. I knew it really wouldn't wash out.

Later I met Austin Glazier, the city hall reporter, for lunch, and as we ate our veal cutlet dinners for $2.95 each at the Andover Luncheonette, we got into an argument about Joe Morgan and the Red Sox. I knew I'd started it mostly to pretend that the morning hadn't gotten to me. But Austin kept saying, "They're deteriorating. We're all deteriorating, we just don't know it yet." I shut up after a while, because I couldn't keep from thinking about that eventual moment — the one when I actually would be able to go to lunch after a morning like that and not have to pretend. When it really wouldn't bother me. What happens when you find yourself on that plateau? When you can watch nearly anything?

At about one, I went to district court and picked up the day's tally of arraignments. When I got back to the newsroom, Maris stared at me strangely before disappearing into a sudden huddle with Doris Flick. I wondered if they were talking about me, but then I got lost in typing up the arraignments. The second I finished, Maris reappeared and tapped me on the shoulder. "Come to Doris's office," he proposed. "We'll have a chat."

How could I refuse? Once I was behind the glass wall, sitting on Doris Flick's meat-colored couch, they spelled it out. "We're making a number of great changes in the assignments here," Doris Flick said, as she tightened her white scarf. "Consequently, we have a need and you fit." She pulled on the lapels of her dark blue suit. With that red hair, she looked like a stuffed French flag. "Our need is for an experienced night reporter and you're it. This will be a permanent change, as of next week."

"There are a number of small chores that go with nights, which I think you know about," Maris genially explained. "Mystery picture editor duties, calling libraries for their most requested books. Plus some of your regular work, which we can move over." He asked if I had any questions and smiled attentively.

I looked at my shoes. I started out as the night reporter. This was a demotion, though they'd never say as much. I knew exactly what it would mean, covering more death and mayhem, all the time. Plus, I'd lose my weekends, as the night reporter always worked Saturdays. I nodded and walked back to my desk, thinking this is what it must feel like to be a pithed frog.

When I left the newsroom for home, Maris called out cheerfully: "Hey pal, remember, you get Monday off. This is a long weekend, for you. Why don't you go somewhere for a change?"

I couldn't say anything, so I waved. But in the car I shouted, "Fuckers, fuckers, fuckers," until I was out on I-93, and with the windows open it no longer sounded like a word. I turned the boom box up loud, but I kept hearing that woman cry as she ran down the street, thinking that her two children might have been inside the burning building. I kept hearing the other mother's scream. How many asphyxiated infants is it necessary to see? I used to think it was important to know this stuff, to understand what was really going on — everywhere. I would get mad at people who didn't know, or didn't want to know. Yet it does start to rob you of something. I don't help anybody. I just write things down. It's irrational. I'm irrational to go on, day after day, sticking my head into the middle of everyone else's pain.

PART TWO

TEN

The driveway was empty when I got home that afternoon, so I stuffed the car all the way in. I took off my tie and knotted it around the steering wheel. In the kitchen, I pulled three beers from the refrigerator and carried these up to the third floor. I turned on the TV and zapped the channels around a few times until I found CNN. There was something on about radio-collared grizzlies in Wyoming, and I tried to focus on this as I opened the Bass Ale. Then I decided I wanted the Molson first, so I opened it as well, and started flipping through more channels. It was all cooking shows and traffic reports. What do you need a traffic report for if you're home watching from the couch?

I'd just switched back to CNN when Sarah came in through the open window. The second-floor roof up there sticks way out and you can use it like a little porch. I'd put a lawn chair and a flamingo in a pot out there a couple weeks ago and forgotten about them.

"What the fuck are you doing climbing in my window?" I shouted. When I stood up, I accidentally kicked over one of the beers. It foamed across the carpet.

"My — there's a pleasant greeting." Sarah took off her wraparound sunglasses. She wore a gray shirt, jeans, and thongs. "I was taking a nap," she said, waving over her shoulder. "Out there. On your nice big chair. Is this for me?" My sister picked up the half-empty beer, wiped the foam off on the leg of her jeans and began examining the amber bottle as though she'd never seen one before.

"How'd you get in?"

"Your housemates. They're sweet. They were going to New Hampshire for the weekend. Janice said, 'If I don't see you again have a nice rest of your life.' You didn't notice the van? Across the street?"

"Van, van, fuck the van," I said. "They moved me to nights, forever, at work. I'm *always* going to have to work on Saturday night."

"Wow," Sarah said. "Poor you."

"This is the last one. I get Monday off, too."

My sister brightened by maybe 75 watts. "Great," she said. "What I mean is — that's why I'm here."

"I wondered as much."

"See, this friend of mine at work wants to buy my dead car. He'll even pay for the clutch. Can you believe that? So — I found a place in Vestal that'll do it tomorrow. But I need someone to drive the van while I bring back the car. Then I thought — what *is* little brother doing?"

"What am I doing?" I asked. The question opened up like a great blank space.

"Thousands have posed that self-same metaphysical query," Sarah announced. "I'll buy dinner and drive — since I've been doing too much caffine. I'm wired already. You — take off your silly clothes. Drink your beer in the shower. I'll pack your stuff and the tapes. You sleep. I'll drive."

"All we do is drive," I said.

"That's because we're good at it," Sarah said. "To be happy, you should always do at least one thing a day that you're good at."

I know, I have this thing about details. Which, as obsessions go, considering what I do for a living, is not all that bad. For my sister, though, details are always sticky impediments. They add up and get in the way of whatever grand theoretical plan she's immersed in. But I see the unassembled all the time. Say I have to do an interview at some- body's house, I always arrive hyperaware, trying to find the kinks in the package. I stay too long and take too many notes, just in case some small unnoticed thing turns out to be crucial later on. It's insurance of a sort, but it's also been like that for as long as I can remember. Cover all the angles and bring everything along. I don't know exactly where it comes from.

When my father would come home from trips, back when he was doing adjusting work for the insurance company, he would tell endless stories. He would go on and on, talking with an odd fascination about little mistakes that had mushroomed into huge and deadly ones. The 30-amp fuse replaced by a penny, the last section of the foundation that was never shored up. Prudent paths not taken, safe routes to the future that only became clear after the fact.

But a love of detail can also lead you past rational observation and straight into the land of omens. I know that, too. For instance, say I did believe in omens, then shouldn't I have recognized that lightning striking my bank machine, just as the card went in, spelled out something dark about the upcoming trip?

We were in the van and on our way to getting out of Belmont when we stopped because Sarah had ordered Szechuan take-out. She did it when I was in the shower but never told me. As she went in to pick it up, I realized that I shouldn't embark on my last weekend of freedom with a cash supply of only seventeen dollars. My bank machine was nearby in one of those storefront ATM deals, so I hopped out of the van.

It smelled like rain, and thunderheads roamed at the horizon's edge. Nevertheless, I slipped my green and blue card into the machine and punched up $100 worth of savings withdrawal. The whirring ching-ching-ching continued behind the steel drawer as I watched Grant's van across the street. The windows were down. And when a silver-burred streak arrived from the sky with a rippled crack, I thought it had hit right in back of the van. The fluorescent light over the ATM winked out as the cash drawer opened.

I snatched my twenties while the thunder rolled on. But then I heard a click, and the yellow letters on the screen announced that my card had been retained. There was a number I could call. For some reason, right then, I started sneezing and couldn't stop. I grabbed the gray phone beside the machine, but halfway into dialing, the ATM beeped violently and spat my card out across the floor.

Minutes later, as huge intermittent raindrops exploded against the windshield, Sarah backed out into traffic. We had kung pao shrimp, General Chow's chicken, and fortune cookies with no fortunes. At the first red light, my sister reached behind her seat and pulled a pair of Rolling Rocks and two sets of chopsticks from a cloth bag. The bag belonged to one of my housemates. We silently traded boxes along Route 2 and then headed south on 128. We were out on the Mass Pike's broad westbound expanse when I finished the shrimp and started looking for some place to start a garbage bag. Sarah lifted the empty white carton from my fingers, folded down the lid with one hand, and tossed it over her shoulder. "Feel free," she said.

My turquoise hay fever pill went down with the last of the beer. Out near Worcester, with the Who on the radio singing about "going mobile," my hold on things began to slip. I was comparatively content, with my right arm hanging out in the cool-running air and my feet on the dash. I was happy enough for the minute, watching us drive ahead into the edge of that scarlet sunset, but Sarah kept rattling on.

"There's another reason we have to go back to Owego," my sister explained. "I forgot the pictures. You know — the red photo book?" I nodded. She'd also forgotten to bring back the slides from Canada, where we twice spent summers on Georgian Bay after my mom died. Our aunts used to have a cottage there, before they moved west and pulled out as active relatives

"Did you know that you have Dad's eyebrows?" Sarah said. "You're also going gray along the sides — the same way he did. Slides are useful. For once our family is totally transparent."

My sister was driving with her elbows couched in the holes of the steering wheel. Even with the beer and the antihistamines, it still annoyed me. Besides, I normally pulled out every gray hair I could find and then regretted the vanity of it.

"Hey," Sarah said, after I told her to drive with both hands. "I don't *seem* to be hitting anything"

"So far."

"OK — while it may not be the perfect time to ask, tell me about this Claire person."

"There isn't anything to tell," I said. "Since we broke up."

"There's always something to tell."

I didn't have the energy to protest, so I let loose with the whole jumbled history. But with Sarah, there's no such thing as a half-confession, and as soon I opened my mouth, I knew I'd be embarking on a journey of endless explanation. I took a deep breath. I told her how Claire and I began as a work romance. How for months on end it was pretty wonderful. How at the start we were both shaky with the idea of having something going on while we spent so much of the day only desks away from each another. How on some level we were always planning ahead to the question: What if it ends? How at first keeping it secret seemed hard, but after a while it turned into a plus, a part of the payoff. Those sweet moments when it seemed as though we could invent our futures and get away with it. Little things, like when she'd call up from across the newsroom and ask, "What's a nice high for Seattle?" because nobody could find the weather box temperatures and she was making them up again. Finally, I got to the part about reaching that point, the one where things always either become real or fall apart, and how I guess I began to distance myself, without recognizing it.

"That could be fixed," Sarah said. "The distance stuff."

"Yeah, but I started making stupid accusations, starting stupid fights. Actually, we were in bed one morning, having another useless argument, and it came out of my mouth like a burp. I said we should break up. It wasn't premeditated."

"And — this was ticked off by what?"

I listened to the thrumming of the rubber dividers between the concrete slabs of the road. We ducked under a bridge with "Tony loves Liza" spray-painted on the side in white, only "Liza" had been crossed out. Then I told Sarah about my dream, the one where I woke up and knew exactly what it felt like to be trapped in a bad marriage.

"You broke up because of some stupid dream?" Sarah said. "Like what? You felt terrorized by the future? So you said sorry and bolted?" My sister took both hands off the wheel and began waving her fingers at me, like she was trying to exorcise something. "You know — that's it. That's it, for the one love of your life."

"Stop," I said. "Mostly, now, I think I blew it. I said a bunch of stupid stuff and that landed me here. All by myself in the middle of a vast blank space."

Sarah frowned, as if that couldn't quite explain it. We passed a "Buckle-Up" public service billboard with two crash-test dummies headed for the windshield.

"How many loves do you get?" I asked. "For life?"

"Oh — two," Sarah said. "At least. It depends on how long you want to live."

It was nearly dark and I was suddenly weary. I began focusing on the guardrails as they streamed by, on the constant parameters of the median strip. About a month before, I'd clicked on to some foreign news show and the picture on the screen had been shot through the windshield of a tractor-trailer on a four-lane highway out in the middle of some city in the desert. Yet everything in the frame appeared with those same familiar and mind-numbing proportions. The bridges were a standard height, the curves a recognizable radius, the mercury lights leaned in from safe and familiar vantage points. It is a border of insulation between you and the landscape, I thought. A tunnel of illusion, designed to create the sense that you're going slower than you actually are. I had no idea where the picture came from, until the announcer said we were in Riyadh.

I watched the Mass Pike stream past and wondered why I'd let things with Claire slip away. Why had I distanced myself? Why did I need to feel safe? I wondered if it all wasn't wrapped up around my job in some tangential way that I couldn't quite see.

Thinking like this wasn't getting me anywhere, so I stumbled to the back of the van and sprawled across the bed. I pushed two familiar-looking sleeping bags off onto the floor, as my sister began dragging down distant AM stations from their high arcs in the clouds. Faint and scratchy voices flickered through the rear speakers — a talk show in Cincinnati; WJR, "The Great Voice of the Great Lakes"; the St. Louis Cardinals, leading two to one at home. I told Sarah to give me a shout after Albany if she needed another driver.

"Sure," she said. "Fine."

It was light out when I woke up. I was sweaty and my head felt stepped on. I propped an elbow under my ribs, as my shoulders remembered the night's vibrations thrumming up through the foam mattress. I had the feeling that we'd driven straight through but I wasn't sure. A flattened Burger King bag was crammed in against the windshield and a green Thruway ticket protruded from the driver's side visor.

When I looked out, I saw that the van was parked at a rest stop. We were at the edge of a forest of trucks and behind a flatbed stacked with lawn and garden tractors in cardboard boxes. The sharp, descending harmonic of the road washed in from beyond the gas pumps. Across the highway I saw a broad cornfield. The leaf tips of each waist-high stalk pointed straight up.

The van's floor was cluttered, almost a mess. Closer to the captain's chairs I saw two large green and white boxes, full of my housemates' camping equipment. A pair of purple sleeping bags were zipped open and twisted around each other. Claire and I bought those together, and she never asked for hers back. A pillow in a zebra-striped case, one I'd last seen on Sarah's bed, rested atop a blue cooler. We'd broken down, I decided, somewhere outside Albany.

It had to be maybe 6:30 or 7:00 in the morning, I thought, as I sat in the passenger seat pulling on my sneakers. I rubbed my eyes. A minute or two later I spotted my sister moving across the parking lot. She carried a large, obviously hot, styrofoam cup in one hand and three plastic-wrapped pastries in the other. The handle of a turquoise toothbrush extended from the left side of her mouth. She had changed into a tank top and was wearing the wraparound sunglasses again, even though it wasn't that bright out. When Sarah caught my eye, her shoulders flicked straight. She piled the Danish on top of the coffee, opened the driver's side door, and began tossing breakfast foods at me. "Here," she said.

I caught one pastry in each hand, but the third skidded against the dash. "Where the fuck are we?" I asked.

Sarah stuffed her toothbrush into the visor pocket and peeled the lid back from her coffee. "Outside Rochester. Ra-cha-cha on the Thruway." She glanced around like a real estate agent. "This is mile 376. Westbound. The Ontario Mobil stop. After Niagara Falls — we're going to St. Louis, because that's where Dad is. I lied about my car. Nobody wants to buy my car."

"What do you mean he's in St. Louis?"

"He's in a nursing home. That's what I figured out from Grant's checkbook." She seemed pleased.

"A nursing home?" I said. "Why is he in a nursing home? Nobody tells me anything. Does he know we're coming?"

"Not exactly," Sarah said. "I almost called, but this is better. I thought he might object, but now I don't know. It won't give him time to assemble an act. You know — to prepare."

I did know. When my father used to come back from claims trips he would sometimes bring souvenirs: a shorn bolt, splinters from a tornado, surreal evidence from the land of disaster. We were the audience, lined up at the varnished dining room table, as he rambled on and on, charming us while recreating the latest disaster he'd just helped set right. My father never seemed tired or worn out when he came back. It was as though the acts of leaving and arriving, on their own, were a source of continual excitement.

"How could he be in a nursing home?" I asked. "He's not old."

Sarah pursed her lips. "There were forms," she said quietly. "Agreements. They didn't say why. I don't think it's a place where you sign off all your savings to stay there. I bet it's St. Louis because of Uncle Stan."

"Did you call him?"

"Stan? Come on." My sister looked ahead at the lawn tractors and back at me. She seemed somehow on guard and waiting for more of a challenge. "Really," she said, "I only just figured this all out."

"Shit." I laced my high-tops tight and got out of the van. The parking lot smelled of antifreeze and the sky was overcast, but it would be hot later. I slammed the door before heading toward the sand-colored rest stop building. I passed two truckers walking out of the men's room, both wearing black T-shirts and unbuttoned flannel shirts over those like sport coats. One guy said, "I've got a camera in the cab if you want to take a picture of it." I couldn't imagine what they were talking about. I couldn't imagine my father in a nursing home. I couldn't imagine that we would actually drive to Missouri.

In the coffee shop I picked up a coconut donut and a giant coffee. This was ridiculous, I thought as I waited in line to pay. I only had three days. You could barely get to St. Louis in three days, let alone back. I have a job. I loaded the giant coffee with extra sugar.

When I returned to the van, Sarah had just put on olive shorts. She was untangling a pair of yellow parrot earrings. I sat in the passenger seat and carefully fitted my sunglasses around my ears. I tightened the bead on their cherry-colored band hard up against the back of my head.

"You know — I could really use a shower," Sarah said, as though we'd been traveling for days and days. As though the reasons we'd stopped at the side of the Thruway were both settled and obvious.

"I can't do this," I said. "I'm employed."

"So?" Sarah half smiled, and I remembered exactly how much I hated that phrase. So. How it was direct from junior high and so —

unanswerable. "A job can be dealt with," my sister said. "Would you really have come if I had told you?"

She stopped combing her hair and tossed the black-bristled brush over her shoulder. It thumped against the carpet. "That's why I didn't tell you. That's why last night I drove part way around the globe, so we'd be far enough out here that you couldn't run back. Come on — I'm counting on your passive acceptance. You could sue me, but I'd still be your sister."

"There's the problem," I said. I sipped my coffee and began slowly spinning in the captain's chair.

"Just how upset are you?" Sarah asked.

"Very."

"Really? You just licked your lips." She held her hair back with one hand. "Come on. It'll be fine. We'll get good suntans. Driving tans — all elbow." She used her teeth to tear a tiny hole in the edge of the plastic coffee cup lid. "Besides — we're heading west. The route of historic optimism. You can call in sick and say you require an adventure. Not having an adventure is in itself a lingering form of illness."

"East to west is the historic route of greed, desperation, murder, and theft," I said.

My sister made a huffing noise and started the van. She backed out from between the trucks and pulled to the side of the coffee shop. I couldn't understand why she'd parked with the trucks in the first place. We could have just as easily parked with the cars. Sarah stomped down the emergency brake and left the keys in the ignition. "I can't go anywhere without juice," she said. "Save my seat."

Through the coffee shop's plate glass window I watched as my sister surveyed the juice bottles and reached for something red. This is stupid, I thought. I'm not doing this.

I undid the seat belt and slipped into the driver's seat. I rested the coffee cup between my legs and placed both hands on the wheel — at ten and two o'clock — as I felt the tiny modulated vibrations working up from the idling engine. I don't know why, but I popped the parking brake and shifted to "D."

Blue, bubble-topped garbage pails, standing like sentries beside the evergreen bushes, slipped past as I accelerated out under the service bay's white canopy. I turned on the headlights. The automatic transmission reached for a new gear. I didn't know where I was going. Then I hit the great dane.

At least it might have been a great dane. Gray, mottled, and almost blue, it could have been a horse. Maybe a small pony. Its owner, a silver-haired man in Birkenstocks, was walking with the animal in the grass beyond the gas pumps. And he, not the dog, yelped, as the animal ran into my peripheral vision. The great dane came on anyway, head down, its canines showing, and made a beeline for the van's front left hubcap.

I skidded right. It was a glancing blow. A tap.

The van rocked to a stop. Scalding coffee sprayed across my lap. Steam rose from my crotch. Things in back kept falling.

The great dane pulled up and almost sat, its rear end quivering an inch off the pavement. It barked once and turned around — as if the day's task had been checked off — and loped back to its owner. The man patted his dog quietly on the head and scowled at me, as though I should have known better.

My thighs burned. My scalp itched. I took my foot off the brake and slowly piloted the van back behind the service building, upstream, past the diesel pumps and the sleeping tractor-trailers. When I pulled around to the front again, Sarah stood beside a phone booth, holding a small second cup of coffee and a bottle of cranberry juice.

She crossed in front of me and knocked on the driver's side door. "Are we maybe a little bit cranky this morning?" she asked.

I pushed down the parking brake and tossed my remaining coffee out the window, as Sarah stepped gracefully aside. I went to the back of the van, searching for pants. "You were saved by a *blue dog*," I shouted.

"Fine," Sarah said, climbing in. "I won't even ask."

I stood in my underwear, holding a pair of green army shorts in my right hand. When my sister accelerated, the edge of the lacquered pine bed frame cut into the back of my knees. It knocked me flat across the mattress.

We were swamped in Saturday morning Buffalo traffic, and the only thing I'd decided was that underneath, at root, all of this was Grant's fault. He'd died holding out on us, and from that moment on, we could charge everything to his account. Belted into the passenger seat and facing backward, I was staring out the side windows using a fully charged Dustbuster I'd found in the cupboard to pick off cars I didn't like the look of. Grant was the last one to plug this thing in, I thought.

"Like my housemates aren't going to notice when I'm not there to write out my Boston Gas check and stick it on the refrigerator?" I asked. We were crawling along beside a tow truck that had a white limousine by the rear axle. The limo's car alarm screamed in protest.

"Your checkbook is here," Sarah said. "I packed it. They sell stamps all over the country. The same ones even."

"I can't. I can't do this," I said. "I have to be looking out for my future. This week I'm supposed to go interview a bunch of religious fanatics about the city's moral fabric. I can't fuck that up. I've got an interview with this guy who works the lift in the Merrimack River. He counts fish, all day. We've already put it off three times. I have to make up weekend coverage scheds for the rest of the summer. I have a haircut appointment."

"This could be your real future," Sarah said. "You'd never know."

"Why are we going to Niagara Falls?"

My sister smiled her serene, older-sibling smile. "Because we're in the neighborhood. Besides — it's faster to go through Canada to Detroit, then south. Have you ever been to Niagara Falls?"

"Not of my own free will," I said.

Some murky green river, probably the Niagara itself, roiled away on the left. There'd been a wreck up ahead and that had backed up the traffic. An ambulance had just finished squeezing through when the yellow Morris Mini ahead of us fired its windshield washers. The one on my side was wildly off target. It squirted over the Mini's roof and splattered against our grille.

"There," Sarah said. "We've been anointed. It's an omen." She flipped the Sugar Cubes tape and crammed it back in, but the music wouldn't start. She frowned. "So I didn't consult anybody," she said. "So I didn't wake you up. But we're already here. I need you along and you need to be along. You can *fly* back from St. Louis, if you want. If you're so worried about missing a few lousy days — fake an illness. Laryngitis. Use that. Get your housemates to call it in. They look like they'd do anything for you. But — if you are that obsessed with removing yourself from this vehicle, I will *drive* you to the nearest airport, any airport, and throw down my Visa."

"You don't have a Visa."

"I do now," she said. "From here on out, any time. Find me the nearest runway." She gave me a stare.

I pointed the Dustbuster at her.

"Tell me, who exactly is it you're letting down?" Sarah asked.

I didn't know, but I certainly wasn't going to answer. I dropped the Dustbuster and pulled down the visor on my side. We were still crawling along in line for the Grand Island Bridge and then the road to Niagara Falls. This is only my sister getting away with more stuff, and dragging me along as an audience, I thought. She always got exactly what she wanted. It's a fact of history.

As we drove on to the island, the traffic suddenly dropped away, but when we crossed over again, I saw that the Niagara had accelerated. There were standing whitecaps, where a mile back the surface had been relatively smooth. We followed a tractor-trailer with a sign that said, "Get On Board." Sarah took a ramp to Pine Avenue and drove quietly through downtown Niagara Falls.

For a few seconds, I kept thinking that the other drivers around us were all headed to work, and a faint, slightly giddy feeling took over, as if I were skipping school. Then I remembered that it was Saturday. I wouldn't have been working anyway, and they were all going off to enjoy themselves.

Sarah turned down a street that appeared to be drawn from a *Saturday Evening Post* illustration. There was a tire store and an old-looking Woolworth's, yet the buildings stopped abruptly as strands of mist threaded up from a hole at the end of the block. I could hear the rush of the falls. Sarah parked the van. The blue-hued buildings on the Canadian side seemed to peer into the gorge. A tower and a distant Ferris wheel glinted. They looked content and happy, forever residing at the brink of a natural wonder.

We crossed the street beneath the "Bridge to Canada" sign, but Sarah kept skipping ahead. I had to grab her arm. "Wait. We cannot get an uninspected, unregistered van in and out of Canada," I said. "Whether the windshield's muddy or not, it's a joke. Canada is a foreign country."

My sister glanced toward the park on the other side of the river. She folded her arms and continued across the street, seemingly deep in thought. "It's not going to be a problem," she said. "It's not. You have to have *some* faith."

Sarah started jogging ahead, anxious to find the river, to locate the roar behind the fresh, ascending mist. "Nate. Come on," she said. "We're having breakfast over there." Her arm arched up, as if she had thrown a flare across the water. She looked toward the falls she could hear but not see. She hopped down a set of steps. "Stop staring," Sarah called. "It's Canada. It's true. You have no choice but to be optimistic."

ELEVEN

Grant here. I bet you forgot about me already. Well, it wouldn't be the first time. But remember, I don't complain — I explain.

So let's get back to the important stuff. Let's get back to talking about my chronology. Let's get back to my specs. Where exactly *was* my story when we last left it?

OK, how about this? We'll retreat maybe fourteen years or so, to when I left the big corporate world and hooked up with this small outfit, Z-mu Tech, in Johnson City. They built test equipment, those machines that let you know whether or not that new computer you're designing — or even the chip that goes inside that new computer — is up to the task. See, for starters — and we should get this straight right off the bat — the fun in engineering resides entirely in forcing objects to work for you. No muss. No fuss. No back talk. Say you can get yourself into a nice big machine and find a way to max it out at some unheard of performance level — that's it.

Around that time Z-mu was still not far away from being a start-up, meaning that they were handing out stock options every few weeks or so, and I had a chance to be your all-purpose technical player. Initially I was dealing with known technology, doing some design work, but that was mostly all cookbook stuff. Later I was able to infiltrate one of those warmer seats, in with the groups designing the better boards for new machines. The job had a tangible, up-all-night, mission-control intensity to it. You spent your hours hunting stray voltages, redesigning through change orders, and always living in fear of accidentally creating a kiss-it-good-bye time bomb. Making the one mistake that would lead to a gigantic redesign. When it's all said and done, when your work is out there doing the job, if you're good at what you do, you never get the credit. Maybe a coffee mug — but never the credit.

After a half dozen years of that, I was starting to find myself shunted away to different, micro-projects. I was designing parts for boards that were never getting into machines. I was this shelved guy, tinkering with piddly stuff and quickly becoming obvious in his isolation. Grant, the nonissue — the big fella who turns into a ghost.

So, one day I met with the managers and offered to move back into creating software, primarily so I could become more of an icon than I already was. They agreed, and that paved the way for my return to the rational world of writing code. I would spend my days sitting at the screen, teasing out the algorithms and writing the instructions to tell those very literal, rational machines exactly what to do. It's a form of total absorption. If you're interrupted, you lose the flow. Real time goes away, it runs on its own merry way. Work like that for too long, though, and you lose your ability to deal with people in the outside world.

Case in point: I was in North Carolina recently, work-related, and way before all this. The big mucky-mucks sent me down to write some clean new software that would terminate this client's installation problem. And I don't know anybody except me who likes getting exiled out to the boonies on applications trips. Wherever you go, they're always mad at you. Me? I love it. I'm always right.

OK, so Acme wasn't this company's name, but that's close to what they were like. I turned out to be unnecessary, which meant I spent three days dicking around, imitating their accents: "I told you fiiiive or niiiine tiiimes how to do it alllready." Accents that left me breathless. But those people were so goddamn polite. Everybody except this one guy I had to work with, an SPS victim — short person syndrome. You *know* someone is short if the first thing you do going into their office is sit down and tie your shoes. This guy, however, was a purely aggressive short person. He disagreed with my very being. We had it out day and night over stuff that didn't matter at all. It was like theater. No matter.

But on that same trip, I'm staying at a Super 16, or 3200, or — whatever. Anyway, there's this hellacious noise outside at pitch black in the morning. So loud it could have been in my room. The largest garbage truck ever created. Urban renewal in Dumpsterville. They might have been taking a few of those tin-foil compact cars along as well. Beep. Beep. Crunch. All making me wake up in a sweat at 4:00 A.M. Sweating in your sleep is guaranteed to make you flatulent.

Anyway, you know how it is once you get going: you look up a little while later and say, How in hell did we get way over here? What I meant to point out was this — the one very good thing about writing code is that it takes a devious mind. Everybody knows that this is a job where it's possible to be a little wacko. There are no discernible consequences. The machine doesn't care. All that matters is the dead-line. After you've done it a while, at a certain point everything you're working on *does* become amazingly obvious. No problem appears impossible. There's nothing the irrational world can throw at you that can't be tamed. Next, you begin to think that this should apply to the world beyond work. If here, why not there? At least that's what you get to believe, until it starts to get you in trouble.

So, what else? I mean — let's clear the record here. In fact, I'm sure you're thinking that I made a practice of keeping life difficult for all concerned. Especially those two children on patrol. Right? OK, here's a hypothetical: Just think how treacherous I could have been. A clean inheritance? I could have sent them on quests. I could have made the *Wizard of Oz* look like a damn day trip. Be happy for small favors.

Anything more? I bet you also have a lingering concern about those stuffed animals in my living room. Most likely you're thinking that I'd have to be pretty twisted to take an abiding interest in taxi-dermy. Point of fact: collecting those creatures was an act of good samaritanship, and typical for me. How'd it happen? See, I met this guy, a French guy, at the dinky driving range near my house. This was the one time I'd decided to use those black clubs of my father's, though he's never played a game of golf in his life. There I was after work one night in July, swinging those clubs for the first time, and swinging them badly. I was chipping balls. Hooking balls. Skimming balls fifty yards straight out, about three inches high. But I paused long enough to watch this guy in the next stall over. He was blasting those suckers off into low spy-satellite orbit. We talked, and he turned out to be a junior high science teacher, as well as a part-time taxidermist. This guy was taking out his quite substantial frustrations at the range because his son had driven their uninsured Oldsmobile through a fence and a plate glass window belonging to some ungracious people in Endicott. My

French pal had lost in court and, as the parent, he owed. I sympathized. We drank a bit — well, a lot. He explained how he'd apprenticed as a taxidermist in Munich. How he'd worked for museums. He'd done some two thousand deer. So, I asked what he had in his collection, and then bought a good part of it, for about what he owed on the fence and plate glass. He was happy as hell, and I had to rent a truck.

You bet those animals work. Prowlers think I've got all kinds of things living in that house. And sure, the neighborhood looks nice enough, but two houses down we've got a nasty conglomeration of students. I don't know why they chose to live so close to me and far away from their campus in Binghamton, but they certainly can slam an amazing number of cars into a two-vehicle driveway. Last fall, months before *my* incident, before *my* fucking occlusion, it was two-goddamn-thirty in the morning and I was having another night of nonsleep because they had to play Pink Floyd's *The Wall* over and over. Then we had chanting coming out of the windows. One kid sat down in an open suitcase in the middle of the street and wouldn't move. The cops showed once, which shut everybody down for about thirty-five seconds. Half an hour later, when I saw a silver Blazer on their lawn rolling more kegs, klang-klang, off onto that porch, I decided that since I *did* live in a Crimewatch community, it was time to introduce a modicum of fear into their souls.

I got dressed. I went to the basement and climbed out the bulkhead. It was foggy out, and I had my chainsaw. I walked past their house, and when nobody noticed, I continued on for a block or so, until I fired that chainsaw up and came walking back through the fog. What would you think? The music went right off. Those lights winked out. They were watching from the porch like kittens, trying to see who was behind it all. It was a good moment. I got my sleep.

But, back to basics. Let's get on track, shall we? Here's another thing currently pissing me off: Am I tired of having my love life maligned — in public, no less. What you probably don't know is that I was close to married. Once. And you're surprised. Marylin, a short, bright woman with silver-rimmed glasses. A pasta person who liked cats. She was a secretary for another group at work, and we met catching softballs. You know, I thought, here is a woman who can *deal* with technology. Things were fine from the get-go, but she had a seven-year-old, Cassandra, who lived with her half of the year and in Richmond for the rest. We got involved during Marylin's half off. But as that whole picture began to resemble yet another family unit, I backed away. Every time some woman starts saying family, I start saying good-bye. Maybe that's a mistake, a fault in the character, but I've been that route once already.

What? Am I still not being useful enough? You'd like more? You'd like some conceptual leaps? One or two metaphysical discussions? A few high points of the cosmic tour? Well, maybe it's not like that. Though I do know that everything I say implies a few further questions.

Case in point: Why didn't I tell those two where Ray was?

Perhaps I forgot. Perhaps I didn't want to. Those two have no conception. Say you're home one night and, out of nowhere, your father knocks on the front door. It's raining and he's soaked. He's been walking, but he can't say why or from where. There are chunks of slush on his shoes and he has a tingling sensation, pins and needles, he says, in his fingertips. He's convinced that you are his brother. He keeps asking what the two of us are doing there. Shouldn't we be in Vermont rebuilding carburetors? Hot-wiring our father's cars? You bring him inside, and he wants to know why your house is full of moths. But these are moths that only Ray can see.

There used to be this saying at work, that with enough talent *every* problem is technical. You can use it if you're so inclined. Go ahead — just be sure to give credit where credit is due.

TWELVE

I couldn't believe my brother. We were on the Canadian side of the planet, at the absolute edge of one of the seven wonders of the Western world — and I was basking in it. Soaking in its misty and magnificent roar. I was quite happy there, watching the sun make a pixie-dust rainbow at the base of Horseshoe Falls. Then Nate asked, again, if I'd taken an "official" leave from work for this jaunt, or had I merely slimed out of it, as usual.

My ancient reputation rides in to haunt me. Oh, but I have patience. I have endless patience. I have to. I said that this was too an "official" day off. Though that could have been more true. I said I was taking a week without pay, for starters. So — could he quit being quite the spoilsport? "What are you," I asked, "a Puritan?"

I couldn't tell, maybe I was imagining it, but it seemed that Nate's really hostile phase began sometime when we were out on the Rainbow Bridge. Or maybe before — say, when I inched the van out of the parking garage and this black cat, fat as a raccoon, gave us a dirty look and crossed right in front of our bumper. "If a black cat crosses your road, does that mean anything?" I asked. I'm not exactly superstitious — but a few tiny spells never hurt.

Nate looked over and said, "More omens?" As if I'd spent my entire life skimming along on hope alone. As if — but no, I saw this for what it was — pure displaced anger about his being kept hostage. I let it go. Kidnap victims can be haughty.

I took my sunglasses off while we were still in line and idling on the bridge. The U.S., United Nations, and Canadian flags snap-popped in the breeze, and the whole bridge bounced when some large trucks went by the other way. That alarmed me, but I tried instead to think about what it might feel like to grow up in Niagara Falls. What would it be like to spend your teen years dodging tour buses full of blue-rinse senior citizens? Would it be truly odd to grow up at the edge of a honeymoon joke? But people can get used to anything, I guess.

Nate's fears aside, I did fine at customs. Simply fine. At the toll plaza, where the road slants down so they can peer inside your car, I looked that cute whiffle-cut boy right in the eye. They're so young, these customs agents. You get the feeling you're entering a country run by children.

First he asked if we were both both American citizens. (Yes.) Were we carrying any firearms, rifles, or pistols? (No.) What was the purpose of the trip? (Visiting relatives.) At that, Nate gave me a glance, as though I'd glossed the truth again. But I hadn't. Our destination? (St. Louis, via Detroit.) Therefore we wouldn't even be in the country for twenty-four hours? (Nope.) Any bottles of beer or alcohol? (I said no.) Anything we planned on leaving or selling in Canada? (I thought for a second, and shook my head.)

"Thank you." With nary a glance at our apparently troublesome registration stickers, his eyes zipped right to the Buick behind us.

Nate looked crushed. Nobody frisked or detained us. Things might actually work out. So he pouted.

Beyond the border, everything you hear is true. The Ontario side is that much nicer. The flower clock, the rose gardens, the black squirrels. We parked and I changed thirty dollars into Canadian. We ate scrambled eggs in a cafeteria surrounded by souvenirs. I broke down and bought several quite nice postcards. I guess I thought I'd bring them along to our father. He was always bringing postcards to us.

When we were done, I leaned over the flat-rock wall and watched the marbled green and white water. The Maid of the Mist boats kept fighting the current and creeping in toward the base of the falls. Intrepid, trusty steeds, one by one they went up to confront the blast of the falls.

Arguing with Nate had gotten so old that I decided to read him a few facts from a pamphlet I'd found. I told him that the waters before us had never frozen solid. That we were watching 700,000 gallons pass by each second. The lip was moving backward at six feet a year. Then there were the people who'd gone over. I explained that the girl where

I bought the postcards had told me she'd actually watched a cheerful woman smile and wave while she floated off in an inner tube — no doubt reenacting some misimagined tradition of sacrifice.

Nate interrupted to say that he was still logy. As if that adequately explained all his evil mood swings. He didn't want to hear facts. He didn't want to see the floral clock. He didn't want to ride the cable car. He wanted to sleep on the grass.

"OK, fine," replied the jailer. I left him on the lawn and wandered along the stone walk up to the edge of Horseshoe Falls. I went way upstream, past greenhouses and several more trinket shops. When I returned, half an hour later, Nate was still out, on the turf. He looked drugged, as if he'd been dropped from a great height. I checked him for a ticket, thinking that some Royal Canadian Neatness Mountie might have tagged my brother for vagrancy. Nate, the responsible vagrant. No such luck.

I sat on the grass a slight distance away and watched while he slept. His eyes were tightly scrunched, and I wondered if he'd taken too many hay fever pills, maybe mixed with a hangover from last night. But he'd had what? One beer? Or was it a kind of depression? Had I in fact kidnapped him?

Last night on the Thruway, I'll admit, I was a little out of control. I was doing all those things you normally do when the person you're driving with is asleep — playing the same song on a tape over and over, scat singing, steering with your toes. I kept thinking how weird it was to be going along like this, with my little brother lost to the world in the back of my dead brother's van.

Then the darker, more hopeless part — the why-draw-this-stuff-out-again feeling — slithered up as I passed the first of the Syracuse exits. I don't like Syracuse. I don't even like the name. It makes me think about everything that's gone wrong in my family. You know, I would like to think of the past as a set of clothes. It's true — an optional weightless wardrobe that you could carry around, yet only certain small items would ever be required. Is that too much?

It got worse when I saw the signs for the Syracuse airport. Because all of a sudden I remembered how my father used to drive us out to a fence by the end of the runway at night. He'd park, and Nate and I would get out and hide in the tall, sweeping grass as the gold and silver planes screamed over with their red underbelly lights winking. "That was a close one," my father would say and laugh. It was like this little game that we all wanted to play. A drama my father had thought up. See — he was very different when we were growing up. He was playful in a funny way. But then that went away. Yes, it had to do with what happened to my mother. But I can't believe that was everything. It's like, when we were older, and I used to think about the things we had done with him as kids, I could never understand why later my father enjoyed being on the road so much of the time. Why was being away always so much better than being around, at least a little? But then, the road does give you a kind of control, I thought. I glanced in the rearview mirror, at Nate's sleeping form in the back of the van.

My father rarely yelled at me, unless I did something dangerous, and usually that involved a car. But there were a few times, and once right after my mom died. We'd just barely moved to Vestal when, in the attic, I found a wardrobe box full of my mom's clothes. They were dresses, mostly. A red silk robe and two suits from the 1940s — one bright orange and the other olive green. I don't know why my father kept them. But when I asked, he suddenly got really mad, and the wardrobe was gone the next afternoon when I came home from school.

Around midnight, when the mileage signs began to list only Rochester, Buffalo, and points west, I'd finally started to slip back into being myself. I even seemed to be the only one on the road, until two dark cars came up in the right lane and passed me very quickly. They were close together and silky looking. They shimmered in my head-lights. I knew they were heading to some place far off and secure. If wishes were road dreams, I thought. Right then I decided to stop feeling guilty about kidnapping Nate. This is good for him, I rea-soned. It's good for everybody. Big deal, if he's not going to be exactly happy.

Nate rolled over on the lawn as two black squirrels crept forward to investigate his sneakers. They were the same as the grays, maybe a little smaller, but with glistening eyes. They couldn't get across the river, so they stayed Canadian — at least that's what the girl at the concession stand said. The squirrels began actually sniffing Nate's shoes, so I thought it was time to wake him up. I was pretty sure my brother had never seen a black squirrel before.

"Ow," Nate said, as if I'd stung him with a tranquilizer dart or something. The black squirrels ran away. I explained that it was 9:50 and we couldn't linger. "Sleep in the van," I suggested.

We bought Dr Peppers and took a path up past an ornamental garden to get to the van. Nate walked behind me like a prisoner. As if he were being towed. This became a trifle annoying, but I decided to take it as one more symptom of his world-weariness. In the parking lot, I unlocked Nate's side first.

"Here," I said, as I opened the door. My brother hopped right in. It is like having a pet, I thought. Short commands do work best.

THIRTEEN

Quite possibly what my sister kept saying was true. Perhaps I might find my brain on the road. Perhaps I might locate a few clarifying revelations out in the great, flat-sky Midwest. But I doubted it.

Out on the Canadian openness of Route 3, I was still annoyed. But I did my turn at the wheel and tried to distract myself by any means possible. For instance, all the cars in Ontario, I suddenly realized, were giant and four-door solid. In the white sedan ahead of us I watched an oval-headed child wedge five bare-chested Hulk-A-Mania wrestling dolls against the back window. He would hide down in the seat and every few minutes or so pop up and knock out a different one with a karate chop to the knees.

The air smelled like fresh blacktop, but the sky stayed white and clamped down. We passed low, musty-green fields of tobacco, dairy farms, and turquoise Players billboards sporting young lasses advertising cigarettes. All the edges — the brick ranch houses and the hard wide cardboard cigarette packs — looked foreign and just different enough to recognize. Occasionally I'd catch a glimpse of Lake Erie, shining like distant slate off on the left. But with all the flatness, I kept losing my perspective. The far-off power gantries and tree islands that hid the farms seemed to stay in place along the horizon until you crept up on them. Only then did they appear to accelerate and move in on you.

Sarah was asleep in the other seat, which she'd clicked back far enough for it to qualify as a lounger. She looked happy, as if she'd become totally accustomed to that sort of rattled slumber. It made me wonder if driving addictions were genetic. My father would always quote this line from somewhere about having an X on your chest, meaning that you could only be happy on the road. I knew he thought it applied to him.

I was staring at a silver Mustang in front of us with New York plates when I began to hear my father's quick voice dispensing driving advice. He was always full of tips. But he'd hand these nuggets out in such a conspiratorial way that you felt like you'd been let in on a secret. I remember him telling me how to get a pace car working for you on a dull stretch of superhighway. A fella starts to pass you, my father would say, but he does it so slowly that you start to wonder if he's ever going to finish up. You increase your speed just as he makes the pass. That means it takes him a little longer to do it. Next, you stay on his tail for exactly two miles, and after that — bingo, you've got yourself a pace car. An escort for life. Count on it. That guy is never gonna let you pass him.

Only after staring at the license plate ahead of me for five minutes did I realize that the three letters before the numbers — RJS — made up my father's initials.

We crossed the bridge from Windsor, Ontario, back into the U.S., as Detroit's svelte blue downtown towers gleamed below on the right. The water was rough. At the wall of U.S. customs toll booths, I sagged into line behind a cream-colored Winnebago. One of the two customs agents in our lane, a red-bearded man in a navy windbreaker, stepped slowly from the camper and nodded to his partner, a petite woman, in the booth. She motioned the Winnebago on with her index finger.

I hadn't even come to a complete stop when the woman in the booth said: "Anything purchased or acquired in Canada that you are bringing back?"

Sarah had made a list, so I handed it over. The woman glanced at it and, above the rush of accelerating vehicles, asked if we were carrying firearms, alcohol, or fireworks. Everything in the van began falling under headings. "No," I said finally.

She returned the list. "How long have you been in Canada?"

"Just today," I said, "from Niagara Falls."

She paused and looked away, as if she might let us go. "Both American citizens?"

"She's my sister," I said. "Yes." I sensed that I wasn't answering quickly enough. That I wasn't on top of something.

The woman glanced across the windshield. "Please put the vehicle in park and step out," she said. "The two of you."

I fumbled with the seat belt as Sarah hopped down from the other side and stood on the concrete barrier. My sister slid a finger across the deep blue lenses of her sunglasses.

The customs woman adjusted her hat and climbed into Grant's van, easing her way across the fake velour of the driver's seat. I tried to keep from staring at the muddy windshield, but I couldn't help it. Diesel fumes swirled. A car door slammed in annoyance several islands over. Through Grant's dark windows I watched her walk the length of the van. She paused to pat down the nest of unrolled sleeping bags on the bed. Up front, she opened the ash tray and pushed through six or seven cigarette butts, left, I assumed, by Grant. As she got out, she gave me a disappointed look and said, "Thank you," before waving in the general direction of Detroit.

My mouth tasted like pennies. The backs of my knees felt weak as I drove away.

"She was searching the ash tray for roaches," Sarah said calmly. "That and for illegal aliens in the back." My sister started to poke through the cigarette butts. "Menthols?" she said. "When did big boy even start smoking? Wow, here's one with lipstick. Think he ever had a girlfriend? I mean — what if? But it is kinda hard to imagine."

At this, the knotty voice of my fearful imagination revved to hyperspeed. "What if," I said. "What if Grant *had* left behind a few roaches? How would we have known? We'd be totally screwed. We'd be tagged for possession and driving an unregistered, uninsured, possibly stolen vehicle. A felony across international lines. We'd never get back."

"Come again?" Sarah began flipping through the road atlas. "We could use some roaches," she said. "I get kind of nostalgic for it these days."

"This is stupid," I said, as all my earlier arguments began coalescing and coming up from the lower depths. "We should *not* be in this vehicle."

"You are amazing," Sarah said. "None of that happened." She showed me her wrists. "Look — no handcuffs. We are not doomed to any particular fate. You're with me, and though it may not look it, I do have a certain reservoir of luck."

"We should not be driving an unregistered vehicle," I said. "It's the same as carrying radioactive material around in your pocket."

"That's good. Ever think of writing copy? No? OK — how about we argue over the map?" She snapped her finger at the Michigan page. "That's what they make maps for."

I clammed up and concentrated on the rowdy swirls of Detroit traffic. Having Sarah for a sister is like living next to a brushfire. You think stuff is smothered but it never really goes out.

It was only when we passed the three-story Uniroyal tire on I-94 and Sarah explained exactly how we were going to get to Missouri that the actual argument started. Specifically, she wanted to drive across Michigan, loop under Chicago, cut diagonally across Illinois, and descend on St. Louis from the top. I wanted to swing through Indianapolis and come in from the east.

"Have you ever been to Indianapolis?" Sarah said. "Not a pretty picture."

"It's just a city." I took the atlas and put it on my lap. I was trying to examine the map and drive at the same time. It is entirely possible for these arguments to last for hours, with every exchange beginning with a "but." And it is much more insidious arguing with a sibling, because you can go so far out, to the point where you no longer know what you're saying. You find yourself mouthing off about half-thought-through ideas that no normal person would bring up in a real conversation.

"Are we — getting back to the root problem?" Sarah said as the road closed in on Ann Arbor. "You don't want to be here, so you've decided to become obstructionist. If that's it — then give me back the map so I can find an airport."

I handed over the atlas and Wyoming fell to the carpet.

"Look." Sarah's finger rubbed a hole in the page. "Half an inch north of here is a place called Hell. If we drove there — then we could have an argument from Hell. Imagine, a whole town from Hell. The high school from Hell. The policemen from Hell, the marching band from —"

"Stop," I said. "You're digressing."

"It's a tactic. But come on, you are due."

"For what?"

"For this. Due to be here. Due — OK, this is my theory. My theory is that one's life goes on just as it is for only so long before there's an eruption of some sort. Then you end up in an entirely different place. It's true. Take you. Your job deteriorates, you've broken up with this Claire person, then there's Grant, and you and I have both let our father off the hook for years and years and years. The pressure builds and whoosh — look where we are now."

"That's not a theory. Things just happen. It's fate. There's no theory to fate," I said.

Sarah hummed. "Yeah well, maybe you can defuse some of this as you go along, so there's less of a reaction when the eruption actually starts. But everything builds and eventually there's this really huge outburst. Like if you don't pay enough attention, that's bound to happen. All these psychic eruptions. Then you have to scramble around and put everything back together. That's just how it works. The problem is — knowing which stuff you really have to pay attention to."

"What," I said, "like Grant dying? Who could have defused that?"

"See — *he* could have defused it. Maybe. But for us, it's like the trigger. That's the thing that propelled us in this direction. Everything works in relation to something else. You are not totally out here by yourself — no matter what you want to think. It's not that the scrambling part is so bad, or that you could even avoid it. Sometimes it's necessary."

"That's *your* life," I said. "The scrambling part."

"Your life, my life—" Sarah's hand waved back and forth. "Wait. You don't even *know* enough about my life to say that. My life isn't all scrambling. Some things, yeah, but whose life isn't 75 percent scrambling? You think you don't scramble? You scramble every day and you hate it. At least I've tried lots of different stuff. How would you know what you wanted otherwise? Maybe *you* should try some other things. But — that's not the point. You need to know which things are going to come back and get you later on. You know, the stuff that will cause massive regret? Things that got avoided? You have to think

-124-

about this so you can pay attention before it does come back to haunt you."

"That shit's endless," I said. "Thinking about everything after the fact. It's like looking in mirrors. We live in an irrational world. That's it. I see that every day at work. I mean, look at what's happened to us."

"If we let Dad float off forever, and pretend we don't care, and never confront him — *that* will come back and get us. Years later, wherever we are, no matter what we're doing, it'll knock us out when it's too late to do anything about it. That's what I mean."

"I'm only trying to keep my head down and out of trouble."

Sarah laughed. "Oh — and things in your life aren't related? There's no cause and effect? How interesting."

"You sound like my boss," I told her. "Maris goes around saying, 'Evil comes to those who leave life unattended,' or crap like that, pretty much constantly."

"You forget," Sarah said. "I am your boss."

The road noise switched from pocketa-pocketa to yeah-yeah-yeah as we skipped across the cracks. The highway sounded like a panting dog. Ahead of us, a dented flatbed truck hauling smashed cars slowed down as its outside rear tire began to shred. Black rubber snakes peeled away, whipping skyward. I watched as a head-sized chunk of rubber shot up like a pop fly. I was sure our windshield was going to catch it on the descent, but the chunk landed in the median and bounced away.

The case against my father had been sharpening itself all day. It was still winding up, even as I drove west against my will. Why hadn't I been in touch with him? It was a big thing, I knew that, but in some ways the problem had gone on so long that it all felt chopped off and distanced. Driving out here to find him, doing that, would never have occurred to me. And I was embarrassed by this. But then I thought, maybe that was only the sentimental guilt, the stuff you'd expect to feel, and not something actually connected to the facts. Had he tried to be in touch with me? It was obvious: He really didn't care.

It is strange, but sometimes, when I dwell on it, the worst part growing up wasn't that my father was away a lot, but that when he was around he was so present. Like when I was small, he'd take me to Syracuse lacrosse games and explain everything, so I'd get all excited.

He'd explain how Jim Brown was even better at lacrosse than he was at football. Or how the Iroquois played on giant fields and the games went on for days. My father seemed certain that lacrosse would be the next big thing. If I was going to play a sport, it ought to be one that I could get into on the ground floor. The odd thing was, I did what he said. My father's attention was a beam of sorts, a focused path of light, one that you missed more than you ever expected, the moment it was gone.

"So — it's like this," Sarah said out of nowhere. "We'll find him and sort things out. What's a little more family dysfunction going to do to us anyway?"

I watched her for a few seconds, so long that she felt compelled to say something about getting my eyes back on the road. "I don't want to build this up," I said. "He's never paid more than cursory attention to us for years. All I really owe him is the chance to ignore him back."

My sister rubbed her lips. "Aren't you supposed to get over these things at a point?" she said. "You know — what's bigger, feeling put upon now, or facing some really sensational regret later on because you didn't do anything when you could? Anyway, with Grant involved — how could you really say what Dad does or doesn't know about us?"

Maybe she had a point, I thought. Half a point.

Sarah shook her head. "I see what you're up to. You go out every day and throw yourself at work like a buzz saw sacrifice. As if none of the other stuff in your life mattered. You pretend you're so busy that you don't have even a second to think about it. No fooling. I know — you brood all the time."

My sister gazed out at the quickly passing fields of Michigan. "Shit," she said. "After I thought you were fine on this — when you stopped going on about everything a few miles back. With me, not talking means there's a big pivotal question floating around. For you, not talking's always this sign that things are way cool."

"Nothing in my life has ever been way cool," I said.

"There's a perception," said my sister.

Sarah drove on through the heat, and my eyes folded down like a lizard's. I woke up outside Gary, Indiana, where the road wind smelled of sulfur. The air was thick and spongy, and you could collect a sweat simply by hanging your arm out the window. Sarah had her window open and the air conditioner blasting. "You should have lain down in back," she said. She gave me a quick smile, something you could barely catch on film.

My knees and back ached. My shoulders tingled as we moved up to pass a liquid propane truck. "The good thing," Sarah announced, "is if one of these things explodes while you're passing it — you're going to make the six and eleven o'clock news. CNN, even."

It was nearly seven and Sarah had decided that we were stopping for the night somewhere south of Joliet. "Don't you know people in Chicago?" I asked, taking back the atlas.

"Yeah, but I don't have their phone numbers on me. It would suck if we did that. We'd have to be gracious tourists. You know — go to restaurants. Chat."

"Chat," I said. "Are you nervous about seeing him? I mean Dad."

"In a way," Sarah said.

"Think he knows about Grant?"

She shrugged. "I couldn't imagine outliving my children. If I ever get to have any."

"All we do is drive around," I said, "spreading bad news like a virus." But as the words came out, I sensed that I'd given in. I realized that I would go along, up to a point. I would go to St. Louis and then fly back. It was like that moment when you're driving and you know you've missed your ramp, and there's no turnaround ahead so you change the route in your mind.

I opened the atlas. "It's like an hour to Joliet," I said. "Unless you want to push it all the way to Normal."

Sarah smoothed a stray hair away from her face and caught the steering wheel with her knee. "You and I could never make it to Normal."

FOURTEEN

Sarah was up at seven. From the floor of the van, where I'd been sleeping on a loose collection of foam camping pads, I watched her glance out the back window. "What a day," she exclaimed. "I wish I had my little pink outfit." She laughed. It was Sunday morning and we were east of Joliet, in a grassy RV campground. The night before, Sarah had begun to get a little loony, which made her first remark of the morning slightly more disturbing than it needed to be. Last night, after take-out ribs near the state prison, Sarah persisted in pestering me about my favorite piece of punctuation. "My old officemate Gala was a dash kind of girl," she said, "and you like semicolons. I've seen that split before. It may be sex-linked, but with a semicolon, you never know which way to go."

I rolled over as Sarah continued to stretch. She stopped to draw a pair of beaded earrings from a plastic container at her feet. She had on a white V-neck undershirt, a pair of men's boxers.

When I woke up the second time, my sister was dressed and in the driver's seat, patting the top of the dash for the keys. Her hair was damp, so I assumed she'd been out to take a shower. The floor shook as she started the van.

"Wait," I shouted. "We can't go until I've brushed my teeth. We can't." Sarah nodded and drove on toward the rest rooms. My back hurt as I stood up. I wasn't used to the rhythm of this kind of travel, and by the time I made it up front everything out in the world seemed far too bright. The sun was already a dense white knob, and when I began rubbing my eyes I couldn't stop.

Sarah coasted up to the rest room door and rolled down her window. Three kids were already splashing around in the campground's aqua-green pool. Their mom leaned against the fence, sipping coffee from a gray mug, as the kids argued about the nature of lightning. The smallest one kept saying, "No, water *attracts* lightning." At first I thought this was funny, then I thought, maybe I should go over there and correct the misconception. I wasn't really awake.

It was only after I'd entered the cedar-paneled shower stall, and had hung my shorts on a chrome hook, that I began to understand that I was actually in Illinois. I was away, and my father sat one state further on, in a nursing home. It was almost more than I could comprehend. I couldn't find a way to fold it into a coherent picture.

Sometimes, when I was small and my father was on the road, I'd find myself in his room examining the artifacts. His closet had shelves and shelves of tweed and felt hats. The hundreds of neckties were all at one end, dangling from a revolving hanger. The dresser, with its glass top, always smelled of Skin Bracer, and the quarters, nickels, and dimes had their own tourist-attraction coffee mugs. There were usually packs of Beeman's gum, half-used rolls of Tums, and a stack of folded, dark silk handkerchiefs lined up in some order across the glass top. My father's campaign ribbons and service medals rested in a tan pocket-watch case that was always closed. A piece of brass with the Chinese characters for the word "crisis" sat under the mirror. The first character, he once told me, stood for danger, and the second for opportunity. I never knew if that was really true or not.

When I finally turned the shower on, I decided that this visit could only be overwhelmingly sad.

We ate breakfast at the Flying Zero truck stop, which was a large, sparkling restaurant hooked to a drugstore. A sign outside announced that they had a fax, and that all the tables in the front section were reserved for "Professional Drivers Only." Blue credit-card phones lined the counter and waited beside the catsup bottle in every booth. The host led us to a table that looked out on the freshly sealed parking lot. Across the aisle, a man in a purple T-shirt, one that came in tight against his brown arms, landed a tired White Sox hat on the table and unfolded his copy of a Christian trucking paper.

I ordered the Early Riser Special, while my sister got blueberry muffins, tomato juice, and coffee. As the food arrived, Sarah asked for a pen and my Sprint number, so she could call the nursing home to get directions.

"Slow," Sarah said. "We'll take it slow." She eased her palm down on a cushion of air while she waited for directory assistance. "Crestwood," she told the operator. "Willow Meadows at Sandy Run? A nursing, I mean, residential home. Thanks." Sarah scrawled the number on the back of a napkin and dialed. "Yes, I need directions from 55," she said, sweetly. The lavender ink bled into the paper a bit, and I was reading upside down as she wrote. Route 44 — west. 270 south. "Oh thanks, no," Sarah said. "We'd like this to be a surprise." She gave me a pained look. "No — really. Blue awning. Fine. I'll remember."

Sarah placed the receiver back in its cradle above the condiments and stared at it for a second. "A bunch of them are going to be trucked to a mall for an art show after lunch," she said. "Well, the woman didn't say trucked, but that's what she meant. If we're there before one it shouldn't be a problem." She tapped my pen on the table three times. "Could this get any grimmer?"

"How long is it going to take?" I asked a little too quickly. As I raised my arm, intending to scratch my temple, I knocked over Sarah's half-empty glass of tomato juice. A stream began to dribble off the table edge.

"Ha," Sarah said as her hands flicked out. "See, I did that. Psychokinesis." She wiped up the juice with a napkin. "How long?" she asked. "A couple hours. Four maybe?" My sister tossed the napkin aside and rubbed the arms of her navy and white striped pullover, as if she were suddenly chilly.

"How long have you had that shirt?" I asked.

"Since I was fifteen."

For a second there I thought, maybe all we really do have in common is this unruly pile of half-junked memories. "You ever wonder about the big chunks, things that somehow got blocked out," I asked. "Like how we got from there to here?"

My sister smiled faintly, as though I were being far too mysterious to actually deal with. "Sometimes," she said. "But it's better not to. We're here and that's it."

My sister and I were back in the van and out on I-55, where Sarah had settled into a flat 75 mile-per-hour groove, leading us on out of the Land of Lincoln. I watched lawns the size of inland seas go by, each one surrounded by acres of corn. I began thinking about how the roads and power lines out there could run wherever they wanted, oblivious to topography. At that, my legs began to tingle, and I found myself again planning ahead only in terms of hours, miles, and bathrooms. It had taken millions of minor adjustments just to get into that loose, state-of-the-road rhythm, to get good and road-brained, and now it was pretty much wasted, as we'd practically arrived.

A few minutes later, as we entered the outer reaches of St. Louis's freeway web, the city popped up as a blue nub of blocky buildings on the horizon. The traffic stream picked up a notch, and soon we were on an overpass, rising above the Mississippi. The river was low and the color of infield dirt as we crossed. Rust-covered barges with turquoise and gray fiberglass tops hugged each other on the Illinois side. In front of the arch, which looked fragile and more delicate than I'd expected, two paddle wheelers, gorged with tourists, were held in place by long thick cables.

Sarah stayed quiet all through the city. And as the exits piled up, I noticed a sign for Clayton, which was where our Uncle Stan lived. I'd been there once, long ago. It was a land of big lawns and cul-de-sacs, as far as I remember.

A few minutes after that we arrived at the nursing home. My sister turned off the exit ramp, and there it was: Willow Meadows at Sandy Run, set into the side of a hill and looking out over a golf course. From a distance, you might even mistake it for a long, cedar-shingled apartment complex. My sister parked just past the blue awning, which was draped in white Christmas lights. A yellow and green windmill, with an accompanying red barn, both looking like refugees from a miniature golf course, sat in the circle of lawn across from the front door. Sarah still hadn't said a word.

We walked in through the push of the air conditioning, and I saw the open double doors of two golden brown elevators ahead of us at the end of the carpeted hall. An antique, glass-fronted hutch waited against one pale wall, beside a locked thermostat. The balcony beyond the elevators overlooked the dining room. A shining banner on the brick wall said, "Summer's Coming Up."

The small formica reception desk by the door had an oversize Rolodex in one corner. A walkie-talkie sat recharging next to a silver phone console, which seemed to control half a dozen or more lines. The red sticker atop the handset said, "Smile."

We stood there for a few seconds, not quite knowing what to do, while a large man wearing suspenders and a brown bow tie shuffled past to peek into the glass-fronted wall of mailboxes. A pair of ladies by the elevator, each with pancake makeup on and pastel-rinse hair, smiled at us, no doubt wondering whose grandchildren we were. They hauled themselves along by the walnut handrails and held the elevator doors for a shrunken man in a black suit. They all moved as though they were under water.

My sister and I wandered aimlessly for several minutes. We looked down both hallways for the vanished receptionist, but no one materialized. I read the canary-colored calendar of events posed under plastic above the receptionist's desk: Bingo, *Caddyshack II*, Learn to Fall Day, Bank Day, Mail Day, Drugstore Day. Errands elevated to the status of events.

When I turned around, Sarah had sat down behind the desk and was flipping through the Rolodex. I leaned in as she reached my father's card. "Raymond Scales, 243 East, 434-6783." Below that I saw Stan's address and phone number. At the bottom, in emphatic red pencil, it said, "Visitors See Mr. Wendall."

"Can I help? You shouldn't —" An Asian woman in a print smock dress appeared behind me. Her voice trailed off as she began reading my Godzilla T-shirt. The caption across my stomach was in Japanese. I had no idea what it said.

Sarah smiled quickly and slipped back to the visitors' side of the desk. "Yes —" she said, as if it had just occurred to her that help might be a good thing. "We're looking for Raymond Scales. We're his children."

The woman took her seat. "I'm sure he'll be glad to see you," she said, spinning the Rolodex to "S" and carefully peeling back one card after another, until her face clouded over. She perched on the edge of the chair and punched the third red button on the phone console. "Children," she said, almost to herself. "Mr. Wendall? Two of Mr. Scales's children are here to see him. Do you have a minute?"

She put down the phone and stood up with both hands in the air, as if she were prepared to conduct a small choir. "You two are in luck.

Mr. Wendall is in today and he will be right with you," she said, before slipping around the corner into a small, brightly lit kitchen.

Mr. Wendall emerged from the dim end of the hall. He was a decade older than me and very tan. It looked as though he'd just tossed on his brass-buttoned blue blazer, because underneath it he wore a teal golf shirt. "Glad to meet you," Mr. Wendall said. "My office. Please."

He held out his hand and led us down the silent corridor. I felt like a parent heading off to the principal's office, all set to discuss the latest misdeeds of a recalcitrant child. "We are surprised to see you," Mr. Wendall announced, once we had settled in the chairs before his desk. "Ah, how shall I put this? We understood from your brother there was a great deal of family friction. But, I am sorry to say, your father isn't here."

Sarah leaned forward and pulled the bangs away from her eyes. "What?" she said.

"Not to alarm you, but your father left us about a month back." His enunciation made it sound as though our father had passed on to another dimension.

"Left us?" I said. "For where?"

"Well, we're not sure."

I looked at Sarah. "But we just found out he was here."

Mr. Wendall narrowed his gaze, managing to look at once both concerned and defensive.

"What's this 'left us' stuff?" Sarah asked. "Like he's missing?"

"He left," Mr. Wendall said, showing us his palms. "He packed and left. We've done every usual thing. Notified the police, filed a missing person's report. Have you spoken to your uncle?"

We shook our heads. Mr. Wendall rubbed his nose.

"I see," he said. "Well, your uncle, his whole family in fact, they are out of the country. In New Zealand for two months.

"What's he doing in New Zealand?" I said.

Mr. Wendall seemed taken aback, but he shrugged. "I'm sorry," he said. "I suppose I should have handled this meeting a little differently."

"No," Sarah said. "You're doing fine — so far." She stood, walked behind her chair and drilled a tiny circle in the carpet with her heel. "It must, of course, be disorienting," she said, "misplacing your residents like this. But here's what we know, and you can fill in the blank spots.

Our brother, Grant — who I'm sure you must have talked to — died several weeks ago."

Mr. Wendall nodded and folded his hands in front of his nose. He looked bored and faintly frustrated. "My condolences," he said.

"You knew?" Sarah said.

"Yes, from your uncle. Your brother's lawyer contacted him. Possibly your father knows too. I believe this sad news came right before he left us."

Sarah squinted. "Stop with this 'left us' stuff. Stop it now. We only found out where our father was through Grant's checkbook."

"Well," Mr. Wendall said, "here is the story as I know it. And this is all I know. When your father first arrived here — and it was arranged by both your brother and your uncle — he was suffering from a moderate to extreme memory loss. Your brother, unfortunately, had a hasty workup done, and his specialist diagnosed this as Alzheimer's, a diagnosis that your brother then began planning for. Your father had perfect recall of many past events, but everyday ones were sometimes difficult. He was easily confused. Once he came here, we changed his diet and placed him on vitamins. Apparently, when he was living alone in Binghamton, he'd gotten himself onto an odd diet — which happens more frequently than you'd expect. With further examinations here, it became clear that your father was suffering from pernicious anemia. We stabilized his diet and his memory improved. You can talk to the doctors if you'd like." Mr. Wendall refolded his hands.

"So — you don't know where he went?" Sarah asked. "No forwarding address?"

"I'm sorry."

"Great," she said. "Can we sue you for this?"

Mr. Wendall frowned. He seemed to have had nearly enough of us. "No, no," he said. "You must understand that we could never keep your father here against his will. He was always free to go. And you've come all the way from —"

"Boston," my sister said, walking closer to his desk.

"Well, I'm a St. Louis boy myself," Mr. Wendall said. He stood up quickly as if to balance the room. "We wish you'd called ahead. Be sure to leave an address and phone number before you go. When will you be going?"

Sarah and I stared at each other for a long and dumb second. "We honestly don't know," I said.

"I'm very sorry that there isn't more for you here," Mr. Wendall said. Then he smiled.

FIFTEEN

Great. Another woe-is-us drama. As if I couldn't live without one for even a few tiny minutes. See — I couldn't think of what to do, so I drove Nate downtown; right to the Mississippi. The whole way in, he didn't once utter a single complaint. It perplexed me, though I certainly wasn't going to ask about it. We parked by the arch, but I was hungry. So — a minute later we were at the river's edge, sitting in the "Dining Salon" of a phony paddle wheeler that was really a Burger King.

"Guess that's it," Nate said. He examined his fish sandwich and calmly pushed some little lettuce strands back in at the edges.

"Guess that's what?"

"It was kind of dumb to figure we could pull this off," Nate announced. "Wasn't it? How many days to get back?"

"What do you mean back? Dear — I could kill you now or wait. This isn't a vacation."

"I know that," my suddenly surly brother replied. "I've figured that much out." He gave me a look that might have steamed vegetables.

"Come on," I said. "Our father's a blabbermouth. We'll nose around and find out who he told."

"Told what?"

"The plan. He's always had a bunch of plans. Kerbillions of plans. You know that. Besides — a plan's never any good if you keep it a secret." More than once when we were growing up my father would explain how he'd barely missed out on some new wonderful invention. These were all plans for improbable things he'd thought up years earlier but never had time to develop. Mint-flavored dog biscuits — for example. We could have been very rich. "Runaways always tell someone what they have in mind," I said.

"So?" Nate said.

"So what? Do you always give up this easily? We could keep going."

My brother's head began wagging from side to side. "To where?" he moaned. "Austin? Vancouver? California? How do we even know if he wants to see us?"

"It really doesn't matter," I told him. "Don't you get it?"

Nate rolled his napkin into a white tube. "I've been pretty good so far," he said.

That one was too ripe. I laughed. I couldn't help it, but really — I wasn't in the mood.

"I've gone along," my brother said, sounding aggrieved. "We've got a fucked-up family. You can't just tape it back together like a snapshot, because it's a snapshot no one ever took. We should forget more things. We should let more things go."

"Wrong, wrong, wrong," I said. "Look, if we do it, if we track him down and it doesn't work out, then OK, we'll feel sad — but not guilty too. That's the problem with this stupid family. Everybody gets their own little way and has a falling-out with someone else. Did we ever know why Dad and Stan had a falling-out after we moved to Vestal? No. Do we now know why Grant did what he did? No. It's a world of petty people where no one talks to anyone, and I'm tired of it. I think this stuff is genetic. It's like a streak or something. It's this selfish, I'm-too-important-to-talk-to-you type thing. So then what? We go on forever not knowing where Dad is? Is that what you want? I'm sorry, but you can't have it. We've got this tiny little window here."

Nate gazed down, out the window. He seemed to be looking across the Mississippi and back into Illinois. He dolefully picked up a plastic knife as a helicopter full of tourists buzzed the tan water. I could have beat him up. Really.

"Why do you think we're here?" I said finally. "Like, on the planet — if we're not supposed to figure some of this junk out. Or at least try. I mean, why do we get stuck with the people we do? Is it random? I don't think so. We have to sort this stuff out. That's our job."

Nate looked weary. Way too tired for someone who doesn't have kids. He spun the plastic knife on the table top and flicked it away.

"I'm afraid we will find him," my brother said eventually, "and he'll be this old guy working in a video arcade or something. The guy who gives out tokens and tells you which games are good."

"Say we find that — aren't you even curious?"

"No."

I didn't believe him. How could he not be curious? "Come on, we'll make this up as we go along. You'll like that."

"We have to go back while I'm still marginally employed. Maybe later I could—"

"You hate work." Nate's face picked up this granite cast. He opened his mouth to object, but nothing came out. Then I said what I still can't believe: "You don't get it. We don't have to go back. Ever."

"Meaning what?"

"Look. All of a sudden, after all this, we are lucky beyond belief. We can do anything we want. We can live out our lives like fabulous lottery winners. Nate — we sell Grant's house and sponge off the insurance. We're having a huge joke, and all at his expense. Don't you see?"

My brother turned his head, but only slightly. It was true — he really hadn't thought of that.

"Go back if you want," I said. "But we're way, way out. Halfway to big nowhere. Across the Mississippi. People *pay* for trips like this. Do you know how many people have died trying to cross that river?" I shut up about there because I was getting a little sidetracked.

A new helicopter scooted back to pick up more tourists, and Nate squinted out the window. I didn't want to let him think too long about anything.

"OK, fine, then just do this," I told him. "Go back there with me and see if we can find out where he went. I've got the room number. We'll infiltrate their next trip to the mall or something. Then — I'll drive you to the airport and slap down some plastic."

Nate opened his pie and frowned. "This is apple and I ordered cherry," he said. But he ate it anyway.

Back at Willow Meadows, though, as I hopped out of the van, this suddenly didn't seem like such a great idea after all. A new failure of nerve on my part. But what choice did I have? I had to pee. It was an excuse — and we were in the neighborhood.

Nate held the door, and as I walked in I saw that — lucky for us — the off-putting receptionist had slipped away from her post. "Bathroom, Nate. Find bathroom," I said, like he was some Saint Bernard. But my brother led me down the hall and around an old smiling couple with walkers — right to the ladies' room door.

When I came out, Nate said, "234 East?" and looked up, as if he could now tell directions inside buildings simply by reading the ceiling. Then he led us back into the lobby, where a woman with wide blue eyes was driving her electric scooter-thing in circles. Smooth as pudding, Nate pulled a piece of paper from his pocket. I knew it was blank, but he said, "Excuse me?" When she jerked to a stop, he double-checked the scrap and knelt. "We're looking for 234 East? We're here to surprise Papa."

Papa?

"Oh?" the woman said. She placed her hand over her eyes, as if she could no longer remember where on earth she was, but she did give us the directions.

We did as we were told and ambled through the cafeteria and past a room full of people watching *Wheel of Fortune*. "Mathilde here should too be on this show," a husky man shouted. In the next hall, we passed endless doors with "Good Morning" smiley faces dangling off their knobs. I peeked into the darkened crafts center. A foam replica of the Statue of Liberty — foil tiara and all — towered over everything from the corner.

Our father's door was at the end of that hall. His name wasn't in the slot, and staring at that blank space gave me a twinge. I imagined his Oxfords denting the gray carpet before the door. Then, for a half a second, really finding him suddenly did seem hopeless.

Nate ran his fingers around the door frame like a spy checking for booby traps. Then he turned and knocked on the door across the hall — though the door next to our father's apartment was wide open. A plaque on it said: "The Kushners."

I stuck my head in. "Excuse me?" I signaled Nate with a finger. The Kushners were watching the Olympic trials on television. Mr. Kushner stood up so slowly that I felt bad for making him move. He was much older than my father and dressed entirely in tan. He used to be blond, you could tell. He smoothed the funny mesh vest he wore over his button-down and eyed me curiously. I smiled. The plaid furniture behind him looked rented, except for the hutch. Mrs. Kushner stayed on the couch. She wore a white shawl and had a vaguely famous face.

"Good afternoon," Mr. Kushner said. He adjusted his hearing aid and swung his hand out to grab mine.

"Hi," I said. I did the introductions and asked if they knew our father.

Mr. Kushner covered his mouth. "You certainly could be his children. Could be indeed," he said, finally. "Margaret, visitors."

I nearly shouted: Nate, they're here. We've found our grandparents. The mythical ones we never really knew. Instead, I blabbed. I began telling the Kushners where we were from and why, but I left out the Grant part.

"Bos-ton?" Mr. Kushner said. It sounded faintly European pronounced that way.

"Originally Vestal," I said. "In New York."

"Right." Mrs. Kushner stood up. "That's where they keep those virgins."

"Margaret, have we used our allotment of guest dinners for the month?" Mr. Kushner wanted to know. His wife shook her head. "Well then, I'm calling down to say that we have two guests for dinner. You two would like to stay for dinner? It's not too late."

Mrs. Kushner waved us into a pair of black loungers. "They have a happy hour first, in about forty minutes," she said, "but it's only orange juice and cookies. That's a snort." Her voice dropped. "We're all a little handicapped here," she said. "Many of us are recuperating from strokes. But I'm old enough now to say anything I want. Get to eighty dear, and people are amazed you're even alive."

Her husband took his place at the other end of the couch. "She's even getting political about the constant use of peas in the diet," he said. "Now, your father," Mr. Kushner began to squint. "Well, I remember him leaving. Which was a shock, until I thought about it. Your father is an able-bodied man and after that adjustment period here with us. Why — your father didn't belong here to begin with. He's quick. A quick study." Mr. Kushner pointed as an aerial shot of the stadium popped up on the television. "He was always reading *The Sporting News* and coming up with new figures — batters faced per game. I don't know. Why is there no baseball on? You two like baseball? You do have those Red Sox."

"I didn't used to," Nate said calmly. "But I got sucked by the World Series two years ago, when they lost."

"Let's get some baseball on here." Mr. Kushner tapped the cushions until he found the remote and soon the Braves were playing New York. "Your father said he was going to Idaho. Margaret? Wyoming? Margaret?"

Mrs. Kushner nodded. "He wanted to get there before the season."

"Oh hell, this was maybe June," Mr. Kushner said. "I'm fuzzy myself."

Nate began grinning oddly. As if he had somehow slipped into an improbable space; one that he couldn't quite believe.

"Your father is a talker," Mrs. Kushner said. "A say-what-he-thinks sort of man. We miss him terribly. We all do, but it's for the best."

"Margaret, you say the same thing every time someone dies."

Mrs Kushner frowned. "Now, Bernie Blyleven — Harold, call him over here. He's fussy, but he'd know."

"Exactly," Mr. Kushner said. They bickered over the phone number until Mr. Kushner ambled off to make the call from the kitchenette.

"Harold likes the replays," Mrs. Kushner confided to me. "Sometimes he forgets they've already happened. But I keep it to myself. That way he gets a more exciting game."

"Ha." Mr. Kushner hung up. "Bernie says he's remembering. I remember everything too, just my timing's off. He would come over himself, but that's too far a walk. Here and back before dinner. He's making arrangements to sit with us. Bernie was the one who told Ray to go west. Read it in a magazine."

Mr. Kushner brought us each a tumbler of seltzer. "Seltzer's good for watching sports," he said. He toasted us, settled back, and smiled. There was nothing more to do until dinner. "Bernie's got the sharpest set of spokes I've ever seen," Mr. Kushner said, after a minute.

I watched Nate squint as the Mets pitcher did his little wind-up. I decided right then that my brother was deep into the game after all.

SIXTEEN

Grant here. I'll bet we're glad to be talking to me again. In fact, I'll bet we're damn near ecstatic to have me back in on the conversation. No?

Listen to those two. A war zone or what? I'm the one accepting the big imposition here. I'm the one having to dog my way through all this verbal self-defense. Those two — they're breathing. They're well fed. I didn't traumatize them *that* much. I certainly didn't mean to. Besides, what's a little trauma anyway? It makes life interesting. Gives texture to an otherwise bland existence. Gives you things to rub up against and figure out later on.

Anyway, and I bet this question has been on your mind for quite some time now: How much of a handful *was* Grant, day-to-day? How despicable was he? I know you're wondering. So hey, I'll recollect. You'd expect that in a situation like this.

Where to start? OK, picture this: I'm about five feet nine in the right socks. I've been known to carry a beard, but I would never stoop to a goatee. Clothing? I'll wear anything handy. A typical Grant day? As always, an assortment of events plucked from the four big activity groups — sleep, sit, run around and sex — yet all within the usual parameters. But you really don't care about that. You're here for the angst. You want Grant's teenage angst. Well, it was the usual: the nobody loves me, I've got craters for a face, I'll never have a date, maybe I'll go eat worms, sort of stuff. I got over it. I lived. True angst? The stuff you never get over? Well, I lost a mother too.

Grant as a child? There's a thought. Grant started out as one of those curious round-faced kids. The kind you'd see chasing a squirrel around an elm tree to see if it went up clockwise or counterclockwise. He spent hours memorizing encyclopedia entries for prehistoric animals, or reptiles, or exotic birds. Only later did he became obsessed with odd logic puzzles and working his way through mathematical minefields. He was always large, a chubster, and a little thin-skinned. In fact, Grant occasionally got the sense that both his parents wondered just how they'd gotten him as their child.

But let's keep up the chronology here, shall we? Take elementary school — that's another thing still pissing me off. For instance, I must have been in fifth grade when this sink in the boy's bathroom broke off. I don't know why. Gravity maybe. But due to my girth, I was suddenly under a cloud of suspicion. Our principal at the time was Mr. Drake, a guy who'd been a police chief in an earlier life. You'd get sent out of class for some trivial reason and be standing there tracing the grout between the wall tiles, when Drake would stroll by and and say, "What now?" Following the sink incident, he had a little lineup in the cafeteria, and I stood out as a prime suspect. "Do you know how much one of these costs?" Shout. Shout. Shout. Even when he lifted me up by my shirt, I wouldn't give in. I went home and told Ray, and that whole scene lit him right up. He started swearing. He made phone calls. He threatened lawsuits. It all went unsolved. My guess is that whoever did the sink probably leaned in on it for a long, long time, just to see what kind of force might cause a structural failure. Only a guess.

But do you think my father ever got that lit up over an injustice involving Nate? Never. By the time those two appeared, Ray had begun to back off. He was restless, and back in some corner of his mind I'm sure he was thinking, "I've been this way once already." My father is not a guy to repeat things. You have to work to get his attention.

In fact, wouldn't this be a fine time for a few quotes from the book of Ray? A smattering of the many things I've picked up over the years from Mr. Aphorism himself. Beauties like: Get up and get into the harness. Do as I say, not as I do. There's no limit to what a man can accomplish if he doesn't care who gets the credit. And my favorite: Know your limits — limit what you know.

There were more, many more, but where did this story get off track? All right, until three or four years ago, Ray kept up an apartment in Binghamton, but then he was still mostly on the road, taking care of disasters and teaching other people in the company how to do it. Ray had also reached the age where his employers thought it might be best to make a move toward buying him out. So they got together and gave him a little parachute. They coaxed him into retiring. Ray took the leap and pulled the cord, but my father could only manage to stay on the ground for about six months. He simply could not adjust to standing still. He turned out to be drunk with the road. So a short time later he talked himself into a part-time job for some hospital equipment company in Philadelphia. He became a salesman, a regional guy with a territory that ran up through Syracuse. At least it kept him moving, and my father has never run across a fork in the highway that he couldn't find a way to accommodate.

The next piece of this saga came after I sold the Vestal house and consolidated myself over in Owego. Ray and I didn't keep in daily touch, but I knew where he was. I knew what he was up to. We'd see each other around. Then one night, when I was on the edge of another project deadline, I came home from work to change my shirt and Ray appeared at the door. Things were getting out of hand, he said, and he needed a place to stay. It was temporary, he said, so of course I agreed.

But seeing him like that frightened me. My father couldn't remember a phone number. He couldn't remember the TV channels he'd been watching all his life. He did know that he was out on the proverbial limb, so that's why he brought it to Grant. People in trouble always bring it to Grant. He didn't want to get checked out, but some nights I'd come home and find him wandering around without shoes because he'd forgotten they were necessary. Or he'd be wearing my sweatpants because he'd decided he didn't have any pants of his own. Here was my father at age sixty-six, his heart still beating. Christ, at that point he'd already outlived all the males on his side of the family, generations of them, everyone except Stan. But here was Ray, walking around my house and repeating himself. "Time goes by," he'd say. "You do the best you can."

It went on for weeks. He would tell me things he'd just mentioned minutes before. He would call me Stan and wonder why the house wasn't in St. Johnsbury. Where were our parents? he'd ask. Then he'd shake his head and go on in crystal detail about the trips his family took to Winter Haven to watch the Red Sox train. He'd talk about memorizing Glenn Miller songs off the radio. Or meeting my mother on a New York subway, when she was a Sarah Lawrence sophomore, and then later, when he took a train with her back to Troy, how she looked so luminous. That was the word he used, "luminous." But he'd ask three times if the Mets had won the night before, after he'd watched the entire damn game with me on television.

Yeah, I convinced him to get this checked out. But I knew, even before they made the diagnosis, that it was Alzheimer's. They gave me books and pamphlets to read. Pathological lesions of the brain. The long haul. The thirty-six-hour day. The funeral that never ends. It rose up like a wall and frightened me to death.

Grant, I said, let someone else pick this one up. Let someone else do the duty. The sibs? I told Ray they didn't want to see us. I said they'd have nothing to do with us. Basically, I didn't want to deal with them. They were useless. They were flounders at large.

Instead, I called on Stan from St. Louis. We sparred a bit, but Stan was feeling some guilt over the falling-out he and Ray had years ago. He was feeling bad about lost opportunities, so I pressured him. Bring Ray on out, Stan finally said, and we'll set things up. By then, I had power of attorney. I was the cleanup son, once again. We closed out Ray's apartment and did the asset shuffle. I researched everything. I found the nursing home. I checked out the staff and confirmed their credentials. Then I started writing out checks for custodial care and felt quite shitty indeed.

Perhaps that particular move turned out to be a bit hasty. Perhaps I left a few details on the cutting room floor. Come on, sue me. I was in a rush. I had deadlines hanging all over my body. Besides, I was also angry. I knew that Sarah and Nate would figure it out eventually — at least Sarah would. So a part of me kept thinking: Why bother? Why tell them? Like he'd been that great a father all along? How would I even know if they wanted to see him? Then, well, this happened.

But hey, let's get back to my clever life. Let's get the next slide up there. This particular episode — one of my favorites — came up a while ago, when I still lived atop that hill in Vestal. I was right next door to the Packers, a family of carpet-store magnates who really wanted to be farmers. Anyway, they woke up one day and decided to get a couple of horses to keep their goat company. Fine. I could live with that. Then they added a few more attractions — ducks, geese, etc. — until I had a goddamn petting zoo spreading out right below my property. I could see where this was heading. Parking problems, squealing children, field-trip buses with cute chaperones that I'd have to keep an eye on with my telescope. Like I needed another distraction. The rooster, though, was the final straw. A big prize-winning thing. That creature got up at dawn or earlier, every single morning. It went on for months, with no solution in sight.

Me? I went mail-order. If you're patient enough, eventually you'll find a catalog where they'll let you buy a weasel. My particular weasel came from California. And when a weasel gets to central New York from California, it's pretty hungry. So the next night after dark, I just dropped Mr. Weasel into the pen. No more rooster.

It's true. Everywhere you go, things are always slightly askew. You just have to look closely. Only from a distance do we think that we're doing fine. You know, at work there's this saying: How small is it and does it do the job?

Well, how small was I? And did I do the job?

SEVENTEEN

In the end, Sarah and I took I-70 straight west, across corduroy hills and into the standard-order heart of Missouri. Headlights twinkled between the guardrails as the thinning stands of trees beside us blurred off into the dusk. Without a kidnapping, I thought, I'd have seen none of this.

I was still far from certain that the traces we'd found of our father were correct enough to follow. It worried me, and with every new song on the radio, I thought again about airports and returning to my life, or what remained of it. I kept consoling myself with the idea that there would be another airport eventually. The faint evidence that we were running west on — and there wasn't a lot of it — had developed at dinner, over an unspiced breast of Willow Meadows at Sandy Run roast chicken. It was an odd meal. From the fruit cup on, people kept shuffling up with their private-stock bottles of salad dressing to ask if we were the Kushners' grandchildren. It didn't seem to matter that we weren't. After each introduction Mr. Kushner would explain our connection to the loquacious Raymond J. Scales, and someone would either laugh and say, "Oh my," or shake their head and announce, "We miss him terribly."

Mrs. Tipperbaum, a tiny woman in green slacks with pastel scarves knotted at her wrists, sat with us until dessert. "Your father was so interesting," she said. "Full of information, and lively. Though you could tell he didn't belong here. He belonged out there." She slowly waved her arm overhead. "We're just glad he improved. It was strange to have someone leave us so suddenly. Usually it's for another reason entirely." She winked. "We're all very happy here."

Only after Mrs. Tipperbaum passed on the no-calorie lime sherbet dessert, and wheeled herself off to confiscate leftover salads, did Bernie Blyleven smile, as though the time had finally arrived to hand over the important information. This was a guy who wore a cotton beret indoors and looked like a shrunken Jimmy Durante. He talked in circles and seemed always on the cusp of some greater revelation. Bernie began his final discourse with a small essay comparing Dan Rather to Tom Brokaw. "If it was up to me I'd finish off the both of them," he explained, before reaching the subject of full-length mirrors. "Those I really don't like."

Eventually, Bernie got around to reporting that Ray Scales had left greater St. Louis for Wyoming. He wasn't entirely clear on how our father would have gotten out there, but he was certain that by now Ray would already be working for one of Yellowstone's concession companies, perhaps even the National Park Service itself. "I saw the ads in those magazines," Bernie said. He rapped the table. "I saw those tiny ads in back. I suggested it to him. A day later — your father had the whole situation checked out."

It did make a little sense, in that I really couldn't imagine my father, even at his age, actually latching on to the idea of not having a job — any job. Even so, Bernie couldn't supply us with anything more specific. Mr. Kushner only remembered helping my father load his bags into a taxi at 5:30 in the morning, and waving as the cab headed downtown. "It was damp out," Mr. Kushner said.

The waitress came to collect our placemats, while my sister and I thanked everyone for dinner. "See you 'round," Bernie said. He set up his walker and started to depart.

With Bernie nearly gone, Mrs. Kushner pointed her pinky toward the ceiling and then brought it down on top of my elbow. "One minute more," she said quietly. "Follow me." She stood and threaded her way between the maple tables and pulled-out chairs, back to the start of our father's corridor.

"Where's my special card?" Mrs. Kushner asked, as we arrived in front of their apartment. Mr. Kushner unlocked the door and groped in the dark for a wicker basket beside the hutch. A minute later he handed something to his wife.

"Only in emergencies," Mrs. Kushner said. She flashed a thin blue and gray piece of plastic. It looked like a membership card you'd get for joining a record club. "They sent this for free, too," Mrs. Kushner explained, as she moved down the hall to our father's door. She looked over her shoulder once, and neatly slipped the lock. Her husband smiled in remembered admiration.

Mrs. Kushner turned on the light, while I investigated the pile of mail on the brown dinette table. I found a *Discover* magazine, something from AAA, two copies of the *Harvard Health Newsletter*, a flier about electric recliners, the *Rocky Mountain Employment News*, and a telephone bill from Southwestern Bell. Otherwise, the apartment looked like an abandoned hotel suite.

"Do you do this often?" Sarah asked brightly. She gathered my father's mail into the folds of the magazine and tucked the bundle under her arm.

Mrs. Kushner smiled.

Several minutes later I took control of the van's keys and drove Sarah east through the droopy air. I pulled into a Roy Rogers and set the emergency brake, as my sister asked what exactly I had in mind. I frowned. I just wanted to get this thing over with. I wanted to know exactly where we were going, and if it was worth it, before we moved a single inch further west. I flipped through the bundle of mail and tore open the phone bill with my teeth. I began checking the itemized calls page for Wyoming phone numbers. My father had made a few calls to West Yellowstone, but the last five calls were to a number in Mammoth Hot Springs. I spotted a bank of phones inside the restaurant and jumped out.

"It's Sunday," Sarah said, following me inside. "You're *not* going to get an answer."

Sarah bought a vanilla shake and settled into a booth. I watched her suck on a red straw as I dialed. After two tries, it became clear that no one was answering at Mammoth Springs. My sister was right.

In that case, I reasoned, we should simply wait this out in St. Louis. We could camp in Stan's backyard. Use the pool. He'd never know. In any case, it made no sense whatsoever to drive blindly west. What if our father had changed his mind? What if he'd decided to try the Everglades? Maybe he'd gotten a better offer driving tourists along the rim of the Grand Canyon? The possibilities were endless.

Sarah pulled her knee to her chin as I rolled on. "Give me those," she said finally, and without thinking, I slid the van's keys across the table. "Thank you," my sister said. She got up and went outside.

I watched through the glass as she climbed into the van. She started the engine and her hand stalled above the steering wheel for several long seconds. When she looked away, it occurred to me that I was being left. I was being dropped off in greater St. Louis. Not freed but abandoned. An instant later, I was bouncing into the passenger seat, before Sarah could even find reverse.

We might have argued half way to Columbia; there was that much material. But I retreated to life as a pensive kidnap victim — the kind of human that deep down I've always strived to be. I sat up front for a while, until Sarah stuffed another Dead tape into the deck. It came up halfway into "Ship of Fools," and that sent me to the back of the van, where I collapsed across the bed. Every time I closed my eyes, I would see this cartoon character of a city following along behind us. It kept lumbering down the highway, trying to catch up. Old people smiled and waved from every window, all slowly mouthing the words, "Come back."

"Another day with nothing to do," Sarah said, sighing heavily. She took both hands off the wheel and reached out the window to adjust her mirror. "Maybe I could knit," she said. "Crochet some curtains. Do a tent."

It was early the next morning, and Sarah had been talking to herself for some time. I didn't want to interrupt, as she seemed to be trying to dispel the leftover vapors of our earlier, map-based argument. We'd stayed the night in the Jupiter-Jet Campground, which was two map inches from Kansas City and still in range of the highway's low moan. It was an odd place, filled with small, Flash Gordon–era rockets. They looked like glinting aluminum sculptures built by 1950s dads with too much time on their hands. As we pulled out, I decided that it was more direct to stay on I-70 across Kansas, and then go north to Wyoming.

"We're going over on 90," Sarah declared. "I can't take Kansas, even Nebraska. Any state where the only topographical feature is the curve of the earth." She traced her fingernail across the atlas, right through

South Dakota. "It's a rectangle, either way," she said. We went on from there.

Some time after breakfast I stopped arguing, since the fact that it was Monday, the final day of my long weekend, kept bobbing up and asking what I intended to do about it. Lately it feels as though I've reached some sort of island, a place where I'm as nervous about leaving things behind as I am about what might happen in the future. But that morning, I just gave in to the finite attraction of insulating myself with small details and dissipating scenery. I began to enjoy the pull of only looking half an hour ahead.

"Can you get a tan through smoked glass?" Sarah asked. "Hello?"

I didn't have a thing to say.

We followed the flat and squalid Missouri north all morning, until we were well into neat and trim Iowa. We hadn't stopped to call Wyoming yet. It was a chore I'd agreed to do, but it had become one more thing to avoid. I had just found a small black dot on the map in northern Missouri called Grant City, and was going to point this out, when Sarah aimed us off the highway and toward a sprawling Texaco service plaza. A scrolling electronic billboard advertised the diesel prices with little animated trucks.

"We only need a location," my sister told me. "You don't have to talk to him." She jolted to a power-assisted stop before the café. I plucked my father's phone bill and some hot change off the dash. I took the calling card from my wallet.

The restaurant's interior was vanilla colored and plastic, and people were ordering chicken-fried steaks for lunch. The phones were off in an alcove, where cloudy Polaroids of giant trucks with sleeper cabs coated the wall. On the plastic-covered map of Iowa, a piece of red tape announced: "You are here!!"

My stomach kept twisting, but I decided to pretend that this was exactly like something I'd have to do at work. This was the kind of call I made every day. I reached Wyoming on the second try, and found that the number from the phone bill connected me to the personnel office of a concession company in Mammoth Springs. After a pause, a woman with a small round voice said, "Raymond J. Scales?" as though there were many to pick from. I knew she was probably scrolling her cursor down a computer screen. "Yes," she said finally. "He is employed here."

I felt a twitch behind my ear. I ran a thumb against the Iowa map's soft plastic cover. "How long has he been working there?"

"Who's calling, please?"

"No, it's OK," I said. "Thanks." I placed the receiver back on its hook.

The still, smoke-filled air clung to my arms. I wasn't sure why I'd hung up. I kept staring at the truck snapshots. "He's there," I said.

Outside, Sarah waited in the passenger seat, listening to some throbbing art rock tape. "Keeps away the undesirables," she said, while waving at the look on my face. She'd already been to the McDonald's next door and bought me a Big Mac.

"He's listed," I said. "He's working in the park."

Sarah's lips puffed out, as though she were about to go under water. We sat there for several minutes, watching blowsy, fatigued travelers wander into the McDonald's. People comforted by the prospect of ordering the same food they could get anywhere. We live in a country stitched together by satellite television and franchise chains, I thought. It wasn't a new revelation, but it felt that way. "We could be anywhere in America," I said.

"We are," Sarah replied.

The interstate north narrowed to a slot on the horizon and I drove straight through. We were out under a sky too far to be real. A sky that turned land to ocean. Sarah was amusing herself by watching crows peck at gravel on the road's shoulder. "Those birds walk with attitude," she explained. "It's like — that car missed us, so the next will, too." The wind made the van sing, and the radio kept talking about corn and soy futures. "You're not listening anyway," my sister told me, as she trundled off to nap in the back.

It was true, I wasn't listening. I was too busy following a long string of thunderheads across the horizon. These were black-bottomed, steel-colored clouds that billowed away through the atmosphere's upper layers as they paraded in from the west. Faint silver flashes flickered at their centers. Ahead of us, crosshatchings of rain faded away before quite reaching the earth. The air had developed an odd, fused quality.

As a rule I never pick up hitchhikers, but when we closed in on the wall of clouds, the temperature began to drop, and I pulled over and backed up for a tall skinny man in canvas shorts. He had a tight red beard and wore new cowboy boots and a yellow t-shirt covered with tiny boats.

"Ja. Ja. Thank you. Thank you," he said, slinging in his backpack and a blue duffle bag. He slammed the passenger door and, with a glance toward the sky, put both hands firmly on the dashboard. "Is this a sturdy vehicle?" he asked. Rolf was from the Netherlands and hitch-hiking to meet his brother in Vancouver. "See America, right?" he said. "Going Wild West? You two are Americans? Then I have one question. What is this Bullwinkle?" Someone had called him that in a restaurant.

The clouds leaned out to cover us as rain curved down from the sky. The light had a peculiar crispness, and rainbow fragments began to emerge at the horizon's edge.

"I once saw the ground end of a rainbow in Germany," Rolf explained. He looked cramped, even in the front seat. "And what are your stories?"

Spare drops rounded up against the windshield. A single bead pushed its way across before breaking into a run.

Sarah pointed to her chest. She had moved up to the captain's chair behind mine. "Me," she said, "I'm a kidnapper, and this boy is my captive. We're not really related. But we did have a distant stepbrother in common. He just kicked off. We're grieving."

Rolf lowered his eyes and squinted at my sister. "You would be very attractive," he said.

"Would be?" Sarah said.

"Well, yes. If we would be in Texas, I should like to take you to fish for sharks. Which is done off the end of a dock. I could take you along." He wagged a finger at her.

"Have you been outside long?" Sarah asked.

The rain began as a curtain. It looked as though we were driving into a wall of sudden doom. I slowed to twenty miles an hour, and pulled in behind a truck with Nova Scotia plates and chrome cutouts of naked women on its mudflaps. Only after the truck pulled off without signaling did I realize that I'd followed him off onto the shoulder. I put my emergency flashers on. Then I was taken over by a hay fever attack. As the thunder folded down around us with an unmeasurable timbre, I couldn't stop sneezing. Lightning drilled the purple and greenish fields. Even with my eyes closed, the flashes still got in.

"This is exceptional," Rolf said.

Between sneezes, I slowly pulled back onto the road. Ahead of us, a cluster of motorcycles huddled beneath an overpass. Lightning continued to brighten the sky like a baby shaking a blanket, and the next wall of rain came on with a harsh clatter. I kept thinking about tornadoes and hurricanes, about birds trapped in the storm's eye and pulled north from the Tropics against their wishes. The noise on the roof climbed in volume. The drops were so big and white — it took a while to realize that we were being pelted with hail. Ice fragments bounced up from the pavement at sharp angles.

We left the gray wall almost as suddenly as we had entered it. But on the other side, we were enveloped in a dust storm, a swirling red-yellow fog that danced stripped-bare clumps of brush into our windshield. The van began to jump sideways, as if it had been punched. After miles of this, the dust storm dissipated into a series of buffeting gusts, and the cars around us began speeding up, changing lanes at will, almost out of relief.

In another half an hour, we pulled off at the Sioux City exit to take a breather. At the end of the ramp, while we waited for a stoplight, Rolf opened his door as though he'd seen enough and that ramp had been his final destination from the start. "I thank you for the shelter," he said. He stepped out as odd-looking steam rose from the pavement in strips.

By evening we found ourselves in Mitchell, South Dakota. My sister and I took the next to last spot at the Lake Mitchell Campground, and with nothing to do there, we ended up downtown in front of the Corn Palace — the world's only Corn Palace. My legs still vibrated from the road as we sat across the street on some cement posts, admiring that fantasy of a structure. It looked like a wonderful parade float at rest, an intricate idea of a building that had somehow made its way into reality.

A white and nameless RV pulled up and idled in the reddish after-supper light as the tourists inside stared at the Palace. High school kids cruised by in muscled pickups with their radios turned up loud. Three boys wearing white T-shirts sat nearby and talked about transmissions and car shows while they waited for certain Impalas and Cougars to circle back around. Everything seemed to be moving extremely slowly, and I realized that I was still velocitized. I was still prepared to receive the world at highway speed.

The Corn Palace itself was under repair. Its outside walls were covered with mosaics created from corncobs, and that year the murals were all based on the logos of different civic groups. But the sky-blue domes, which should have towered down from the corners, rested in a side street beside an orange crane. Above the Corn Palace marquee, the legend "In Service To Others" had been written in corn.

Inside, we discovered that the palace was part auditorium, part basketball court, and part souvenir shop. I bought a deck of Corn Palace playing cards and told my sister I had to locate a phone and call Maris, since I obviously wouldn't be at work the next morning. I found the phone underneath the stands and next to a fenced-in exhibit of stuffed animals. A gazelle's head gazed mournfully down from the wall beside the lit Coke machine. The giraffe had been cut off at the shoulders and mounted on the floor. Its head cleared the top of the fence.

I couldn't decide how much to tell Maris, but it did seem like the more of this I explained, the better chance I'd have at staying employed. I was sure that if I simply called and said I wasn't coming in, he'd fire me on the spot. It would probably make his life simpler, and I wasn't certain what it would do to mine. I don't know, a couple years ago, when I started reporting, the work itself seemed so much more important. But in those last two days, I'd begun to wonder if I was actually helping anyone much at all. There were occasional moments when you could focus attention on a problem and watch things change, but that was rare. Wouldn't it all go on without me, and pretty much exactly in the same vein? Or was it only working on that particular paper? Combined with the fact that I was so tired all the time.

I dialed directory assistance in Massachusetts and a man on the other end with a compressed twang said, "One moment," before that universally calm, recorded voice gave me Maris's home number. I dialed instantly, another work reflex. After a couple of months on the job, I found myself developing this unnatural fear of phone calls. I would let the numbers pile up on my desk, until there was nothing to do but fire out all the calls in a burst. I thought at the time this might be a sign that I wasn't doing exactly the right thing with my life.

Rache, Maris's wife, answered on the second ring. "Is Reggie around?" I asked. Actually pronouncing his first name felt both wrong and too intimate.

"Nope," she said. "He's at *Roger Rabbit* with the kids. Back in maybe an hour. Who's calling please?"

"Naw, thanks. I'll try again." I hung up before she could ask anything more.

Beside me, a small towheaded boy in a black baseball cap began lunging up between the bars to bat at the giraffe's neck. But he couldn't get his arm in far enough through the fence. "Stop that," I said, and the boy looked up as though I were a piece of talking furniture.

The No Hope Goat Ranch Lounge was a small building attached to the left side of the Lonely Bison Motor Lodge. The interior was mostly done up in red leatherette, and along the walls, in places where there couldn't have been windows to start with, little boxes of imitation stained glass were lit from behind. An older couple sat at a round table drinking beers with ice. They'd been coming there for years. We'd taken our seats at the tiny bar and were watching *Wheel Of Fortune* when Sarah said, "Time to shoot the wounded."

The waitress at the end of the bar sprayed cheese-in-a-can on a line of Ritz crackers and began eating them one at a time. After a second she said, "Hiya," and walked over. The bartender, an older man whose black belt buckle read "Walter," looked away from his paper and pushed a pair of brown-rimmed glasses up onto his nose. Sarah smiled and ordered two Bud tallboys.

"Seven ounces of beer a day gives you breast cancer, but you won't get heart disease," Walter announced. "You folks are from back east."

"How'd you know?" I asked.

"You've got those tired, driving faces. That, and the only other people your age we get come in after softball, which isn't over yet. You could be from California."

"Not me," Sarah said, "I'm too worried to be from California. We're from Boston."

"That's a ways," Walter said. "You getting any rain? We're dry here. And about the name — because I know you're gonna ask — it was a ranch I owned over in southwest Colorado. One that didn't pan out." He rubbed his chin. "Probably because of the name, if I were to guess."

"I was there," the waitress said. "I mean Massachusetts. I did three semesters at Smith," she said as she handed each of us a cracker with a crown of Cheez Whiz. "I never got used to all those trees. It took a while to figure out that's what it was, but they all felt so sinister. Creeping in and blocking the view." She laughed. "I finished up out here."

Walter seemed ready to ask if we were on vacation, but then he glanced up at the TV. "That last word's skunk," he said, solving half the puzzle. "I should be on these shows."

"Everyone should," Sarah said. "Once."

Our host rearranged his forearms on the bar. "I had this guy in here last night telling me that skunks are vampires," he said. "Could you believe that? He's sure this is true, he says, because a skunk got into his chickens and sucked five of them dry. They toppled over, one by one, with little tooth marks in their heads. Plop, plop, plop, all in a row. Lined up, drained, and ready to ship. The reason that skunks are vampires, this guy tells me, is because they contract rabies and that turns them hydrophobic. They're so thirsty, they go for blood instead." The waitress laughed. "Wendy believed him too," Walter said. "You like it out here?"

"Yeah," Sarah said. "I like the wind. It's real loose."

"It's the one part of the country where you can sit on your front porch and watch your dog run away from home for two days straight." Walter smiled and leaned back, letting a line he'd used before head out to work.

"We came from St. Louis, through this gigantic storm," Sarah explained.

"Any hail?" Walter asked. "We've picked up pellets here big as softballs. There'll be people selling off hail-damaged cars after that. Not bad, if you don't mind riding around with a few dents."

I nodded and asked where I could find a phone.

"Local call? Charge call?"

"Yeah," I said, and he pulled a heavy black phone up from below the bar.

The call went right through, and thousands of pearled pulses later, Maris picked up. "Hello," he said. It sounded like he was next door, but asleep.

"Maris?"

"Yup."

"This is Nate. I won't be in tomorrow."

"Why not?"

"I'm in South Dakota."

I thought I heard pillows moving and sofa springs releasing in the background. "You're not in South Dakota," Maris said. "I don't want you in South Dakota. This doesn't sound to me like you're in South Dakota."

"But I am."

"Nope."

Sarah had moved closer, trying to hear. She looked a little buzzed. I glanced at Walter and handed him the phone. "Could you please tell this guy that I'm in South Dakota? He's my boss."

Walter frowned and took the receiver. "He's in South Dakota. He's in Mitchell, South Dakota. He's in my bar. The No Hope Goat Ranch Lounge." He handed back the phone and looked pleased.

"I'm not fooled," Maris said. "You could have gotten anybody to say that." His voice was measured, the verbal equivalent of the eye roll he uses while trying to think his way around some obstacle. "OK," Maris said. "I'll play. Why are you in South Dakota and when are you leaving South Dakota?"

"We're looking for my father."

Maris didn't answer.

"In Yellowstone," I said.

"That's in Wyoming."

"Yeah, I know."

"Then — you're chasing him?"

"Not exactly. We didn't know where he was. Kind of lost touch." For an instant, I worried that Maris would see a story in this and assign me to cover myself. "Inept Reporter Hunts Down Hallucinating Father."

"Really," Maris said, though it was hard to tell if he sounded intrigued or tired. "You drove there? How long will this take?"

I looked at Sarah and mouthed: A week? She shrugged. "Yeah," I said. "A week."

Maris eventually agreed, but in a way that made it sound as though he had some sort of payback scheduled for later. "Officially you can be on vacation," he told me. "Are you reachable?"

"Nope."

"This really screws me up," Maris said, clicking off.

I closed my eyes and imagined Maris staring at the mess on his coffee table.

"Well?" Sarah asked.

I rubbed my chin and smiled at her.

Walter pulled the phone back under the counter. "Always wanted to do that," he said, "but I can't just run away from myself."

EIGHTEEN

Well before eight in the morning, when it was a mere 90 degrees out, my sister and I were already driving deeper into South Dakota. At that point, we were still passing occasional fields with crops, a few dusty cottonwoods, and the infrequent burr oak. But as we closed in on the 100th meridian, the rolls of hay in the median strips disappeared and the landscape turned suddenly minimal. Stale, yellowed grasslands wandered off into open rangeland, which seemed to bend down completely at the edge of the sky. I found myself wanting to locate the exact moment in the landscape, the spot where one set of attitudes tipped over into the next, the place where an old way of thinking could no longer apply.

At my feet, confused cellophane wrappers from a bag of sour apple candies spiraled away on the overheated breeze. A trio of used Band-Aids formed tiny rings on the open edge of the glove compartment's door. A Diet Dr Pepper cap, a red fist-size rock from Canada, and an empty box of Archway cookies were lined up on the carpet beside my toes. The blurred nursing home directions, written on a napkin, rested atop the "Spend the Day, See It All" map of Niagara Falls. In the pocket on the door, I found a flier from the North American Loon Fund and a brochure for DYNAMO — "The only mystery gravity area that's family approved." Balled-up plastic shopping bags from several states rolled like caged tumbleweeds behind my seat, skipping across the scrim of cinders, stones, and rice kernels that covered the carpet.

"We are piloting a garbage scow," I announced. "A rolling landfill."

Sarah gave me a look. "Oh — come on," she said. "It's all useful. Or most of it is."

The New York pages of the atlas had slipped their staples and plastered themselves down against the floor. I pulled these away and stuffed them back into the book. With the atlas open across my lap, I noticed that the maps got smaller as you went farther west. The scale for South Dakota was thirty miles to the inch — up from the twenty the day before in Missouri. I flipped to the continent map in front, and watched as the rungs of the blue-veined interstate system climbed (70-80-90) across the northern half of the country. But when I glanced outside, it all began to seem like a cheap attempt to impose order on a landscape that had already sprawled beyond the range of anyone's imagination.

We are riding on a big cement chute, I thought, as Sarah flipped the tape and the Clash came up on the other side. We are riding west into larger and larger pieces of sky. What might all this extra space do to your thinking? I wondered. Would your problems become less significant, or would they expand like gas, filling all available space? Say you did adjust to this vast change in scale — would you then, in some small way, become a different sort of person?

I plucked a Corn Palace postcard from a crack in the dash. It was a picture of the building at night in 1985, when the domes were all on and properly lit. Walter had written his address on the back. I remembered him giving this to Sarah at the bar, and asking that we let him know how things worked out. It had been a long night. After I'd called Maris, I decided to call my housemates, mainly to let them know that I wouldn't be there on Wednesday to take out the garbage. No one answered, and my own taped voice bounced back at me from across the plains. I really didn't want to have to explain this trip to anybody.

Next I called Claire, first because I thought she might get a kick out of hearing that I was in the No Hope Goat Ranch Lounge, but really it was more that I missed talking to her. I got her machine, so I left a rambling communiqué, clotted with environmental details. I said I'd call back, but that sounded like a fragment from the way things used to be. I really don't know why we broke up. But back when those fissures started opening, I only watched. I couldn't even envision how to sew anything back together. A total collapse of the imagination. A failure to think that things could ever work out in any halfway decent fashion. The effects of a long reign of inertia, I suppose.

Around then, I left Sarah at the bar and began piling quarters into a driving game I found beside the pool table. After forty minutes of cruising the bright video landscape, dodging land mines and decimating all the slower traffic in my path, I started to feel a little better. I listened in as the people nearby talked about irrigation dilemmas and walleye limits. It made the East seem distant.

When I went back for another tallboy, my sister had Walter and Wendy's full attention. She was in the middle of running down our tired family saga, though Walter occasionally looked a bit dubious, particularly when Sarah tried to explain our father. "You know, I like you two," Walter said at one point. "It's not for me to say, but have you ever thought that maybe he wants to be alone? When you lose a child, even a troubled one —" Walter shook his head as if to redirect the thought. "Being found though, that can be a pretty frightening experience."

On the map, I spotted a road in North Dakota where it was possible to travel 121 miles in a row without making a turn. This amused Sarah, who suggested that with a little string you could hook your thigh to the steering wheel and not have to adjust anything for hours. We were closing in on Rapid City, and it seemed wise to start some sort of a conversation, since a few minutes earlier I'd caught Sarah closing her eyes for long stretches at a time. It was a game. She was trying to see how long she could go and still stay on the highway.

Several minutes later, Sarah began touch-typing road signs on the bottom of the steering wheel. Your Speed Clocked by Aircraft. Visit the Pioneer Auto Museum. About then I had to turn down the tape, as a soft, intermittent clacking seemed to be coming from somewhere in the back of the van. Though the more I listened, the more it sounded like someone was on the outside, tapping and trying to get in.

"Do you hear that?" I asked. "That clacking?"

"Nope," Sarah said. "How far back can you remember?" she asked suddenly.

"In general? Or do you mean like being small?"

"Small." She pulled out to pass a tank truck and typed the words "Liquid Air" across the steering wheel.

A cricket smacked into the windshield and its exoskeleton glanced away on the hot wind. "OK," I said. "I'm sitting in the blue high chair and I can't count past twenty-five. It's a Saturday morning. Mom's there and Dad has on a blue work shirt and his elbows have black grease marks on them. I've got a plastic bowl with gold sparkles in the bottom."

Sarah drew her front teeth across her lower lip. "I can barely get high chairs," she said. "I remember Mom coming to get me in the crib once. I was standing up and reaching for her. I think it was sunny. It's almost like looking at a photograph — you know, the way I see it. I remember her hand around my wrist once, when I was crying on a sidewalk. Something about the feel of it made me stop. I calmed right down." She smiled. "Did we have a floating lily pad in the bathtub?"

"With black spots," I said. "It held soap. There were plastic boats you could sink."

"What do you think caused the differences in our ages?"

"Between us?"

"Nope." She passed over an open bottle of raspberry seltzer. "Between us and Grant."

"A mistake," I said.

"You mean Grant was a mistake?" She laughed. "What — like they didn't mean it when they had him?" I shrugged and Sarah made a low humming noise. "Did you ever think we'd get to a point with Grant — say, years from now, where he'd just admit that he was wrong? Like things would have settled down between us? I sort of did. It kind of shook me up. You know, that the chance for that was never going to — be there. It made me mad."

I pulled my bare foot across the dash and stuck it out the window. "He could never admit that he was wrong about anything," I said. "His whole purpose was to control things and be right. That's what he did all day at work. He wrote directions on how to run systems. That's what he wanted."

"But what made him that way?"

I shrugged, though I thought I knew. "Grant had this deep fear of the irrationality of the world," I said. "That's what he kept fighting against. He kept trying to carve out little corners against it. Which was how he could keep up the I'm-staying-between-the-lines-so-you'd-better-too stuff." A big heavy bug smashed into my heel. It stung, so I brought my foot inside. "I know the world's a weird place," I said. "I see that all the time. Look at what's happened to us. That's pretty irrational. It doesn't make sense to try and control too much of anything."

This last part seemed to annoy my sister. "But you have to control some things," she told me. "Besides — you've got some of that law-and-order stuff in you, too."

"You're not supposed to defend him," I said.

"I'm not," Sarah said. "Really. I was only wondering."

As the Black Hills bubbled up in the distance, Sarah eased into the passing lane and began battling her way around a caravan of five silver Airstream travel trailers. The last one said, "Let Me Tell You About My Grandchildren" on its license plate holder. Sarah scoffed and told me we had to get off the highway and find lunch within five minutes or she might do something drastic. We took the first Rapid City exit and found ourselves downtown. It was a very medium-size place, which amazed me, considering how long I'd been hearing about it from the road signs. Everything out here is bigger and smaller at once, I decided.

When we pulled up at the first stoplight, I closed my eyes, but those road stripes still ran through the edges of my vision like threads. How many miles a day do we cover just by standing still? I wondered. We're rotating. We're carried along in the planet's giant elliptical orbit, so what would that be in miles per hour?

At a Taco Bell, we picked up burritos and switched drivers. Then, right in front of a Safeway, as I was preparing to reload us onto I-90, we got pulled over. I saw the flashing lights behind us before Sarah did. I signaled and coasted off into a parking lot.

"What will this be?" Sarah asked. "Attempted speeding?"

My mouth started to itch. I checked the mirrors and felt around under the seat for my wallet. "Fuck," I said. "How come you're not driving?" I finally found the wallet under Sarah's seat and pulled out my driver's license.

For a few crisp seconds, I could see exactly what would happen. Someone, maybe Grant's pesky neighbor, had probably reported the van stolen. There were most likely APBs out on us all over the place. If not, at the very least we were still unregistered and uninspected.

The van would be impounded, and within hours, Sarah and I would be in holding cells, trading menthol cigarettes for favors, unable to make bail, and getting homemade tattoos that said, "J. C. Is Lord."

The cop unloaded himself from the cruiser and left the flashers on. Behind his silver sunglasses, he looked like a defensive end gone to seed.

"You two are a long way from home," he said, tapping the van's door twice with his fist. "Know why I pulled you over?"

"Nope," I said. "I mean, no, sir."

He glanced back at the flashing lights atop his cruiser. "OK," the cop said, "you've got a dangling gas cap." He smiled like a Good Samaritan. "Didn't want you to have a spill. You two be good now."

Sarah hopped out, recoiled the chain and screwed down the gas cap. She waved, but the cop was already accelerating away.

"I don't believe this," I said.

"Believe what?" My sister jumped back in. "That you're still breathing? You should believe it, because it's true. See — we're doing the next great thing. We could have been nailed — again — but we weren't. Look at you. I saw your face. I saw your eyes. Oh no, they got me. God, finally, it's such a relief. You really do go around thinking that. You go around all day wondering, What else wrong could happen to me? You shouldn't," she said. "It makes a difference."

"Yeah?" I shouted. "Then how come we're having all these close calls with authority?" It came out sort of high and whiny. "I will not succumb to ridiculous optimism."

"Optimism is never ridiculous," Sarah said. "I'm still the boss. So — you can drive over to that hardware store beside the Safeway and put it in park."

I did and she got out. A minute later she returned with a screwdriver, a paint-stirring stick, and a can of that tarlike stuff people use on trees to cover fresh wounds. Sarah popped the lid and watched it roll away across the blacktop. She slathered a glob of the black goo onto the right-hand corner of the windshield, neatly covering up our out-of-date stickers.

Instead of getting out and grabbing her arm, I slid across to the passenger seat. Was I really so disappointed that we hadn't been picked up? It would have stopped all this, I thought.

Sarah climbed back up into the driver's seat and wheeled us out past a bank with a twirling time and temperature sign. I looked at my watch and found that I was still on central time. I'd never set it ahead to mountain standard. As I spun the hands forward, I saw that we'd at least caught up with our father in terms of time.

NINETEEN

Three days. I counted. Three days ago, my little brother gave up shaving. The funny thing was, each morning it did make him look a tiny bit more like a hostage. But he seemed to be reveling in it. At least that's what I wanted to believe.

So — it was way past dark, and there I was, reduced to thinking about Nate's beard. I was quite tired and killing time outside the campground laundromat, totally unable to face anything more complicated than that. To be exact about our location — which I'm sure Nate would prefer — we were in the middle of Wyoming, barely north of Sheridan, and staying overnight at the Bighorn KOA. By then, Nate was probably already asleep in that tiny blue dome of a tent he'd been unfolding as I wandered off with the laundry. He found it somewhere in the van, and right away decided that he wanted to sleep under the stars.

I knew we'd been driving a lot, but sometime late in the afternoon, Nate started hallucinating. I noticed it around dinner time, as we rolled into the deep folds of Wyoming. I was steering us alongside some pretty purple mountains when, out of nowhere, my brother said: "Look! That man is riding a really fast horse. He's in our lane!" I laughed but then felt bad, because Nate was so completely serious. It freaked me out a little when I saw the fictional man and his horse a minute later — just a motorcycle off in the other lane. This whole episode struck me as odd, so I decided to interrogate Nate a little. After a while, he admitted that on his last driving shift, he'd thought that a jet on the horizon was really a smooth-flying silver bird. "I was convinced," he said. "I almost woke you up to say, 'It's a bird, it's a plane.' Then I figured it out, pulled over, and made you drive. I'm not used to being this wrong about stuff."

Indeed. Nate obviously needed a sustained rest. A long sleep. We both could have used one. I'd been sleeping badly all along. Like, as soon as we entered South Dakota I started having these odd dreams about getting places. Tiny transportation dramas. Last night, I had to learn to be an engineer. The train kind. Someone kept explaining that a freight train was in the wrong place and it had to be moved. So I thought — I could do that. I could figure out how to drive an engine. I did, too — in that easy dreamlike way where things just work out. The best part was that, along the way, I kept stopping to visit people I didn't know. First they'd give me snacks and popcorn. Then they'd show me videos of how to work the train's controls. It certainly felt like I was making progress. I think I'd know otherwise.

Outside the dreary campground laundromat, I sat on the top rail of a white fence, breathing in the high summer night and waiting for my quarters in the dryer to run down. I could have waited inside the laundromat itself, except I'd been forced out by a bumblebee the size of a pony. It kept buzzing me — just me. Which didn't seem fair, considering I'd only gone to the laundromat to do the necessary shirts and shorts. While I was inside, piling the dirty clothes into the machine, I did feel — for a little bit at least — like one more campground mom on the road. Driven by sheer pity, I'd even included a bit of Nate's wardrobe in the load. Mostly it was mine — because in the frantic rush to head west, some of what I'd packed was not exactly pristine.

As I sat on the fence, I started wishing that I smoked — because it did seem like a good time for a cigarette. At least until this pudgy, sullen child wandered past. He wore a huge "Super Dad" T-shirt. So — I asked if the shirt belonged to his father. The child looked down at his chest and said, "Yeah," as if we were about to have a fight over it. Then he went inside, probably to tell his dad about the weird woman outside and get him to come to the rescue.

I gave up on rescues long ago. Not that I wanted to. I mean I was once held hostage by a giant Saint Bernard, and nobody bothered to rescue me. It's true. We were sledding at this park in Syracuse. Emily Fursberg, me, and her two older sisters. But in the middle of everything, the Fursbergs' incomprehensible dog, Fatso, carted me away. I was eight and my father was at the top of the hill. I saw him, leaning against our station wagon, sharing a thermos of Irish coffee with Emily's stepfather, and watching it all happen.

When we first started sliding down the hill, Fatso would canter along beside the toboggan. But he'd get really upset every time we crashed, which we thought was the best part. The dog kept drooling and barking until, when he couldn't take it any longer, he decided that I needed to be rescued — just me. After the next really bad crash, Fatso wrapped his soft mouth around my left leg and carted me thirty yards away into the woods. My mom's too-big navy ski pants made a soft scratching sound as I bounced over the dead burdocks. Fatso eventually stopped and put a paw on my stomach to hold me in place. He looked pleased. I was in shock. Emily finally found me and screamed. But when everyone else caught up, my father laughed. Almost a cackle, as though I were nobody's daughter. I didn't talk to him for weeks, or maybe it was only a week. I'm sure he never understood why. Later he said, "That dog may be uncoordinated, but at least he's got good instincts."

There was this other time in high school, when I was in a bar way before I should have been. I was with Alex, who was older and, I knew even at the time, was pretty dubious, and my friend Karen Valentino. We were doing some dumb game with quarters and beer for about a half an hour until I realized that my father was up by the television with his friends from work. They were watching the Mets, but my father was also watching me — the whole time. But he didn't come over and make a scene, as I was sure he would. He didn't do anything. We left first, and the next morning, my father nodded at me and said, "Have a good time?" We never talked about it and I didn't get in trouble, but I knew I shouldn't have been there.

There are times when I think it's stuff like this, the things you expect from other people, that throw you off. What if you could just expect less? If your expectations didn't have to rest on everyone else's idea of normal? What if I just didn't expect anything from my father? That could be a moment to strive for.

I was still on the fence, wondering if it was time to divide up my already spinning load of damp laundry and stuff half of it into a second dryer. Was there a free dryer? Could I make more efficient use of my quarters? That got me moving. When I threw back the laundromat's screen door, the child and the bumblebee were both, thankfully, absent. There were eight dryers in that concrete building — and all occupied. On the TV up by the ceiling, the eleven o'clock newscasters were wrapping up the escaped pig update. A giant pig, who had been heading peacefully off to a fair, broke out of his trailer at a stoplight and ran amok in a Cheyenne suburb, assaulting ranch houses. This went on all afternoon, until they netted him in a cul-de-sac. After that, the little news they had about forest fires in Yellowstone seemed almost like an anticlimax. I did like the shot of the silver bombers raining buckets of flame retardant down on the woods. It looked like a wall of falling tangerines.

I sacrificed a five at the bill changer and made a fist around the cold quarters. I bought a second Dr Pepper from the machine as the TV news wound down to the stockman's report. When that got dull, I went to examine the map of Yellowstone up on the other wall. We were still 150 miles away, but this campground had maps of the park everywhere. It felt like we were following the tire tracks left by generations of Yellowstone pilgrims. I ran my fingers across the map and tried to divine exactly where my father could be. Would we find him in Mammoth? In West Thumb? Grant Village? I stared as if I actually could see him. As if I were the eye in the sky. He would be energized. Happy, in a familiar and disaster-awed way. Fires could do that to him.

I rubbed someone's lost barrette with my thumb, and started tapping it on my soda can in time to a car ad on TV. The room smelled like fabric softener, and everyone else was either younger or older than me. It was your basic mom and daughter crowd — with some stranded fathers and an elderly couple thrown in for diversity. I was my own demographic niche. And I should have been backpacking.

A pair of young fathers squinted at the baseball scores. How would Doug fare at this? I wondered. How was his pluck? I hadn't done much about Doug over the past days except to buy funny postcards that I would probably never remember to send. How patient could he be? How much patience could I put up with? He was right. It was a shame about us. It could have worked. I think. But saying that made everything around me seem even more and more absurd. The fact that I was in a campground laundromat, contemplating Doug from Wyoming. I felt guilty about putting him off and disappearing so quickly. Yes, I was not sure why he kept popping back into my thoughts at such odd moments. Though I knew that, back in my real life, I might not see any of this in the same light. Or was this my real life? Either way, it made me restless. And that meant what? I wondered. Was restlessness simply another symptom of fear? Fear of what? Loss? But what was I afraid of losing with Doug? Too much endless speculation always ends up seeming somewhat sinister. Stick to postcards, I told myself.

What postcard opportunities we resisted that day. We had failed to visit "The Universe's Largest Animated Cowboy Ghost Town." Nor did we stop to see "Incredible Trained Animals" operate a be-witched village at Reptile-Land. There were others, too, but Nate nixed every opportunity. He kept calling these attractions "the snares of nothingness." To me, that was the most intriguing part. There is nothing out here but space, sentiment, and free time. Those roadside-attraction people were clever enough to bring RVs to a brake-searing halt. All for the satisfactions of strangeness. I did, however, coax Nate off the interstate in time to see the Badlands. I found them very odd. Disorienting, even. The plains paused and the Badlands erupted, like ancient molars. Big Foot Overlook. Dinosaur Playland. Vampire Valley. It went on for miles. So far that I had a problem getting my mind around it. We have entered an entirely foreign place, I thought.

Then, after we'd stopped at a turnout and started climbing around, I suddenly began seeing us as the littlest tourists. I mean, for the briefest of instants, it seemed like an experience that I should be saving. Something I should be doing later, with those imaginary kids I'm quite possibly never going to have. At least that was my first thought — before I watched a blond preteen in cycling shorts scale a nearby ridge with all the energy of a pent-up gerbil. He clambered up and shouted back: "Mom, I don't need to do drugs anymore. My foot went off the edge of a 300-foot cliff! What a *rush!*"

They all count, I decided. Even the smallest epiphanies, even the ones created by tourism. And without geology, tourism itself would be practically impossible.

As we left the Badlands I dropped off, relying on Nate to pilot us on through the middle of that bright nowhere. I don't think he was hallucinating quite then, but I didn't wake up until we were well into Wyoming. I opened my eyes just in time to see a few hammerheads in a nearby oil field slowly rise and fall in the hot air. I was still dozy when I thought I saw a lone horse standing among a cluster of black cows. Did he think of himself as simply an oddly shaped cow? Or was he just making do? We are indeed passing through a strange stretch of the planet, I thought, as Nate pulled over to change drivers. The land around us had picked up a surreal, haunted, and lunar look. Dirt roads disappeared into scrubby little gullies. Two-wheel tracks seemed to head off into nothing. As we got back on the road, Nate began talking about how you could design the world's biggest book on land like this. You could lay it out on the ground, he said, and read by helicopter.

I chose that moment to ask how he was doing with all this — meaning the quest.

Nate looked at me sideways, as if I'd dropped an intriguing word problem in front of him. "I don't know," he said. "Sometimes I'm OK. Then, with all this empty scenery, I get anxious. I get embarrassed almost, having to do this."

Embarrassed? I thought. How could he feel embarrassed about a trip like this? It was simply a requirement. That and nothing more. A part of life, even if it was a little unexpected. "Well — don't," I said, which I can see now was a little curt. "What I mean is — if he doesn't want to see us, well, I don't care. That's his problem — after all. We'll arrive and he'll just have to adjust."

"It's our problem if we get there and find that out," Nate said. He kept looking ahead. "I mean, if we find out that he doesn't want to see us. Besides, these big reconciliation scenes are always a recipe for disaster."

How so? I wanted to ask. But the thought disturbed me enough that I kept the question to myself. What if we did get there and he scolded us? Or sent us away? Then I saw this for what it was. I had begun to absorb my little brother's thought patterns. It's true, I thought. Maybe, after sitting next to him for so many hours, they were beginning to soak in.

I shook my head. "How would you react if your kids hunted you down across the country?" I asked. "Wouldn't that produce even a little guilt? Wouldn't that make you behave fractionally differently in the future?"

"It might not even surprise him," Nate said. "Remember how — what I mean is, people always cut him enormous amounts of slack. He talks around things and eventually they smile, like they've even forgotten what the problem was. Remember how he used to talk up wrong numbers?"

"Yes," I said. This was an old story. My father would keep people who called our house by mistake on the line for hours. It was a trick. A kind of solitaire. A sort of improv thing that he did for his own amusement. He once even sold a little life insurance that way. And for a few months, we got calls from students looking for some SUNY Binghamton math professor who had our last name. My father would happily hand out all sorts of misinformation. "Oh yes," he'd say, "chapter five will most certainly be on the exam." Grant thought this was funny.

"I've been thinking," Nate said. "He shouldn't have saddled Grant with us."

"Yeah, but Grant also did a lot of things to Grant," I said. "He wasn't saddled. It wasn't anyone's fault."

Our tires suddenly sounded really loud as they clacked across the ripples in the asphalt. I pulled out to pass an eighteen-wheel horse truck. There was no other traffic, and I hung my arm out the window. Suddenly everything became terribly sad. Maybe it was that eerie landscape. We are out in space, I thought. Just us, sealed in our dead brother's van.

You have to push back. You always have to push back. Otherwise the gray stuff comes in while you're sitting around the house. It crawls across your living room and eats the plants like a fungus. That, I know. I stuck the first tape my fingers touched into the deck. I turned it up loud.

"Nate." I shouted. "You never used to be like this all the time. You used to be this happy kid. Even in high school. Now, it's like you're beginning to believe you don't have a lucky life. Like if they're going to spray paint someone's car on the street — it'll probably be yours. Am I right? You should be visibly happy."

Nate looked over and frowned.

"You're worried about Dad because of the way he's always been," I said. "That's not our problem. How he takes this is his problem."

That was hours ago and way out on the highway. But as my brother folded his arms, I could tell that he was thinking about it.

TWENTY

Grant here. Once again. And to tell the truth, I am starting to lose interest in all this defensive posturing. I am starting to think that this is all taking far more energy than it's worth. Especially now.

But anyway, while I was out on my journeys, while I was out doing what we might call my work, I came across this particular pressing question: What would our mother have thought of this? What would Alice Sally Scales — excuse me, what would Alice Sally Harkness Scales think of us now? What would she think of my brother's inertia? Of my sister's career wandering? Just to bring it up. Just to make it a topic of conversation. Isn't that my job here? Isn't that my primary function? To extend the range of the conversation?

Sure it is. So, what would Alice have thought? In short, my mother wouldn't have understood them at all. Squandered opportunities, one after another, that's what she'd say. Having that many choices would have seemed the greatest luxury in the world.

If I work at it, I can take myself back to one fall afternoon in Syracuse when my father was downtown, working away as a draftsman, and Mom and I were at home. I was kind of small and standing on a table, dancing to a Tito Puente record, while she scorched a shirt on the ironing board and started to swear. She had to pull up for several seconds, to regain her composure — all because of an article she'd finished a couple of minutes before about corporate wives. Actually, the article was about companies interviewing the wives — before they hired the husbands — to see if the women were going to cause problems later on. I could tell, even then, that my mother thought the whole idea that a housewife had a life of tremendous privilege was total crap. She had ambitions. But were they realized? Of course not. "You don't know how lucky you're going to be," my mother used to tell me.

While we're at it, let's go back even more. Let us go back again to Grant as a child. A quick flip through. Look — there's Grant in kindergarten, getting Vitalis rubbed into his scalp before scampering off to school. His mom is smiling and giving his hair that "sixty-second workout," because Grant's been eyeing the bottle his father uses every morning and wondering just what it did for him. There's Grant having breakfast in that high chair. He's reaching for that heavy glass bottle of milk, getting his small paw inside the rim, tugging once and experimenting with fluid dynamics. There are dusty copper molds of roosters and fish on the kitchen walls. Orange St. Joseph's Aspirin for Children crushed between two spoons. And my mom spends her afternoons entering jingle contests, just to keep her mind engaged.

Enough? That's enough for me. You know, I've found that if you work at it, you really can go nearly forever without thinking about your early childhood much at all.

It's true. But let's get back to Alice. My mother was a minister's daughter who grew up in Connecticut. She had to be good, and she hated it. Her father, Hal Harkness, was a Protestant, and an arbitrary Protestant at that. Certain boys were off limits — military boys especially. Curfew times were sacrosanct. Alice could be a majorette, but cheerleading was forbidden. Hal had started out as an oil burner installer, but he had a furious sense of right and wrong, and after the Depression, he decided on the seminary. "Some people do and some people do nothing." I heard that one from him all the time. He was the busy, stubble-haired guy with a big, shielded heart. He married Alice and Ray in his own church in 1946. There were tears all around.

My grandmother? Sally Harkness. A minister's wife even before she got the job. She found her niche. Then again, her ideas of life in the world came direct from the nineteenth century. Quiet down. Wash those Sunday-supper dishes. Respect silence. Make the home serene. Let Hal minister in peace. The woman happened upon a life with no obstacles in it of any importance at all. Don't get me wrong. I liked her fine. She was a fine grandmother.

But my mom learned shorthand and typing on her own, so she could always be self-sufficient. She won a scholarship to Sarah Lawrence, and after college ran away to work in a New York City bank. She met my father on a train. He was freshly back from Europe and smiling all the time — happy to be there and not underground with most of his buddies. Fear of Hal Harkness alone put off my father's proposal until well after the fifth date. They were gloriously happy, my parents. So happy, Ray told me once, that it used to scare the shit out of him.

Anyway, they moved to Syracuse — and I arrived. Grant as an infant? Oh yes, he was a cranky and difficult child — but he grew up. You know, my mother always believed in schedules. She believed it gave one a sense of place and responsibility. And it did. I can attest to that. Later, when Grant was old enough, she went to work part-time in a bank, spending her afternoons sorting out loans. "Un-happy mothers at home cause more problems for their children than happy ones at work." That would be her. But this bank job, even if it did help cover the bills, was not what you could call satisfying. See, my mother was a woman who could always do several things at once. It wouldn't stress her a bit. She could keep her eye on a whole room. "I work on the theory that we go this way only once. So leave things better off than when you first found them." That would be her. "The TV belongs in the basement. The living room is for living."

The kids made their entrance during a stretch of years when my mother was unusually restless. By the time Nate appeared, she had raising us pretty much down pat. She was volunteering for political campaigns and taking over the PTA. She was even considering a run at law school. And on that last item, Ray, to his credit, was nearly all gung ho. Let's make a plan, he'd say. Let's figure this one out, he'd say — and they did. Nate was in kindergarten by then and Sarah was obsessed with the upcoming, all-encumbering universe of fifth grade. I'd be-come a freshman at Troy. Alice, at forty-three, began work in a tiny legal-aid office, one staffed by retired judges and S.U. law students. She checked people in. She heard their stories. She kept them from crying. She worked the switchboard, and came home to tell Ray, "My nerves are all jangling, but it's nice."

As part of the plan to amass capital for law school, my mother shifted over to bulk food. She bought in restaurant quantities. She froze things. She brought home peanut butter in the half gallon size. Breakfast cereals were poured from nine pound plastic bags. My mother sold this to the kids as part of a great and progressive adventure. And they went along.

That's it. That's where things stood when, one November morning three years later, while waiting for Ray to come home for lunch, my mother decided to go for a walk.

OK. That's enough from Mr. Historical Perspective. Remember, pal, when you get right down to it — we're all history.

TWENTY-ONE

It was after breakfast, and we were rolling up Wyoming's Route 14 as it cut into the eastern flank of the Bighorns with a series of yellow and red switchbacks. The rearview landscape was the twisted, rolling benchland of yesterday afternoon — much harsher than the plains. That odd sense of displacement had settled over me again. Something I couldn't find the proper word for, a feeling that made me wake up each day not fully understanding how I'd made it from there to here. It had stayed with me like a shadow.

Earlier that morning, before eight even, I'd climbed out of the tent and discovered that the campground had already emptied out. As I stood in my bare feet on the damp grass, still wearing the shorts I'd slept in, the empty campsites on either side of us somehow began to piss me off. It was like we were late and all those retired tourists had beaten us to something valuable. I slapped the outside of the van, rumbling around it like an omnidirectional force, until I heard Sarah groan.

Twenty minutes later, we were eating breakfast in Sheridan at the Big Spur Café. It was a tiny place. Sarah and I took seats at the counter as Dot wiped away a stray hash brown — "That's something you wouldn't ordinarily find on your table at home," she said, snapping the rag.

We both ordered blueberry pancakes, though I thought twice about it because the night before, in a different diner, Sarah had attacked my range of recent menu choices. She claimed I'd barely eaten anything in weeks not based on grease or sugar. "What have you had lately that wasn't — brown?" she asked.

When the coffee came, Sarah plumped the sleeves of her badminton sweatshirt, placed both elbows on the counter, and gazed into the mirror above the wall of miniature cereal boxes. It was that infinite look my sister regularly gives the world when she's not fully functioning. Or that's what I thought. In the past twenty-four hours, as we'd begun to close in on Yellowstone, she'd been all over the place. I was never exactly sure where on the emotional arc I'd find her.

An older gentleman settled onto a nearby stool and asked for a half order of hash browns with white gravy. I sipped my coffee as voices from work started running through my head. I glanced at my watch, factored in the time difference, and saw that they would have been coming up on the first edition deadline. In the equivalent of that seventh-grade, wouldn't-they-all-be-sorry-if-I-died fantasy, I began to wonder what sort of story might be circulating about me. Would they be taking bets on the date of my eventual return? Would they even care?

A guy close to my age, but heavyset and with a beard, claimed the stool between the older gentleman and myself. He tucked in his blue polo shirt and ordered the special. "Frank," he said to his friend, "you walking much?"

"Every other day, till I build my legs up," Frank replied, before launching into an animated soliloquy on VCRs. "You have to be smarter than a park bear to run mine," he said. "A goddamn electrical engineer. You can watch movies, but I can't program the thing worth a damn. *Victory at Sea*, you seen that? I got all hundred and eight episodes."

"Vietnam in there?" his friend asked.

"Nope. It's all World War II. Boom boom, bap-bap-bap." Frank worked at his breakfast for a bit, and then began talking about his time in the Pacific, right before the war. "We had these Navy training films," he said, "for combat, where they showed how you could use bodies to block holes in a sinking ship. One guy would put a body in the hole, and the other guy would brace him with a four by four. At the start, you saw this sailor coming along with another guy on his shoulder. I thought he was taking him to an aid station."

"Guess not." His friend glanced at me and back at his scrambled eggs. Frank used his last hash brown to draw a thin bead of gravy along the plate's edge.

It stuck with me, because I'd never been able to get my father to talk about the war. When I was younger, I'd ask all the time, and he'd say that I didn't want to know. Which only made me want to know more. Eventually I stopped, and the subject spread between us like another silent lake. These days, whenever I see a bit of old newsreel footage on TV, a part of me imagines him there — floating pontoon bridges in the rain, or directing heavy equipment beneath the sound of distant shelling, or whatever it is that I imagine he did. My mom used to tell me that when they were first married, he would have nightmares all the time. She had to be careful waking him up, even from a nap, because he'd still be dreaming it, even if he never talked about it.

As we climbed the eastern slope of the Bighorns, the peculiar sharp light of the morning fooled me into thinking that I could see tremendous detail at great distances — down to the bark on individual stumps in faraway clear-cuts. We drove alongside scalloped cliffs and small alpine meadows, as acres of Ponderosa pines washed around the caramel-colored outcroppings. On one rare straight stretch, I overtook a laboring RV, but at that moment Grant's van began making a lower than usual growl. As the temperature needle inched across the red H, I turned on the blower to suck heat away from the engine. When that didn't work, I coasted into a turnoff, got out, and left the van idling.

I next found myself standing on the edge of a soft cliff, while the landscape below me rolled on like atmosphere. The road we'd been traveling coiled up to the turnout like an ascending river. Beyond it, a white and tan expanse spread east for hundreds of miles. Thin racks of close clouds skittered across the light sky, propelled by a gangly wind that reached down to slap my face. It was a wind that hadn't run into anything for days and days.

Sarah followed me out, as a light green Impala pulled in next to the van. The older woman in the driver's seat draped both wrists across the top of the steering wheel, as if her hands alone could say, "That's it." She left the car running and smiled at the thin, bearded man who was arching his back in the passenger seat. Both doors opened at once, but only the woman got out. She smoothed the front of her azalea-print blouse and walked toward us.

"Hi," she said. "Saw your plates. You from New York?"

"Yeah," Sarah said. "Binghamton."

"You're overheating too?" the woman said. "This is as good a spot as any to cool down. Has it been wet in the east? We're from South Dakota and we're dry." Her name was Lana, and it turned out she was from Mitchell. She'd gone to high school with Walter, our friend the bartender. "That's my stomping grounds," Lana said. "It's smaller out here than many people think." Lana and her son were heading to Idaho, where they had a cabin. We talked about farming, where in Iowa they'd once lived, and how bad the corn looked as we drove through. "Iowa's always been such a good corn state," she said. Her son waved from the car and Lana nodded back. "I guess we're cool," she said. "You pass through some pretty meadows up top, then it's a narrow canyon with hairpin turns all the way down. This range drops right into a desert, but it's the quickest way to the park."

Sarah buckled into the driver's seat and backed out without using her mirrors. That last bit didn't even bother me, because I was suddenly feeling small about making fun of the Corn Palace a few days before. I looked back out over the cliff as my sister waited for a break in the traffic. I wanted one last view of the east. It was true. Over the last day or so, I had started to think of this trip as a guilt-producing errand of revenge. I was even beginning to enjoy the prospect of suddenly reappearing in my father's life. A kind of payback, almost, for the times he'd reappeared in ours. Thinking like that tended to narrow down the psychic horizon, and I wasn't used to the view.

We'd left the Bighorns and were down in the following desert, but at the exact moment Sarah drove off the road, I was not thinking: We are having an accident. Or even: This streaked windshield will be the last thing I see on earth. Instead, as the road curved gently left, and the van knowingly propelled itself straight ahead and on over the shoulder, I thought: Here's a view I've never seen before. Sarah kept smiling, but her eyes were closed. Her hair streamed around and into her face as we headed at sixty-five or more miles per hour toward the faint outline of a rutted dirt road.

I made a loud but totally unintelligible noise.

Sarah pumped the brakes, missed the start of the dirt road, and winced as our right front wheel slammed into a large rectangular hole. We lurched. I heard a clank, and the van tilted, grinding into the dirt like a stunt horse shot in the chest. A loud, tearing vibration rode up through my feet. The back wheels lifted, and my knuckles smacked the windshield. The shoulder belt bit in, and as the rear of the van bounced back to earth, the engine stalled.

A faint cloud of orange dust caught up and drifted over us. Country music droned on from the speakers.

"What the fuck *was* that?" I slapped the dash and reached around to undo the seat belt. My right shoulder burned. My knuckles stung. My knees began to shake. Something smelled like burned oil.

Sarah seemed stunned, but her face finally worked itself into something of a grin, as if she were trying to hide her shock at being so far from the road. I turned off the radio. We were a 150 yards away from the highway's edge, maybe more, and halfway sunk in a long ditch. When I unlatched the door, it swung open by itself. A puff of cream-colored dust, the kind you'd expect if you'd just touched down on the moon, rose as my sneakers hit the ground. I could feel the heat through my soles.

Transparent olive dots of oil had sprayed out through the van's grille and splashed down along the front bumper. Our right front wheel was so far underground that I couldn't even get a look. It was splayed out at an unnatural angle. I kicked through some loose gravel at the front of the hole until I unearthed a half-buried chunk of metal. It was a three-inch-thick cast-iron plate the size of a table, and we'd hit the corner of it. I told Sarah to make sure the ignition was off, because our oil pan had been scraped away and something might catch on fire.

"Hey," my sister said, meeting me by the bumper. "We're having a big day, and it's not even lunch."

"You drove *off the fucking road*," I shouted.

"No, in the cosmic sense, we're still *on* the road," she told me. "We've just — meandered onto another literal path. There is a difference."

"You drove off the fucking road because you're an idiot," I said.

"Oh yeah, that's it. I forgot."

I went to get a handful of paper towels from behind the seat and marched around to the front, where I held them stupidly in my hands. How could we have hit a metal plate in the middle of a desert? Who would have been dumb enough to leave a metal plate here for us to hit?

I dropped to my knees and the paper towels blew away. We couldn't back out. We'd lost all our oil. I kicked the fender in movie-style disgust.

"Think of this as a test," my sister said, trying to sound calm. She scanned the sky. "Besides — no vultures."

"Test," I yelled. "What kind of fucking test? This is an ac-ci-dent. An accident that you planned. And why? Because it would be *fun*? Spontaneous? You're always doing shit like this. When I finally have things, this whole string of events, under control in *my own mind*, you go beyond the stupid envelope. You're fucking incomprehensible."

I slugged the driver's side door with the heel of my palm. The panel dented in and quickly popped back, like something from a cartoon. My sister folded her hands. She seemed amused. I could have hit her. "Stupid, stupid, stupid forever," I shouted.

Sarah drew a line in the bright dust with the toe of her running shoe. "It's OK," she said.

"What's OK? What?" I turned and walked out to the edge of the highway before she could answer, and sat on a warm, crumbly rock. Two cars went by — a Crown Victoria with Pennsylvania plates, and clothes racks filling the back seat, then a guy in a yellow T-shirt driving some subcompact from Ohio. The first guy ignored my wave, and the Ohio man waved back. It was hopeless. Then I remembered that Grant did have a CB. Or at least I remembered seeing one in a cupboard.

But when I got back, the CB was already sitting on the seat and its wires had been tapped into a jack on the dashboard. Sarah sipped from a bottle of orange seltzer and gazed at the abandoned dirt road we could no longer follow. She calmly pointed out that even though the CB *did* light up, it did not in fact *work*. I played with the squelch knob for a while, and when I concluded that she might be right, she began to recount some ridiculous story about a retired couple in Arizona who were driving the back roads without a CB when they had an accident. The husband had a heart attack. He died, and his seventy-nine-year-old wife had to walk out. She survived by breaking into a cabin and eating canned peas. Why was she telling me this?

As my sister spun her seat in circles, I squinted back out at the empty highway. "Well," she said finally, "the only other explanation has to do with the law of big numbers. I figure, the longer that something illogical doesn't happen, the more likely it's going to happen — eventually."

"This isn't about logic," I said. "This isn't about the irrational world. You drove off the fucking road."

"Well — perhaps my reservoir of luck is finally running dry," she said. "Wouldn't that be something?"

Big numbers. I got out of the van again because I had to walk somewhere. I took the rutted path, the one right in front of me, and followed it up over the rise and down into a broad, dry gulch. Fine, I thought. I'll starve. I'll dehydrate in the desert. I'll leave behind a full set of bleached and picked over bones. They'll never find me.

Twenty minutes later, I came upon an abandoned one-story house, something that might have once been a ranch. It only had part of a roof, but I jogged toward it anyway, without even knowing why. When I got close I saw that what was left of the building was half timbered and half stone. The initials JX had been carved into the flecked white rock at the foundation. It was even hotter inside. The door frames were gone, but a few of the long rectangular window frames were still in place. I found two nests made by some kind of small animal in the fireplace. I even located a scrap of wallpaper. It had a baroque pattern with large, faint diamonds, and was still attached to a strip of lath. I picked at the wood a few inches below this, and behind it discovered layers and layers of old newspapers. They had been used for insulation, and I tore out a few pages.

On a scrap from a paper called the something *Boomerang* I found this story: "Will Hang Himself — Gab Ferris Will Not Be Hanged By Sheriff of Laramie County — But Will Hang Self." The rest was unreadable, except for a description of the mechanism. "The device to operate the drop will be located below the platform on which the doomed man will stand. As the doomed man steps on the trap door, a cork will be removed from a tank of water. The water will slowly run out until a counterbalance becomes heavier, and swings down to release the trap. The doomed man will then drop into eternity."

I sat on the front stoop and stared at the flattened tin roof of a nearby shed. Behind it were odd pieces of beat-up wood and rolls of rusted barbed wire. A set of concrete steps in the middle of nowhere led to a semicircle of shot-up cans.

The doomed man. Wonderful, I thought. It probably happened, too. That's probably how he went. You see, that is the thing — say something is true and you still take an unnatural interest in it, what does that make you? A voyeur? But say it's false, simply a story, and then we can all watch. We can dismiss the parts we don't like and stay safe at the same time. I've probably written hundreds of stories with dead people in them. All true. And what will they be? Historic scraps? Dropped into eternity?

My shoulder started to ache from where the seat belt had held me back. What minute string of decisions had led me to this particular spot? I wondered. Then again, how many actual decisions had I actually made? I'd been pulled along for what felt like ages in a sort of slipstream.

I began to think of how I'd feel if I walked back and found the van gone. Would I blame her? Of course. It would be the last yawning gap between us. The unforgivable action that led to our final falling out. It would also be a relief. I'd stand there staring at the spot for a while, then I'd hitchhike east, or south, to Casper, where there would be a bus. Then I'd go on to Cheyenne and find the airport. I'd charge a flight to Chicago. I'd sleep on the gray carpeted floor of some vacant airport lounge and take an early morning flight to Boston. I wouldn't even call anyone to pick me up. Instead, I'd take the T from Logan. I'd ride the Blue Line into town, change at Park Street, get out by Harvard Square, and find a seat on the 73 bus to Belmont. I'd walk those last few blocks, and unlock the kitchen door as if it had been only a very long day at work. Then I'd climb to the third floor and sleep this all into eternity.

TWENTY-TWO

"Oh, Christ — bikers," was the first thing I said. It's true. Word for word, the instant I heard them. Even before I knew. Honest.

By then, Nate had sulked away over that dull-orange hill, ready to suffer the solitude of the desert. Which left me all by myself, staring into the pale sun. Until suddenly — swoosh — the bikers arrived. It was so unexpected. It felt like a cloud of pandemonium had pulled right up on my doorstep. Their leader, a big guy with a white wrap-around helmet to match his beard, appeared first. Sixteen other motorcycles followed, two by two, in a little parade. Their headlights sparkled like hot jewels.

Make no mistake, these were giant touring bikes. Metal-flake Harleys and Hondas with sidecars. These people had CBs, stereos, and televisions, and stuffed animals swinging from their aerials. I stood on the back bumper, slightly at sea, and squinted as the parade circled our crippled van once and muttered to a stop.

Only after they unplugged their helmet intercoms did I recognize this motorcycle gang for what it was. A gang of retired bikers. The Lord's Team Riders from Albuquerque, they announced, and nearly in unison. They were on their way to Glacier, via Yellowstone, when they discovered me — a dame off the road and in deep distress.

"Golly, we needed a break," sighed a heavy woman with shiny gray hair. "My bottom was getting tired anyway." A bald eagle was embroidered on the front of her shirt. Most all of the other bikers wore thin leather vests. Some were studded with little patches and rally pins.

I jumped off the bumper and explained our dilemma to Herbie — since he seemed like the guy, the leader. When he couldn't locate Nate, he asked eagerly if there were any other casualties? No? Then did I need a lift? A tow might be helpful, I replied. Herbie smiled and smiled. "Good to go," he said. In an instant, I imagined those hearty motorcycles all harnessed up like a team of sled dogs, towing Grant's van out of its hole in the desert. Herbie tugged at the microphone cord on his palm-size CB and dialed up some emergency channel.

The Lord's Team Riders, it turned out, wanted to know everything. They were especially curious about how a girl, like me, could find herself so far off the road. I skipped that one. I told them Nate had been driving and that *he* fell asleep. Everyone nodded as if that could be expected from any younger brother. From there we jumped to a discussion of crashes in general, skin grafts, the trials of witnessing for the Lord, and which were Yellowstone's best bearless tenting grounds. Herbie finally established contact with a voice from somewhere, who put him through to a wrecker service in Cody. At that moment, a square-chested guy said, "Praise God and protect us from the idiots on our roads. Let us have a hymn." They sang "For the Beauty of the Earth." It sounded nice.

The bikers varoomed away shortly after that, but not without making sure that we had enough Gatorade and Slim Jims to last for days. Nate did finally return from his desert walkabout. But as soon as I finished recounting the story of our rescue, he started checking his watch. He was worrying again; no doubt imagining that our wrecker had abandoned us.

Then — bingo, just like that, just like before, I heard another low roar. A rumble, shivering up from out in the desert. Festooned with violet fog lights, jade-green side panels, and turquoise light strings spiraling up its bristling aerials — ten wheels larger than any tow truck I'd ever imagined — the mythic wrecker of our future appeared.

The skinny driver hopped out and sang, "Have you driven over a Ford lately?" as he ambled toward us. "You the folks I got a call for?" he asked. "Looks like." He wore a white Western-cut button-down.

Before Nate had a chance to speak, I leaped into the short version of our story, and the driver nodded. When he touched the brim of his hat, I knew he thought it was time to survey the damage.

"What you've got is an outfit with a busted oil pan and some solid front-end difficulty," he said, eventually. "How again did you get all the way over here?"

I explained patiently, eloquently I thought. At least I did a good enough acting job to sell my version of reality. (Although in this one, I did the nodding off.) "Road rapture," I explained. Not, if truth be known, that I'd closed my eyes again to play chicken with the curves.

The driver gave me a wily glance. For an instant I thought, this might be a guy who'd appreciate the full account. He might even get a laugh from it.

The driver circled Grant's van a second time, as though it were a tethered piece of livestock. "This'll be ninety for the tow to Cody, once we get her out. Unless you still got the Triple-A, like it says on your bumper."

I looked over at Nate. "He does," I said. We discussed this after my brother returned from the desert. All he had to do was sign Grant's name on the slip, but he didn't want to because it wasn't legal. The driver returned with the form on a little plastic clipboard, and Nate scribbled angrily away.

Good boy. I smiled and tried, for a change, not to say anything.

On the way to Cody, I sat the middle of the tow truck cab and looked down from a great height on a big green car in front of us. Its license plate said, "BOOK-EM." I decided we were following a librarian. Les, our savior, believed it was an out-of-state cop on vacation.

"You can always tell," Les said. "People's cars are like their houses. Take your long cars. Your Caddies. There you've got a hood and trunk, like your front and back yards. Most people keep all their stuff in the back yard. The same as putting suitcases into your trunk. If you think about it, cars even have doorbells to let you know when you're getting in. People with expansive personalities drive Caddies. People who live in apartments drive compacts," he said. "It's natural."

The green car slowed to twenty, so Les tapped his horn. "If a guy's hair in front of you don't go up a bit, then you don't have a horn," he said. "I want them to wonder what I want. I like to move 'em up a little." The car pulled over.

Les had already decided that the place for us was Elias's Auto Hospital in Cody. He listed our symptoms as he radioed in the reservation. A sheared spindle assembly, in need of a wheel, a tire, and so on. When the happy voice on the other end, possibly even Elias himself, asked how many miles the van had on it, Les said, "Lots."

"What are you two doing out here again?" Les asked. "Vacation? Or that open-road-sets-you-free, running-on-down-the-highway crap?"

"Something of that." I offered him a Slim Jim.

"Run it out here a while, and things begin to look so much the same you'll think you've slowed down to a stop," Les announced. "We've got all those rendezvous people in town now. Would-be mountain men. They want to recreate the past. No blue jeans or zippers. They're all born in the wrong century, as far as I'm concerned. They're all for the past, these people, making it out to be so spiritual, but they can leave after a weekend. I think we ought to leave the past exactly where it is. Let's not drag everything around with us all the time. But I talk too much. What brings you this direction again?"

I ticked off the highlights, plus a bit about our dubious family. The van dangled behind us like a captured fish. Nate frowned and pulled his arm in from the passenger side window. "My brother has a bug," I said. "A cold."

"And don't you hate a summer cold," Les said. "Lost my Dad early on," he said. "It's never the same, but what can you do?"

In a small yard at the edge of Cody, I saw two girls lassoing each other behind a fence. Nate had perked up enough by then to explain that at the turn of the century, Buffalo Bill had envisioned Cody as a starting point, a place where you'd pick up a last few items before trekking away into the wilderness. Les nodded, as if my brother had done his homework. The town did have that last-gasp kind of appeal. All the traffic seemed to be either going to or coming from Yellowstone. A passing RV parade that stopped to buy.

Les and Elias's Auto Hospital seemed to count on each other for patients. We were in luck, it turned out, because Elias had a freshly wrecked van, almost like ours, in back, so there were plenty of parts. But it would still take a day or two to get everything fixed. I didn't care, really. I'd started cooling off about this whole trip as soon as we began to really get west. I wondered why that was happening, since it was all my idea in the first place.

We walked to a Wendy's on Sheridan Avenue, my brother's idea of dinner. A young man entered the place wearing only chaps, spurs, and a loose calico shirt. Eyes popped wide across the franchise. Living history at its best! The man picked up two big white bags of food and sauntered out. He handed the food to a bearded buddy who was driving a Jeep. They were pulling a small trailer loaded with gear. The bumper sticker said, "Custer got the point."

A plump woman gently tapped my shoulder. "Dear, did we get his number? Where's he from?" All Wyoming license plates, she explained later, had numbers in the corner, saying what county they came from.

"Nineteen," I said.

The woman put both hands on the table. "At least it's not from around here. He's one of those buckskinners going to rendezvous in Montana. We're glad to have seen him and glad he didn't stay."

Elias finished off our front end a day later. He seemed pleased by the result. I charged the result. Elias said come back any time.

We had another fifty-two miles of National Forest to go. Nate and I, by then, had pretty much ceased talking. Beyond the accident, and the fact that he'd had to sign for the tow truck, he was annoyed because I'd used Grant's credit card for the repairs. But come on — that card only had his first initial on it. I simply signed, "Gail Scales." Like I'd been doing all along. Of course — it was yet another felony in the big book. The big book that would always be open.

At Yellowstone's eastern border, I watched a gray cloud billow in against the azure sky. It fascinated me, somehow. But, oddly, this cloud looked like it was attached to the top of the pine-covered mountain in front of it.

"It really *is* burning," Nate said. The air tasted like smoke.

A few minutes later we pulled in at Pahaska to get gas. It wasn't anything you could call a town, only a sort of motel-restaurant-gas-and-grocery combination. Inside at the register, people were saying that the fire on the mountain behind us was only eight miles away. No one appeared too worried. They didn't think it would cover that much ground overnight. At least that's what the boy behind the deli counter told an MBA-type in safari shorts, after he forked over two dollars for a bundle of firewood. I wasn't so sure.

As I buckled up, Nate asked if I wanted to call Dad. Right there. It was around 4:30 in the afternoon, and that call was the last thing I felt like facing. I shook my head.

"OK," my brother said. "That's cool." He seemed suddenly jaunty and confident, and I couldn't figure it out. "We'll set up in the park," Nate said, "and nail him at dawn."

Nail him? We really have shifted, I thought. I was all for wandering around for several days and *maybe* finding my father when we got around to it. Or at the very least putting it off for a day.

Dark pines flicked by. We quickly climbed a long hill and arrived at a National Park toll plaza. They had a little A-frame house in the middle of the road like a toll booth. A wooden board at the side listed the campgrounds. But they were all full or shut down by the fires. Our entrance fee was good for a week.

"Your best bet is to go back and try the National Forest campground in Pahaska," the woman in the booth said. "Really. It's your only bet."

I thought the campground there was a little too close to that fire on the mountain — given a choice. But Nate picked a site right beside a frigid stream. He set up the tent and took the van somewhere without telling me. There was nothing more for me to do. So — I waded into the stream. It was ankle deep and numbing. I had trouble keeping my balance. Finally, I sat down on a knocked-over pine tree and skimmed the soles of my prickling feet across the quickly moving water.

I took off my sunglasses and everything seemed way too bright. Washed out, even. I tried to console myself by watching the smoke billow off the burning mountain next door. I dipped my toes into the frozen stream and it hurt. I knew I'd have to immerse them whole, to get back. For some curious reason, that set it off.

I had felt this one inching in earlier. I had. As we came through those gigantic blank lands around Cody. But then we were moving, and motion alone can sometimes keep these things at bay. Nevertheless, it was hard to keep from feeling that I was losing myself in the face of all this. Maybe it had to do with the oppressive scale of things out there. Maybe I was overwhelmed by scenery. It can make you see how insignificant you truly are. We were only out to collect more and greater rejections, I decided. We were very away.

That morning, I'd had another odd dream — a vivid and strange sequence with blunt white captions. One said something about me running off to find the family I'd always been running from. But the annoying thing was, when I could almost read what came next, the words jumped to another language. None of this worked out in the dream. The trip, nothing. In the dream, Nate and I drive back empty-handed and my brother won't say a word to me. In the dream, my job is to apologize endlessly and return the kidnap victim. All through this, everyone's faces were bigger than usual — like giant puppets. I wasn't sure what this was supposed to demonstrate.

I know — I always act as though everything is well sutured, and at the last minute, take a big dive. But what can anybody do in the face of deep patterns? I mean, wouldn't it be oh so simple to actually be someone with incredible resolve? To follow through, all the time? And not be the stubborn screw-up I always turn out to be?

I stayed on that precarious log, facing the burning forest, thinking those useless thoughts for the longest time. It's just a mess, I heard myself say. One brother's dead. My father might as well be on another planet, and this mountain is on fire. This hopeless mountain has picked *now* to burn itself up.

My fingers tingled. I wanted to be home. I wanted to be back in my life. In my apartment and taking a nap. I needed a vacation from big holes. It had been light-years on end of big holes. But I had to stay and watch that goddamn mountain burn. At least until I could stand to put my feet back into the freezing water.

At some point when I wasn't looking, Nate had brought back the van. He'd left a white plastic bag of groceries on the picnic table and started to scrub the windshield. He smiled as he wiped away the bug bodies and smeared cricket legs. He moved down to the headlights. This is how he deals, I thought. This is how he gets through. He turns meticulous. I watched him collect a handful of trash from inside the van. There was nothing frantic or angry in the way he moved. It was calm and chorelike. A contained series of repeated motions. How wrong was it to describe any of this as happy? I wondered. Could that word even apply, out here in the burning forest?

I should know these things about my brother, I thought. I should know what he's good at, while he's still here and while there's still time. He is good at attending to the small daily tasks, even if he leaves the large things unresolved. Aren't those small tasks part of the reason he clings to that all-consuming job? The daily trial?

Nate's bare legs wiggled out from behind the open passenger side door. His head was under the dashboard. I looked away and then back, as he sat up and tore a piece of electrical tape off the roll with his teeth. He caught my eye and stared for a long liquid second. He took the small piece of tape from his mouth and stuck it on the outside of the door. He walked to the bank and waited for an entire minute, with his arms folded in judgment. Like he couldn't decide whether I looked like I wanted to be left alone or not.

Nate splashed into the stream. He stepped resolutely through the current, as if it had no hold on him. Once he stumbled, but finally he settled in beside me on the pine log with a bounce. His sneakers dripped and he slid a casual arm across my shoulder. I shivered. I couldn't remember either one of us ever giving the other a hug. It had never been a part of the vocabulary.

"I know," Nate said. "We'll make this deal, from here on out. You be my sister and I'll be your brother."

TWENTY-THREE

Grant here. And you thought you were done. You thought I'd be out doing some fresh celestial navigation. But I'm still around — if not for long. See, I'm running out of patience.

What I'm getting to is the fact that this entire adventure is beginning to interest me less and less. Especially now, as I am coming to you from the land of infinite regret. You do see that you are only receiving a part of the story. You do understand that what you're getting here is a mere fragment. Which, after all, is probably the best it can be for any of us. But in this particular case, with the tyranny of perspective hovering at my shoulder, you might say that I get the point. I understand. Now, there are things in the offing that I don't particularly need to see. I've already got it — if you catch my celestial drift.

So let's get down to it. Aren't I a horrible person? Isn't that the upshot? You know how horrible I am? I'm so horrible I ought to be dead. It's true. What would you expect from a family of eccentrics, all complaining because nobody ever explained any of the big stuff to them? See, I've always said that the best way to win an argument is to be right at the start. If you can't do that, then be right at the end.

And I'm right, here. Though, as I've said, when viewing the landscape from a distance of this magnitude, well, you adjust, you readjust. Perhaps I held on to certain images, to certain ideas about the way things were and should have been, for a little too long. Far too long, in fact. But it's far easier said than undone.

Suffice it to say that when I made my pact with Ray, I was not fully aware of the ramifications. It's true, I could have had a different life, but I picked one route and kept to it. So what made me the hoarder of information? Why did I keep everyone away? Think location. Think accumulation. Think about the things I believed I was missing, day by day, because I had that mantle of extra responsibility to carry around.

The piling on in the world that makes you fidgety-small and mean. The mountain of triviality that becomes the final argument. The break-off moment, after which no one can remember the original why of the problem.

Besides, I always had the keys to their pasts, or to parts of their pasts. I knew things they all would want to know eventually. At a certain point, yes, they would come in to collect. It should have been another way. I can see that now. Possibly those two out there are even correct on some points. Possibly they're right about my trying to control and compensate for an irrational situation. Possibly they're even right about my sliding into the groove, the one you can't quite see until you've been down in it for far too long. The job I couldn't think my way out of. The inexplicable trick of herding my siblings into a semblance of a family life. I shouldn't have gone along. I should have picked up help — from Ray. I should have forced the issue. Were I there now, yes, it would be different. I wouldn't settle for the little house and the lone life. I wouldn't keep everyone at arm's length. I would make substitutions. I would allow for changes en route. If they can still be figuring things out — shouldn't I be allowed equal latitude?

All right, go to it. Drive my van. Charge what you like. You always need a scapegoat. I mean, hell, I already *have* these goddamn broad-as-the-universe shoulders — so why not?

TWENTY-FOUR

I once interviewed a guy who hiked the entire Appalachian Trail, but when he got home, after months of spending every night on the hard ground, he couldn't sleep in a bed. His entire concept of comfort had changed. By morning, I'd come to see that I could use a change of that magnitude. It even felt like one might be coming up.

The night before, as I had spread out across the dirt of the National Forest campground, under the blue tent's dome, sleeping on the ground began to feel somewhat luxurious. It had started to seem, more and more, that I spent too many hours worrying about hardness, worrying about growing scales over my reactions. I was beginning to feel as though I'd been taking notes on myself since the start of time. But then, it's not as though I slept perfectly that night. I was up for hours, because a gang of mule deer with respiratory problems kept nuzzling the tent walls. It had to be an entire inbred pack, and each one had a deviated septum.

As the 7:00 A.M. sun cut through the dew on the tent's fly, I was awake, wired, and ready to go. None of that slipping in and out of consciousness stuff. I was propped up and propelled by straight-ahead, leg-shaking adrenalin, as if I were expecting an important call. We should be up and moving, I decided. We should be out there, jostling our way among the rented trailers and RVs, staking a claim to some campsite territory.

That was my litany as I pulled on the light green T-shirt with the Navajo circle design that I'd picked up with the groceries the night before. Sarah was asleep inside the van as I collapsed the tent and shook the ground cloth clean. When I peeled the dew-laden map of Yellowstone away from the picnic table, it stunned me, again — that we thought we could locate my father within 3,471 square miles of national park. Before that trip I'd always carried along a wrong idea of parks as contained zones, with hikers, happy wildlife, and lots of blacktop paths. But none of that could accommodate the state-size wilderness we were about to enter.

I heard chainsaws in the distance. Or maybe it was the drone of heavy aircraft, bombing the nearby fires at first light. The air held a faint tang of smoke. I gave the campsite a final policing glance and it felt like such an inherited thing to do. A Grant sort of move. I probably spend half my life trying to please people who aren't even around to notice.

My sister wasn't awake, so I slipped the tent and the sleeping bag in behind the driver's seat, started up the van, and backed out. The lone road into the park was empty, and the van shuddered as I accelerated up a long, steep straightaway cut into the edge of a nameless mountain. Sarah rolled over twice, until her sleeping bag hit the rear door with a thud. "Whoa," she said, again and again, until the word sounded like a command sprung loose from a dream.

"What the hell are you doing?" Sarah walked unsteadily to the front of the van. She wore boxer shorts and a sleeveless purple shirt. The windows were open, and the breeze was thick with the smell of pine. My sister slipped into the revolving captain's chair and squinted. "What's all this fucking energetic military shit?" she said. "I have to pee."

"We have to dash for it," I announced. "Or we'll *never* find a campsite."

"Dash?" She covered her eyes. "Do you know the word 'hotel'? It's a nice word. We could stop all this needless dashing."

I shook my head, because somehow staying in a hotel didn't seem like the right option. Maybe if we were older, or part of a tour.

"OK," Sarah said. "I take it back. This is the new me. Starting now."

The night before, while cutting thin, chewy steaks with clear plastic knives on my housemate's worn camp ware, we hashed things out. I'd confessed to having heard a reassuring voice in the back of my head all during our slow-motion glide off the highway, promising that I was not going to die with a head injury from a rollover in the Wyoming badlands.

"That — you could have told me," Sarah said.

"Well, I don't know, I'm flawed."

My sister nodded and, to my surprise, said a whole raft of things that I used to think. She told me we were taking a big risk in trying this at all. She said that it was possible that our father might not want to see us. She ran through all my well-tempered complaints of a thousand hypnotic miles back. The strange part was, they didn't seem to apply. Or I didn't care. It was hard to say.

Part of it, I think, was because I was still a little angry about having to sign Grant's name on the wrecker's slip. But when I did it, I felt as though I had crossed some line, as though I had arrived at another place. We were going to do what we had to do, I'd decided. Sarah's sudden change of heart puzzled me. But this is Sarah's primary problem — whenever she gets close to something, she makes a sudden retreat. Usually by moving to another part of the country.

Sarah started in on how the two of us were in fact the only functioning family we had left. "We might as well acknowledge it," she said. "Have you ever wondered why we're not *more* screwed up?"

"What do you mean?"

"There are people who've had a lot less bad stuff happen to them, and they're a mess, not even functioning — in the smallest sense."

"I don't know," I said. "I mean, we both sort of had other places to go. You got out. I was pretty much adopted by the Costellos for a while, in high school."

"You think that's it?" Sarah asked.

I shrugged, not in a dismissive way, but more because I couldn't explain it.

For an instant there, we both seemed ready to map out exactly what we thought might happen when we went in, all armed with familial duty, to find our father. Because planning that part out, in detail, would have been a sane thing to do. But we also both had this idea that we'd drive into the park and somehow find him waiting by the gate. We'd slow to twenty, open the door, and he'd hop in.

Instead, I ended up repeating some old line about how every family is screwed up in some indescribable way, and as families went, we happened to be stuck in a really obtuse one. Those things never sound quite so obvious when the words are actually coming out of your mouth.

"Exactly," Sarah said. Then she got up, went into the van and fell asleep.

The East Gate tote board showed only three open campgrounds. The rest were closed by fire or full. I asked the blond, college-age guard in the booth for strategy suggestions.

"Get as far north as you can," he said. "But don't speed. We had two fires jump the road last night, and they evacuated a couple of campgrounds. If you don't need hookups you've got a chance. Indian Creek?"

I accelerated and handed Sarah the map. Within minutes we were climbing into Sylvan Pass, but also stuck behind a slow camper. I reached for my sunglasses and decided that this guy in front of us was not one to worry about. They were hookup people. They'd never take a tent site. You could tell, just from the cautious way they drove.

"Indian Creek is way, way up," Sarah said. Her fingernail wobbled along the map. "Fifty miles." She hung her wrist out the window. "Remember — I'm hungry. It also might be time for different clothes."

In the heart of Sylvan Pass we found ourselves surrounded by vast slides of gray, plate-size rocks. The bare mountain overhead topped out at 10,000 feet, and appeared to curl back in toward us. On the other side, the valley below opened around Yellowstone Lake in a panoramic scene that should have come with cherubs. I couldn't decide if the stripped-in clouds below us were fog or smoke.

The road wound down a few thousand feet, and by the lake the wildlife began to emerge. We saw mule deer, elk, two shaggy moose in a marsh, and several bison at the edge of a meadow. I watched as an oblivious coyote on a hillside pounced on something small.

The trading post at Fishing Bridge turned out to be a grocery store crammed into a broad-beamed, 1920s-style lodge. It was crowded and filled with the hint of emergency. It seemed like the last free hours before a blizzard, when people feel compelled to stock up on Froot Loops and toaster pastries. I collected some day-old blueberry muffins and a bag of Goldfish crackers, before locating the coffee in a brew-pot up front.

The two older men working the register smiled as they slipped groceries into square paper bags. They were both balding in different ways and wearing brown-rimmed glasses. Their name tags, the white-lettered kind you'd make in an industrial arts class, read Jim Arizona and Jack Arizona.

As Jack Arizona herded my muffins into the bag he said, "Breakfast? I gotcha." He winked.

"You two brothers?" I asked, absently waving my finger toward the name tags.

"Sure," Jack said. "Sure thing." He smiled and handed over the bag. "We've come to Yellowstone for a little light lifting and to pick up a few new languages. Have fun now."

I took the bag and thought, OK, they've got an odd last name, but it's nice, two brothers working side by side, all these years later.

As we sat in traffic, I watched a pair of bottom-heavy pelicans skim the Yellowstone River. They lifted over the bridge's dark pilings and began to glide north, like small cargo planes. The traffic jam up ahead seemed to be caused by wildlife posing by the side of the road. On Fishing Bridge itself, only a photogenic family of four could actually be seen fishing. The two tiny kids were padded out in life jackets. The father reared back to cast but hooked his red and white striped lure on the side of a passing travel trailer. He whipped the rod toward the water and the line broke. The kids pointed as the lure drove away, and fell to the ground in spasms of laughter.

For the next hour we headed up the Hayden Valley, but with all the traffic, we didn't get far. Sarah spent most of the journey reading aloud parts of the hot spring and fumarole field guide she'd picked up at the trading post. Stale sulfur smells from roiling mud caldrons, bubbling just off the road, slipped in through the open windows. We bickered over whether or not we had time to investigate the passing natural features — Dragon's Mouth Spring, Cooking Hillside, Sour Lake, Mud Volcano — and decided to wait.

At Canyon Junction we veered away from the line of traffic and raced west through thinning lodgepole pines to Norris, the first campground that might have openings. When I didn't see a "Full" sign by the edge of the road, a bubble of elation worked up in my chest. But at the office, a man who might have been Santa in a ranger suit rested a hand on the van's mirror and said that signboard by the road was wrong. He'd just given away the last site.

"Double damn," said Sarah.

"Don't I know it," Santa replied. "I was going down right now to flip over that board. It's these fires. They're driving people around like animals. What you two need to do is keep going. My radio says Indian Creek's OK. But that was a good five minutes ago. Don't speed."

My sister and I screamed north toward Indian Creek. Right then, somehow, everything felt fine, even though I was getting pissed off at the nature of our campsite quest. How could we be having an urban, no-vacancy sort of crisis in the midst of a vast wilderness? I kept a close eye on the cars in front of us, checking their rear windows for coolers or rip-stop duffel bags, any of the telltale signs of future tenting.

The Indian Creek Campground was on the left, in between two small swamps. The red-brown status board in front of the tiny office showed only a handful of open sites and three cars were in line ahead of us. Eventually a tan woman in a too-large ranger uniform stepped up on the van's running board. She calmly suggested that we drive around, decide on a site and come back. Or we could pick blind. I took site 69 and filled in the card.

"Finally," Sarah said, as she hopped out to slip the envelope with the money into a locked tube that stuck up from the ground. "An excellent decision," she said, sounding relieved.

Our site was on the campground's outer rim and up against the woods. A couple one site over began to argue loudly in German, though they were going far too fast for me to follow. Yet another language I gave up on in high school — it always annoyed my father. It was the language of science, he told me. It's something you'll regret later in life.

Sarah returned from the rest rooms with a jug of water just as a redheaded, bright-eyed ranger who had been making the rounds with a clipboard materialized from nowhere. He'd come to tell us that there'd been a bear in the area, and that we had better keep all of our food locked in the van. All garbage had to go into the nearby bear-proof trash containers, which he located with a stern wave of his arm.

"You two," he said cheerfully, "get our special warning, as this tent is on the bear's route. He's been ambling through here every night.

You've got a hard-sided vehicle right here, so I wouldn't think twice about sleeping inside."

"How's this?" Sarah asked an hour later, once we were back in the van and driving again. She rattled a park service map at me. "We'll go south, then — east to Canyon Junction. We'll find food, take showers, and — assuming we're still ready — decide if we should start the hunt." There was a kind of false bravado in everything Sarah said. But I nodded, though I was still a little sleepy. After we'd set up the site, my sister and I had both suddenly fallen asleep. Naps, in my world, have always been a well-known response to stress.

As we pulled into Canyon Junction, Sarah proposed her bargain. She would buy lunch if I would call the concession company and try to find out where our father lived.

Canyon Junction was a series of newish, sandy-brick buildings. Two gift shops, a restaurant, a sandwich bar, a visitors' center, and a brigade of blue mailboxes. I applied the parking brake in front of a line of pay phones and got out to make the call. The concession company picked up on the first ring, and I think I got the same operator I'd had last time. I explained who I was, and why I was looking for Raymond Scales. I said we were visiting, and that I'd lost his number because my address book had gotten soaked in a storm and then run over by a truck.

"Oh," the woman said, "now that *is* a problem." Next, she reeled off our father's address and a phone number. He was at Mammoth, she said, living in an employee barracks. According to her schedule, that afternoon Raymond Scales should also be working at Mammoth, in the general store. I scribbled this down, pretending it was simply some piece of disconnected information.

Sarah was fending off ground squirrels from her perch on a picnic table beside the sandwich shop. I left the open notebook with our father's address and phone number on the bench beside her. It was a little dramatic, but it did feel as though we were somehow movie-bound, with the final crucial evidence now plainly in view.

She glanced at the pad and slid a white paper bag with half a ham and cheese sub in my direction. She had already fed most of hers to the gathered squirrels. I fed mine to the squirrels too. I only wanted to look at T-shirts, take a shower, and then think what to do. I knew the order was absurd, shop first and perhaps find your father later, but Sarah agreed immediately.

The gift store was also a hardware store and a camping supply emporium. And everyone working there — from Elwin Connecticut to Ruth Wyoming — had a state for a last name.

A tidy-looking father nearby began hectoring the twelve-year-old he had in tow. "Come now," he said, "is the right T-shirt really going to change your life?" Only half of the shirts on the racks were passable, the rest were too cute by half. Because of that, I guess, I somehow decided that I needed to buy a four-inch-tall brass hiking lantern.

My sister flicked through larger and larger circular racks of shirts. We were only several thousand yards from the Grand Canyon of Yellowstone and yet browsing had a far stronger appeal. Sarah pulled out a cream-colored shirt with a rainbow trout on the front. Above the fish it said, "Yellowstone," and on the bottom, in small script, "Catch and Release."

"You like?" She drew her finger over the letters. "It's the romantic motto of my life."

"We've got to go," I said.

"I know." She slipped the shirt off its hanger.

At the register I stood behind Sarah, looking out at the parking lot, as an odd copper light rained down on the roofs of the collected campers and rented cars. I thought the strange light might have to do with all the smoke, but I wasn't sure. The man at the register pulled Sarah's T-shirt around to examine the tag. He had a silver crew cut and wore a raven-black bolo tie over his checked shirt. His name tag said Joe Montana.

"Let's see." Joe held up the shirt. "Oh yeah. I like this one fine. Have all season. It's new. Wasn't here last year."

"That's good," Sarah said. "We weren't here either." She handed over Grant's credit card. Mr. Montana smiled and ran the slip through the machine.

The stocky man in the tan, short-sleeve, many-pocketed shirt who was working next to Joe stopped gazing out at the oddly glittering parking lot. He turned and cupped both elbows in his palms, the way my brother used to stand. Sarah's shoulders rose a fraction of an inch.

The man's large hands splayed out on the counter. He leaned forward, eyes wide. The name tag read: Ray New York.

"Well I'll be," my father said. "You two — I've been expecting."

TWENTY-FIVE

It was all quite strange. I stood next to Nate, in awe, as my brain tried to come up with the proper chemistry to tell me that my father was right in front of us. There, on the other side of the counter. This can't be, I kept thinking. It can't be this simple. But I stared anyway, like we'd come across an exotic foreigner who claimed to be related to us. Still — it was him.

He seemed OK, at first. I think part of it, the strangeness, came because he was wearing contacts. They made his face look even bigger. Expansive. All that new terrain to ponder. But my father looked older, too. His hair had turned a brilliant white against his deeply tanned forehead.

See, I'd prepared for a sudden flash of anger. I'd expected it to go off right when I first saw him. A how-could-you-run-away-and-not-tell-us thing. Instead, I was struck dumb with irrelevant and unanswerable questions: Why are you wearing contacts? Why are you selling T-shirts? How could you be *expecting* us?

My father seemed glad to see us. True, he stared cryptically for a second or so, but a minute later, like a host who'd forgotten to introduce his guests, he touched Joe Montana's elbow. "These are my kids," he said. "Nathan and Sarah."

Joe's eyes moved poignantly from Nate's face to mine. "Why, so they are," he said. It felt like we'd come all that way only to have our features pass a sort of test.

"Ray," Joe said, "you've got interesting-looking kids here." He began clasping our hands. It felt like a parody scene in a movie, the one where everyone gets the parents they deserve. Parents who are always happy to see their children and spend time baking cherry pies in their honor.

"Yes," my father said. He smiled, but he seemed troubled. He couldn't really look either of us in the eye. "This one could use a shave," he said, shaking Nate's limp hand. "Don't you think?"

My mind went as blank as a chalkboard. All those pivotal questions I'd been storing up skipped away. I had nothing to say. As if finding him was enough.

"What are you doing here?" I heard Nate ask.

My father looked around a little sheepishly. "Oh," he said, "well, I'm selling T-shirts. Is that OK?" He glanced away.

"You look different," Nate said. I could tell by the way my brother's hands slid around on the counter that he was not comfortable.

"I look surprised," my father corrected. "But I do feel different." He folded his arms and tapped his temple. "Got rid of those glasses in St. Louis." His hand swerved up and squeezed Joe's shoulder. "Cover me here a few minutes. Can you, Joe?"

Joe's gaze roamed over the racks of unsought souvenirs. There was no one else in the store. "Sure," he said. "It looks safe."

My father sidled out from behind the counter. "Usually Joseph and I are working over at Mammoth," he explained. "But today I'm a floater. You know, people get sick, can't take the altitude, the smoke, whatever. So — I float. Joe and I, we're both floaters, going wherever the operation needs us."

We waited in a huddle by the end of the counter. I was suddenly very cold. My father leaned back to pick up Grant's credit card from beside the register. He checked the signature and handed it to me.

"Are you camping?" he asked. "Remember, in these woods, you have to observe bear discipline. Sleep under a good climbing tree." He pointed toward the parking lot. "They have excellent showers over there. Really excellent. A dollar and a quarter. How did you get here? Fly?"

"We took Grant's van," Nate told him. "It's in the lot."

He squinted at the plate glass windows and turned back to face us before he could have spotted the van. "You haven't seen *my* vehicle but — candy anyone?" My father reached into his pocket and took out a half-empty package of butterscotch, each piece wrapped in silky foil. It was eerie. This was a gesture straight from when we were kids. My father would hand these out whenever Nate and I fought. Nate plucked a piece and slowly unwrapped it. He smiled when he put it in his mouth.

My father skimmed my T-shirt to the end of the counter. He held it up and examined the lettering. "Look at that." He pointed to a tiny extra dot of white above the trout's tail. "A defect." He frowned and muttered something.

"Oh, I don't care," I said. "Besides — it was the last one."

"I have discounts," my father explained. "You wait here. I'll zip into the back and hunt up a better one."

"No, it's OK. Really —" But he was away, with my "Catch and Release" shirt sailing behind him like a pennant. My father disappeared behind a swinging chrome door.

Nate and I milled about for a long time. We browsed in circles, farther and farther away from the counter. I was over by the window, staring into the parking lot, when a dark blue limo pulled away from behind the building and drove off. Who would bring a limo to a national park? I walked back to the counter and Nate looked puzzled. "Where do you think he went?" I asked.

"I don't know." Nate quickly folded his arms. "We should just go back there and get him."

"You can't do that." My brother looked somehow annoyed and relieved at once.

"At this point," he said, "I think we can do anything we want." He walked to the chrome door and I followed. There were bright fluorescent lights in the storeroom. Stacks of brown cartons, items in plastic bags.

"May I be of assistance?" a voice behind us said. It was Joe.

"Yeah." Nate turned around. "Where did he go? We were out there for hours."

Joe looked concerned. He put his hands on his hips and called down an aisle or two. We followed along, until he paused at the open loading dock door. I asked Joe what his real last name was. "Levy," he said and smiled. "I like that tag. Just to see how many people pick up on the football connection."

We scanned the parking lot together, as Joe shaded his eyes.

"Some mystery," he said. "You two know his car? It's a midnight blue limo. Quite a car, but I don't see it."

"What — you mean it's not here?" I asked.

"It's gone," Joe said. "Since nobody would steal it, this means your father must have gone for a drive."

"A drive," I said. "Why would he do that?"

Joe folded his arms and sat on a stool. "Between us, I think your father's been having a rough time of it lately. I'm sure he's glad to see you, but it might be more of a shock than he bargained for."

"What sort of a rough time?" Nate asked.

"You know that your father and I were both in the war," Joe announced. "We were both in the same part of England, for a bit anyway. Only he got sent to France as a replacement, and I got sent back to the U.S. to pilot escort tugs up the East Coast to Greenland. I had a bumpy ride of it. That's all. But I know those years have been on his mind. I'm not sure why, but it happens that way when you're older. When there's room to think things over."

"He's talked about that with you?" Nate asked.

"Like I said, it's been on his mind." Joe brought his large hands together. "You know, we got a zinc penny in the register here a week ago. Had a lot of those during the war. After that, your father and I started talking. That was the jump-off point. He said that, with all the smoke and the 'dozers working the fire lines out here — and we went out to watch for a while — it started him thinking about the war again. He began remembering things he hadn't thought of in years." Joe stood and led us back through the storeroom.

"Well," he said, after we arrived at the counter, "I can't find that zinc penny, but here are some things to do. And you can't miss his car. There's only one like it in the park. First, go check the barracks at Mammoth. I'll give you the address. If that doesn't work, he's been talking about his geyser list. Your father is a man of fascinations, and he was going on today about cutting out early to see the Lone Star, which is a geyser that's a ways off from the Upper Basin. I'd try there. Be careful with him. He's a good man. I don't have to tell you that. He's having an adjustment, that's all."

Joe smiled, as if he'd solved a word problem. He reached under the counter. "I'll loan you a good map," he said. "Just don't mark it up. You can give it back the next time I see you."

In the van I was overcome by an unfortunate failure of nerve. "This is a mistake," I said, as Nate drove. "We should forget this. We should just go home. It would be much more simple."

My brother, to his everlasting credit, laughed. "What do you mean go home?" He grinned like he meant it. Ever since that scene at the store, he'd become the calm and rational guy. Cool, almost, as though he'd started to see things in a very different way. He was acting more like he did the night he told me about Grant and we fooled the state troopers at the roadblock. I could have admired it, if I hadn't been so rattled.

"I mean it," I said. "This is my worst nightmare. He doesn't care. He just walked off. That's it. He obviously doesn't want to see us. We should — go home."

"Nope," Nate said. "It's not so obvious. What I think is, we've flushed him out. He couldn't deal with it. He didn't know what to do, so he ran away. After we find him, we'll have the upper hand forever." My brother smiled. "I think he looked pretty good, don't you? Older though."

I didn't know what to think. I leaned back and watched the pines and mountains and mountains of smoke, as they passed by beyond the tinted glass.

Mammoth turned out to be a bust. Nobody at the barracks had seen him, so we drove south for maybe an hour until we passed the Upper Geyser Basin and the giant parking lots for Old Faithful. Nate pulled off the road a little ways after that — and there it was. The dark blue limo, parked all alone in a little turnout near the trailhead for the Lone Star Geyser. I couldn't believe it.

"That's it," I said.

We parked a little farther on and started in at the trailhead. It wasn't a real trail but paved, so you could bike on it. The trail went beside the Firehole River and was a mile long, maybe two. I don't remember, but it felt like we were walking for hours. What if he isn't there? I kept thinking. How could we keep tracking him down? What if this went on forever?

By the time we arrived at the geyser I'd broken out in a fine, prickly sweat. The geyser itself was in a clearing, all alone beside the river. It was a cone of white-streaked rock, nearly twelve feet high, with steam coming out at the top. The air was thick and had a strange, warm sulfur smell.

Here's the part I still can't believe — as we came into the clearing, there was our father. Sitting on a rock. On the far side of the geyser, with a little notepad on his lap. He had a big patch of gray mud on his left knee.

"Dad," Nate said. My father looked up as if — again — he'd been expecting us. He seemed pleased, but regretful. Sheepish, maybe. Or at least it was a look I rarely saw. But part of me wanted to go after him — right there. Chew him out. Until Nate put his hand on my shoulder.

"When's it going off?" my brother asked. He glanced around. "Nothing much seems to be happening."

The geyser started making tiny gurgling noises. Little splashing sounds.

My father looked at his pad. He tapped his wristwatch. It was a black, digital thing with a million buttons and dials. "Well," he said, as if nothing unusual had happened, "it's supposed to go up every three hours. But my sources say this one's been a little unreliable recently." He clicked his pen. "It's one I haven't seen before, so I arranged to take off early. Nice of you two to come out here."

Nice, I thought. Nice. "What if it's already gone off?" I said.

My father shook his head. Then, with no warm-up, he started to tell us about a dream he'd had the week before. He'd been getting these dreams nearly every night now, he said. In this one, he'd watched as Nate and I bounced along in the cab of a monstrous tow truck. He couldn't hear what we were saying, but as the truck sped off into the red sun, my father watched Nate fly a small model plane out the window. "Funny thing was," my father said, "this truck cab was filled with bags of bread. White bread. Sliced. Even up on the dashboard." He offered us his palms, as if the bread was the odd part.

Nate and I traded dubious glances. I once read that the man who invented the demolition derby first saw it in a dream. He woke up and thought — people would like that. But before we had a chance to say anything, we were engulfed by information.

"This is a wonderful place." My father spread both arms, as if he'd inspired the view. "Except of course for these fires. You know, dry lightning is responsible for almost every one. A day ago, both the Shoshone and Red fires made major runs. This windstorm came up and pushed them on with hurricane force. Sheared the tops right off some trees. Now, plenty of people think fires are evil. They may be ferocious, but there's nothing evil about them. It's part of an ancient cycle. You need a good fire to clear out the deadwood. You know — nature's way of getting back on track."

"Dad," I said, but Nate's glance waved me away.

"So why am I here?" my father asked. "I know you're wondering. Well, this geyser is on my list, and I had an appointment. I'm sorry, but you two were something of a surprise. You know some people here are quite serious about geyser watching. They treat it like a science. They've got time charts, checklists, monthly activity sheets. They bet on eruption times. They do. Did you know there are 10,000 thermal features here? And some of these geysers are huge. There's Steamboat, nobody's seen that one go in decades. Four hundred feet. Think of the pressure required for that. This one here could go anywhere from thirty to fifty feet —"

"Dad," I said. "We went to St. Louis." The words felt weird and sticky. They seemed to take a million years to come out.

"So you did. So you did." He looked almost annoyed. "That place I escaped. They're probably mad as hell about it. But you reach a point — well, I don't know." He gazed at the geyser. Steam at the sides began to come out in small white clouds. We were the only ones there.

"Ever hear this one?" my father asked. "That in skating over thin ice our safety is in our speed? No? How about this: People wish to be settled, yet only as far as they remain unsettled is there any hope for them. I've been reading Emerson lately. Just picked it up. He's got a lot to say that really applies."

"Do you know about Grant?" I asked.

My father's gaze snapped back. "Yes," he said, quietly. "Your uncle told me. He stopped on his way to the airport. On his way to New

Zealand. He won that goddamned trip in a contest. Can you believe that? But I was on the tail end of my recovery. There wasn't much point in going back to Owego. I didn't know where you two were. Grant used to say he didn't, either. As a matter of fact — he told me you two didn't want to have a thing to do with either of us. That you'd decided to lose touch."

"He lied," Nate said. "He knew where we were, or he could have found out. We went to his house. That's how we got here."

For a well-placed second my father did not make a sound. Then he smiled, as if commenting on our cleverness. He hummed. A bass note. "I lost a boy," he said. He took a deep breath. "First your mother, and then — what a mess. No one's supposed to outlive their children." My father smoothed his eyebrows with his thumb. "Besides, how could I be mad at your brother now? Even when there's a death, someone has to get up the next day and mow the lawn. And how are you two?"

Nate moistened his lips. We lied. We said we were fine. The wind shifted to blow the strange-smelling steam into our faces. The sky was copper again. Tenacious bits of ash, tiny wicked fragments from a distant fire, fluttered toward me.

"I have to say, though, when your brother dropped me off at that place, that rest home, once I came to enough to figure it out, I was livid," my father said. "So — I disappeared. I came out here, where it's another story entirely. Make yourself necessary. That's something I've always believed in. I've worked with people all my life."

By then Nate and I were sitting on the bank, beside him.

"Which gate did you come in?" my father asked. "East Gate? Then that was the Clover-Mist fire you saw up on your left. Unbelievable."

I ran the word across my tongue. Yes, I thought, this was all pretty unbelievable.

"Well," my father said, "you two look fine." His hands rose up. He checked his watch. "OK. Let's go." He seemed to be talking to the geyser. "Look at how white that steam is." He shook his head. "Looks like a smoke barrage. It does. I saw a lot of those in the war. They used them to cover us from the German guns when we had to put up a bridge in daylight. Did I ever tell you two about that? About the dud shell?"

"No," my brother said quickly. "Never."

"The fall of '44, after the breakout, in France, when we're trying to get across the Moselle only it's flooding. Never been that high in twenty years. We're trying to set up a treadway bridge, which is on pontoons, but they're shelling us. Wham-wham-wham. So our guys lay down this wall of white smoke to hide what we're doing. We move our position a little, and the wind blows it all away. I'm trying to get a float lined up, and this shell comes in. Skips off the float at a strange angle, goes up ten feet in the air, and clips the guy next to me in the shoulder. Knocked him over, and I think broke his collarbone. But the shell didn't explode. It clanked down and twirled in a circle on a flat section of the bridge, not five feet in front of me." My father shook his head.

"We finally had to build the bridge in the dark. Everything went across in the dark. I hadn't slept in days. I don't know why these memories are coming up now."

"You never talked about any of that," Nate said.

"With good reason. I didn't want to think about any of that. I didn't want anybody to bring it up. I couldn't listen if they did. That's why I never could take you to those Cub Scout meetings at the V.F.W. Had to have your mother do it, but you never knew why. It was much better to keep busy."

A fountain of scalding water sprang up from the geyser. The noise from the steam had been getting louder the whole time. My father touched the timer on his watch. The eruption cascaded on for about ten minutes and ended in a loud roar of steam. I don't know what Nate was thinking, but I looked over my father's shoulder to check the time. His shirt smelled vaguely of Aqua Velva, but he wasn't watching the geyser. He seemed to be concentrating on something else. Something far away. When the eruption ended, my father stood and swatted at the caked mud on his knee.

"Look here," he said. "Had a little mishap down at the river earlier. OK, I've got to go back and get cleaned up. You two can stay, or go off on your own. You could even hike a little further on. There's a lake up the trail, you know. I'll meet you at Canyon, at 5:30, at the cafeteria. I can explain everything then."

Nate laughed but he wouldn't stand up. I knew he thought the concept of everything explained was total lunacy.

"Go on." My father waved at us over his shoulder. He was already walking down the trail, back to his limo. "Explore," he called out. "You could learn something out here. You could."

Twenty-six

M y sister and I arrived at Canyon late for dinner and fresh from
$1.25 showers. My father paced in front of the gift store–
restaurant complex. Hands clasped behind his back, he was doing the
Dad-walk beneath a line of slack American flags.

"About time," he said, when he saw us coming across the parking
lot.

Was he angry or merely hungry? My father frowned at us and
squinted into the sun, which looked like a falling, bright orange
quarter. He led the way into the cafeteria, and we took our place in a
long line of tired families, all waiting to pick up that evening's entrees
on trays.

"Did you hike?" he asked, as Sarah and I scanned the chalkboard
menu.

"No," I said. "We went back." I almost stuttered a little and it
surprised me. I could look at my father and be unable to locate even
the simplest words.

"You know," he said, "we've got a thousand miles of trails here.
Literally."

"We were tired," I explained. "Besides, there's time." We could be
any family, split up for the day and reuniting to review their misad-
ventures.

My father shook his head, as though we had missed out on yet
another opportunity. "I'll bet you two don't know," he said, "but this
was a park before it was even a state. That's right. Montana entered in
1889 and Wyoming a year later. It's a damn good thing those fellas
didn't know about geothermal power back in 1872 or we'd never have
the park we do now. They thought big game hunting was going to be
their main attraction."

"Didn't know that," I said. I decided to just let him go on talking.

For some reason, I found myself less concerned about what had happened in the past and more interested in simply seeing him as he was now.

"Meet many Europeans yet?" My father then told us that everyone in Germany gets six weeks of vacation, so they fly to the Pacific coast, rent cars, and drive east. "And their economies are doing fine. We could all use the time off. We'd be more productive. Working the counters here, you know, we get the French, the Japanese, all accents of Commonwealth English. And your trip? How's that going?"

"What do you mean?" I asked. He seemed to think our visit was only a stopover. Sarah, too, looked surprised.

"You've got to pace yourself on the road," my father said. "My bet is the pair of you just rushed on out here — hurtling on ahead. It'll catch up with you. Many times I've found myself somewhere interesting, only to be too tired to look around. But you've got to ask, When will I ever be back? Remember, in an unsavory hotel, keep that television on while you're away. It's the best crime dog you can rent."

He paused to ask an aproned, bearish-looking guy, who was busy stacking trays, how he was doing.

"I'd rather be doing something else," the guy said.

"Wouldn't we all," my father said. "Wouldn't we all."

I ordered meat loaf and kernel corn. I picked up two different kinds of cake for dessert and a beer. My father lagged behind, inspecting every possibility. Sarah and I carted our trays out to a circular table near the plate glass windows. We decided to let him pay.

The room could have been a college cafeteria from anywhere, except the fluorescent light fixtures on the ceiling formed giant wagon wheels. A minute later, my father settled in with his tray and leaned across the table. He motioned over his shoulder with a glance. "They're here," he said. "The family from hell."

"What — us?" Sarah said.

"No. That blond group behind me," my father explained. "They were in the store twice yesterday and once this morning — right before you two showed up. Every week at the counter we have a new one."

I turned to stare.

"They're screamers," my father said. "Arguing all the time. And they're bookworms. You know, people who memorize the guidebooks and contradict the guides? They're impossible."

They looked like a normal enough family, I thought. Two girls somewhere in middle school, a distracted, Clark Kent-ish father and his well-exercised, ash-blond wife.

"Foolish families should not go on vacation," my father declared. "Keep them locked up at home until they sort everything out. Then let them go off and enjoy things. It's a shame, allowing people like that to ruin everyone's experience of a place."

I reached for my beer while Sarah smiled unkindly. "Dad," she said, "don't you need a drink?"

My father unfolded his napkin. "Now," he said, "were I a betting man, I would guess that you wouldn't know that each one of these fires is named for a particular geological feature. The Fan fire? Named after Fan Creek. I could go on —" He finished his tomato juice in one swallow. "Here are some fire terms you'll be wondering about. A snag is a tree that's still standing, but dead. They go up like candles, and the place is chock full of them. Thanks to a mountain pine beetle infestation that went through some years back—"

"Dad," Sarah said. He waved her off.

Grant could be a snag, I thought.

"Fires," my father announced, "move in a skip-and-run pattern, called spotting. If you're fighting one, and you stay in one spot even fifteen minutes too long, that might be a mistake you'll never recover from. You've got to know your geography, too. Get lost, and you could find yourself facing a 300-foot wall of flames."

He paused for a few mixed vegetables. I thought I heard classical music rising up in the background. A big dramatic Russian symphony, but I couldn't locate the source. A minute later, I realized that the symphony was filtering down from several tiny speakers up by the lights.

"Many fires spread by crowning," my father continued. "This is when an airborne blaze moves through only the top of the canopy. At that point, you can kiss those bulldozers and fire lines goodbye."

"How do you know all this?" I asked. My father shrugged, as if knowledge of this sort was simply at hand, waiting to be remembered.

"You don't have to explain *every*thing," Sarah said. "Only what we want to know."

My father frowned. He seemed wary of what might be coming next. "A lot of your fire suppressionists out here have degrees in combustion science," he said. "The pay is quite good, so I'm told. Long hours, though. They all wear these Nomex suits and carry fire shelters. Or, you can escape by going into the black. That's fire talk for jumping back through the wall of fire. You'd call that jumping to a charred space. You have to remember — fire is part of a natural cycle of chaos and disruption."

I found myself thinking about the doorway of that burning duplex in Lawrence. I looked around at the room of happy families and tried to shake it off.

"Dad," Sarah said. "We don't care."

He squinted at us.

Sarah shook her head.

"Well, let's eat then."

I looked at my food and couldn't think of the things I knew I had to ask. How could it be so much easier to keep anger up at a distance? I wondered.

"Why are you two looking at me?" my father asked. "What's going on? Fill me in."

"Yeah?" Sarah said, gathering a dangerous gleam in her eye. "OK. Fine. Why can't you quit unraveling long enough to listen to anybody? You and Grant never listened to anybody."

"Watch your tone," my father said. "For heaven's sake, this is an interesting moment in natural history. I'm doing my best to fill you children in on what's going on — right in front of you."

"We're right in front of you," Sarah said.

My father nodded. "So you are," he said. He tapped the table. "So tell me."

My sister and I began to comply, at least to a point. The story of the trip tumbled out, and we backed each other up along the way, adding in the forgotten details. As I listened, though, I wondered how close we actually were to our stories. I explained my life at work, but only in the most distant terms, and that seemed entirely appropriate.

"In truth, we are a little tense," Sarah said. "It's been a while since we last saw you."

My father sat up, but Sarah glared at me, as if it were now my turn to crank out the larger issues. "We traversed the country," I said, but it sounded small and plaintive.

He gave this a quick smile. I couldn't decide whether he thought the situation was funny or simply strange. "So you did." He spun his section of Cornish game hen with a fork. "I knew you'd show up. Didn't we go through this out at that geyser?"

"Wait. Just wait," I said, a frazzled edge began to encircle my voice. "You disappeared down this big hole. You should be glad we bothered."

My father put down his fork. "I am," he said, quietly.

"Then — what are you doing here?" Sarah asked.

He drew a deep breath and looked slightly sideways at us. "Have I ever told you two about fracture zones?" he asked. "How about subduction? How much do you know about plate tectonics? How we were all once part of a super-continent, Pangaea? Then that broke up, and the continental plates have been drifting away from and into each other ever since. Now, where two plates run into each other, that's where you should find volcanoes and geysers. But think about this park. This whole park sits atop a caldera, which is essentially a term for the crater you're left with after a volcanic explosion."

My father made a church with his finger tips and simulated a collapse. "Whoosh," he said. "The last time it blew was 600,000 years ago. It blocked out the sun for a year. Anyway, we've still got all this subsurface heat here and we're, what, 500 miles from the nearest continental plate boundary? Five hundred miles from where you'd expect to find hot springs." My father spread his hands, marking the mileage five times over from thumb to pinky. "Now, what would you do with those facts?"

"Nothing," Sarah said. "Not one thing." She got up and started toward the cash register. "You're nuts."

"Come back here while I'm talking to you."

"You're not talking to me. You're not talking to anybody."

"Hurry back." My father cracked his knuckles while I maneuvered a mountain range of kernel corn across my plate. "See," he said, "at the *edge* of a continental plate, that's where you'd expect to find this kind of heat. Any place else on this continent, you have to go ninety miles down to hit molten rock. But here, they think it's only seven miles away. And why? Because something is eating away the underside of the continental plate. The continental plate we're riding on is sliding across an intense thermal plume. This plume is a narrow funnel of heat, rising up from the center of the earth and spreading out below us like a thunderhead."

My father's hands were out wide, like a defense attorney's in midsummation. "A hole in the plate, that's what we've got," he said. "The thermal plume is burning right through the continental plate, expressing itself in the geyser life all around us. This is a hot spot. One of the hottest spots on the planet."

If I'd had him in an interview, right then I'd have slowed down. I'd have stopped taking notes, and watched from that little lifeguard perch in a corner of my mind. How could he be immersed in this geology when there were so many other things to talk about? Maybe that was the point.

Sarah returned, holding a bottle of Coors against her forehead. "Forget all this," she said, waving the beer at him. "I want to know why you moved us from Syracuse. I want to know why you disappeared. How come nobody ever explains any of the big stuff to us? Start with the business of why you're here."

My father shook his head. "Because it's beautiful. What else could you expect?"

"Not good enough," Sarah said. "We don't know what to expect. That's the fucking point. It's *all* entirely incomprehensible."

People around us were leaving. They were standing and looking over their shoulders, as if trying to confirm their suspicions about us before they reached the door. A different, more rugged-sounding symphony began to float down from the speakers.

"I'm here because it's beautiful," my father said. "This is where I found myself again. In a hot spot."

My sister hung her head back for an instant, contemplating the wagon wheels in the ceiling. Maybe he was telling the truth, I thought. Maybe that's all there is to it. I glanced at Sarah and saw a familiar glaze building around the edges of her eyes.

"*Tell us* what happened," she said softly. "Tell us what you remember about getting to St. Louis and here, or you might not see either of us again."

My father appeared puzzled. As if he had just recognized that he didn't know what we knew. "What are you two tanglefoots so steamed about?" he asked. "Look at yourselves. You've turned out fine. Both of you. Do I have to say that? The time to be a dad is when the kids are little, and I did that. You've got to let the kids grow up on their own. When are you finally going to have your own damn Copernican revolutions? There are other orbits in this universe aside from your own."

"Grant never told us what happened to you," I said. "And the things he told you about us were all bullshit."

"Watch your language," my father said.

"How can you worry about our language?" Sarah snapped. "We had to figure this whole fucking thing out ourselves. We had to go to Grant's house. We had to dig through all his papers. We get to St. Louis and you're *here*, watching elk and bison and fumaroles. If we hadn't done all this deranged driving, would you have bothered? I mean to find us?"

"That place." My father stopped eating. "That place in St. Louis."

College students cleaned the nearby tables. They glanced up at the speakers, as if something were on louder than normal.

"What a boy your brother was," my father said with a billowed sigh. "I don't know. Really, I don't. Smart as a whip in some ways and dumb as wallpaper in others. But you two — you don't know what I went through." His left elbow came up to the table. "I was going crazy. I'd lost my memory and I had to watch it happen. You tell me — where do you go when you can't trust your own mind?"

Sarah closed her eyes for a long second. My father jumped his chair a tiny step closer to the table.

"Around that time, I had the apartment in Binghamton," he said. "You knew that. We even had dinner there once. At any rate, my problems began small — forgetting my keys, not remembering when your mother's birthday would have been, the plate number when I bought gas on the card. It got worse, until whole chunks of time disappeared. A fluke thing, really. Actually, when I think of it now, it was sort of liberating in a strange way. All these things I carry around and can't get rid of were gone. But it reached the point where I couldn't even trust myself. I would remember some things perfectly and others not at all. Christ, I remembered a hell of a lot from the war. Little things, like the Nescafé we made one night from puddle water. We boiled it in our cups over K-ration boxes. Things from before you kids were around. Your mother in the early days. But I couldn't see what was going on right in front of me. It was infuriating." He pointed to his forehead. "This is all chemistry," he said. "That's all we've got up here. One cup of coffee and you're a different person. I wouldn't have said so before, but now — what the hell."

Another college kid in a white apron, his hair held back by a green bandanna, edged closer, focusing a determined eye on the plates piled atop my father's tray. As he took them away, my father said, "Sorry the tip's so small." The kid smiled. There was no tip.

"So there I am," my father said, "living my life in my increasingly unfamiliar apartment and having these spells. I couldn't even follow ball games on television. I couldn't follow the newspaper. After a while, I went to your brother for help. I thought being there would give me some structure, with these vivid dreams I had coming in on me every night. Then more memories of things I had to do in the war. Sweeping for mines out in front of the tanks. Guys screaming in the snow. Artillery fire breaking through the trees. My god, you should have seen me. I'm yelling at your brother's chairs. Insulting the table. People yell at their TVs every day. They're just not expecting an answer."

He laughed quietly. Sarah moved her hand over her mouth.

"For a while," my father said, "I kept seeing moths around lights. Even inside, whole clouds of them. Black ones with white stripes. Zebra moths. These were delusions, sure, but what would you expect, given the things Grant had on those walls? I never understood any of that. Other times, I'd see duplicates. I'd see two of things. People. That, or piles of laundry could be animals. A car backfires across the way, and I'm in the service again, thinking that was an artillery blast and scared to shit. Auditory hallucinations. I don't know. It was almost wonderful, at times. If I could have known what was happening. But I didn't want to tell anybody."

My father looked at our nearly empty plates and threaded a napkin between his fingers. "Of course, there were more tests that your brother should have had done, but he agreed with the first diagnosis. I mean, hell, I had enough of the symptoms, only they got it wrong. I'm lucky when it comes to my health. That's the difference. That's always been the difference."

My father took a deep breath and patted his stomach. He seemed relieved.

"What caused it?" I asked.

"Now," my father said, "before this got started, I came up with a sound rationale for not eating red meat. Think about the advantages of staying low on the food chain — what with all those pesticides and bovine growth hormones we have now? The rest of the world eats nowhere near as much red meat as we do. So why not? Except, with my particular body chemistry, I ended up with a vitamin deficiency. A B^{12} problem. This B^{12}, this cobalamin, is what you need to build a sheath around your nerve fibers. Otherwise it's like having a lot of uninsulated wires hanging around the house. The wires get crossed, and you're left with these hallucinations. But now they think I also had a second problem, because when you get to be my age you can't absorb B^{12} as well. So, with the meatless diet, I wasn't getting enough. I ended up with pernicious anemia."

The symphony swelled again and abruptly cut off. My father's voice seemed suddenly louder. "So — I got to St. Louis, they gave me B^{12}, and I started creeping back into myself. You can't imagine that. It was like I'd been on another planet. You know, one ounce of B^{12} would do the entire country of England for a day."

My father winked and I wondered if this wasn't a speech, a monologue he'd been working on for just this moment. It would help if I knew him well enough to tell, I thought.

"Your brother and I made an arrangement long ago involving the Vestal house," my father said. "It was his because I knew that, with my work, I might not be available for long stretches of time. There were accounts set up in case something happened to me."

"You mean you paid him off," Sarah said, "to take care of us?"

"It was something for the shared responsibility," my father said. "I thought you knew about that. Besides, that family deferment kept him out of goddamn Vietnam. I was glad of that."

My father looked out the windows for a long second. "And yes," he said, "I do regret selling the Syracuse house. We shouldn't have moved. It was too soon after what happened to your mother. At any rate, I woke up in St. Louis where I didn't belong — so I left."

"You had the dream about us in the tow truck when you were in St. Louis?" Sarah asked.

"No, no. That was last week. I had other dreams, about here, when I was in St. Louis. Steam and smoke dreams. Who knows? Should I have sat around there and made pot holders? All due respect to some of the fine people I met, but — everyone's allowed to escape once in their life."

Sarah laughed. "Once?"

"It's true, I escaped from the war," my father said. "I could have taken my last breath in France, any number of times. You two know that. My helmet was hit twice. Once, in the hedgerows, right off my head. I was driving a 'dozer at the time. Another time by a sniper when I was towing dead cattle off a one-lane road. Finally, toward the end, Noel Little told a joke and wrecked the jeep and that got me out."

"You should tell me all that someday," I said. "You never have."

My father seemed surprised. "That's how I got out," he said. "After everything else, and I still don't know why, when all those other guys didn't. But the jeep — it was after we'd recrossed the Saar and were moving north, in the end of December, to what was going to be the Battle of the Bulge. My feet were a mess. Almost frostbitten, but not bad enough to send me back. It was at night, after Christmas. The roads, and they weren't much, were iced up. Noel drove with only the blackout lights on, but there was enough moon, and he told me a joke about a camel. We both laughed. That's all I remember. That and the Jeep rolling over an embankment. I had three broken ribs and my left leg was fractured in two places. Noel jumped clear. They sent me to England, and one day in the hospital I woke up with a ZI tag on my bed. That meant zone of the interior. The States. After my discharge, I took a bus from New York to Vermont and walked up to your grand-father's house in the dark. I couldn't believe I was there. I never found out what happened to Noel. That joke saved my life."

"You have to tell me more about all that," I said. I looked at Sarah and wondered at the fact that we existed at all.

My father nodded and leaned forward, as if to continue a previous conversation. "With Grant," he said, "your uncle Stan didn't explain right off that he had died. My God, Stan and I had a hell of a falling-out over that."

"We weren't there either," I said. "We didn't know about Grant until later. His lawyer called me at work, and I told Sarah."

My father made a small leveling sound.

"Did you know where we were?" Sarah asked.

He looked faintly annoyed, as though he'd explained this already. "I depended on your brother to take hold of matters," my father said. "I suppose I didn't really believe that you two didn't want to have anything to do with me, but I wasn't sure."

"But back then — you were away and just sent postcards." Sarah's voice kept sliding up. "We had to deal with Grant. We were dumped."

"You two were fine," my father said. "You had friends all over town. You had places to go. Your brother did an admirable job — given the circumstances."

"Which were none of our choosing," Sarah said.

"Be honest. Was it really so bad? You weren't abandoned. I wasn't away all the time. A few weeks here and there." His arms were out again. "I used to think you two and Grant were amusing. You were educating each other. I knew all his systems were never going to work. Powdered milk. You remember he used to make up powdered milk, mixing it in, to make the real stuff go farther. Your mother did the same thing for a while. God, I'd see that stainless steel pitcher in the refrigerator and I couldn't drink the stuff. But I stayed out of it. I thought it was good for you. It made you self-reliant. Read a little Emerson, for cripes' sake."

He leaned back, folded his arms, and stared at us. "You don't understand," he said. "I didn't want days off. There was nothing to do standing still. Standing still, I had too much to think about. Far too much that was going to catch up with me if I stayed put. My giant follows wherever I go. Ever hear that line? It's probably not the best way to live your life, but I'm mature now. Hell, I'm old."

I picked up a fork and rubbed the back of the handle with my thumb.

"Are you two going to carry around these apparently horrible childhoods I've saddled you with for the rest of your lives?" he asked. "No, you are not. Look at my life. Look at my losses. None of it adds up. This not a rational world. But you've done fine."

"How would you know?" Sarah asked. "How would you know what we've gotten over and what we haven't? Tell me about the things you've never gotten over."

He rubbed his cheeks and looked first at me, then at my sister. "Your mother," he said. "I never got over that." He covered his mouth and then took his hands away. "I doubt now if I ever got over the war. I tried to forget about it. I never contacted anyone from then, and maybe that was a mistake. And then your mother. After all I'd been through. It was a body blow. I never believed I'd have to face such a thing."

My father spread his hands across the table, covering the space where his tray had been. "People have such ideas about themselves," he said. "I didn't want my life laid out for me as it was, but that was my responsibility. Not yours. When you two were off in college, I tried to get your brother to see that, how he'd built himself this safe little place, while the whole world was out there. He could have done something better. But he always had excuses. A dream thwarted stays a dream. The thing goes under and burrows like your thermal plume. Your brother's the one I really failed."

I wasn't used to hearing my father talk like this. In fact, I'd never heard him talk that way. Yet I kept thinking about the miles of things my father didn't know about. How could I say that we were both almost happy, or at least relieved, when we heard about Grant. How would we ever get to that?

"There's too much death in this damn family," my father said. "It keeps changing everything forever. Should I suffer a stroke, which is a distinct possibility considering our history, do nothing to help me if I cannot tell you otherwise. A paralysis of that sort would be more than I could take."

I decided then to tell him that Grant had left us the house in Owego. I suppose I did it to change the subject, but I explained how we broke in, and asked if some of the money was his.

My father shook his head. "No," he said. There were bank accounts and stocks he'd forgotten he had, things that Grant never knew about. When his memory returned, there they were. "To come back to the world remembering money you didn't know you had, it was like getting the lottery. You know, this job was an idea I got while I was ill. For some reason, I decided I could be a ranger. The way I thought about it, age wasn't even a problem." He laughed. "Then someone got sick and they had an opening on summer job list number three. Now, I'm not a ranger — but if you think about it, who cares where your ideas really come from?"

My father absently tapped the edge of his coffee cup with a spoon, but not hard enough to make noise. It was more of a caress and something he'd always done. We are built by accretion, I thought, one layer of detail at a time. But in this family there are huge dormant periods followed by times of uplift and fracture. A pattern set in semisoft stone.

"We'd better be getting along," my father said. He looked around with birdlike eyes. The heavy dusk made the room appear brighter than it really was. "Get to my age and you start to know things," he said. "You've got to stay on top of it." He pulled his index finger across the table and traced out a small X. "It all goes by very quickly," he said. "You're lucky you don't know this. Be glad that you don't know this."

TWENTY-SEVEN

Grant here. A few quick and final observations, and I'll be out of your way. Really, before I even have a chance to get cranked.

So they found him. And aren't we glad? Look at Nate, for instance, smiling and believing he's got Ray in a spot where the guy'll slow down enough to listen to him for once. I have my doubts, but little brother does certainly have some brand spanking new wide-open horizons out there to investigate. Distant landscapes crowded with exhilarating possibility — and all courtesy of my generous endowment. Isn't it true? Even from this vast distance I remain influential.

Sisterwise, go ahead, accuse and accuse. All the way back, if you want. I don't care. So I occasionally exploded in a prepositioned rage. I'll admit to past theatrics. Sure, but there's a difference — I've always had a purpose. Case in point: that one time when Sarah was in high school and I refused her the keys to the Camaro and she simply hot-wired the thing and rode off? When she did finally return, I made it clear that I'd reported the whole incident to the state police and she was damn lucky that no one spotted her out on Route 17 driving a newly minted hot car. I even had a guy from work call the house and impersonate a detective. The things my father missed. But I had no choice. I had to puff up like a baboon and stomp about, when all I really wanted to do was laugh and congratulate Sarah on her ingenuity. All early management techniques, every one. And what person ever impersonating a parent hasn't acted?

I could go on, I could, but the time has arrived to move to larger issues. The time has arrived to take the long view. So let us talk about momentum and inertia. Let us talk of celestial mechanics. Let us discuss the red giants and dark stars, like myself. Let us examine the globular clusters, those fantastic, crowded balls of stars out in the void. One million celestial objects, all in the same general area, but with slightly unstable orbits. A series of stars, orbiting one another in an ever-changing balance. Yet once in a while a single star will gain just enough energy to achieve escape velocity. And when it goes, it goes forever. But in the space behind, the rest of the cluster contracts, ever so slightly.

I have to go. It's true. There are many things for me to do.

Besides, who can say this wasn't all without effect? Then again, who's to say that you're not all a part of my dream?

TWENTY-EIGHT

On Tuesday morning the wildfires jumped the road, closing off the park's south entrance, so that afternoon, to get to Jackson Hole, my sister and I went via Idaho. We left my father at work, and suddenly it was just us, driving through the intense sunlight and on beneath a sky too wide to be real.

For the whole drive down, scenes with my father kept rethreading through my thoughts. Only they would pop up as single flashes and not the smooth, explainable film I'd hoped for. I had driven into Yellowstone with a reservoir of righteous anger. I was pumped taut and ready to wing into my father for all his accumulated wrongs and absences. But when I saw him, and he seemed so much smaller than I'd remembered — with his hair that odd, bright white, all that energy — everything I'd been carrying along blasted on out into space, wide of the mark. In the end, I was more intrigued than angry. I knew we'd gotten to him, but beyond that, I couldn't tell what he was thinking.

Last night, when we sat down at dinner, I understood that these things would never sort out into obvious categories. It perplexed me in a way, to discover myself at that much of a distance, when I'd spent so many years imagining the parental history I should have had. But Sarah's question, when she asked about the things my father had never gotten over, I don't think I could have brought that up. I don't think I had ever stopped to understand how those events had marked him. How could I not have seen that? It suddenly seemed too convenient for me to have gone on for so long believing that he couldn't care, when maybe he did, even if it was beyond him to make that clear. I wondered what other ideas or parts of my life I'd held on to for so long that they no longer appeared to require examination.

Early that morning we were out on a trail beside the Firehole River. Sarah and I sat drinking coffee next to some other new geyser, watching clouds of pastel steam swirl past, as my father talked up the geyser watchers. They were mostly older folks in lawn chairs. They compared checklists and tossed around mineral trivia as if we were at spring training in Florida. My father talked with concerted wonder about the deep and narrow vertical pipes, about the water that circulated down for miles and boiled back up through the earth's crust where the pressure was less intense. "It's the change in surface area that does it," he told us. "All that open space as you get to the surface. The expansion causes a chain reaction — and you're in a new spot. It's a terribly delicate system. You don't fight nature, you know."

I watched and thought, he's always going to sound like this. And I remembered the almost cautious way he shook my hand the night before, at Mammoth, after I drove his limo and he drove Grant's van up from Canyon. My father and I stood under the moon, quietly looking up at the steaming Jupiter Terrace. There's more going on here than I once thought. It only requires something large to bring it to the surface.

Sarah and I crossed the Continental Divide and headed over into Idaho as the Grand Tetons rose in the distance. A half-jaw of gray incisors, breaking out from the golden fields. We were rolling along the backside of the range when Sarah changed tapes. Some loud symphony, raucous Beethoven, came up, and the music and the scene beyond the windshield recombined in an astonishing way. I might have had a jet-pack strapped to my shoulders. Levitation seemed entirely possible. It felt as though I'd crossed the point of a fulcrum, to a place where the shape of the present might be more powerful than I had first imagined. "This is it," I said.

My sister looked over. "This is what?"

But I couldn't articulate it, even though it did feel like I had come to a conclusion.

Sarah grinned and read to me from an orphaned Wyoming guidebook we'd found on a bench. "French Canadian trappers called these mountains the three breasts," she said, folding down the page. "Geologically speaking, the whole region is rising, but the valley on the other side is collapsing." She tapped my thigh. "What we've got here is a big scenic climax."

*   *   *

In Victor, where Idaho 22 went left to climb through a notch before dropping off into Jackson Hole, two cops waited on the side of the road. A blaze orange "Local Traffic Only" detour sign had been strung across the highway to Jackson. My sister bounded out to ask what was up. A minute later, she returned to report that a pair of semis had slid together in the pass, leaving the road slick with smashed fruit and petroleum products.

To reach Jackson, we had to loop south, past the Palisades Reservoir, and follow the Snake River back up into town. I occasionally caught glimpses of the green and rushing water far below, and sometimes yellow and red rafts stuffed with life-jacketed tourists. Empty raft trailers towed by white vans bounced past on their way down to the pick-up points. The drivers were tanned and grinning, and I thought, there's a job.

At the base of the Tetons we paused on the stone beach beside Jenny Lake. I was getting mildly buzzed by the violence of the scenery, that odd combination of geologic order and disorder, resonant and apparently stable. I didn't want to leave. On the way back into town, I kept slowing down in front of used car lots. I was scanning the prices, which were drawn in big numbers on the windshields, though I didn't know why. Eventually we parked near the square, beside one of the arcs made of white elk antlers, and strolled. It was indeed a tourist town. You could feel the currents of free-flowing vacation money in the air. But it also seemed somehow comfortable.

We stopped for drinks in a dark cowboy bar, where the stools were saddles and you could spin as long as you liked. When that novelty wore off, we wandered to another place, where the polished furnishings looked as though they'd come straight from the 1950s. Sarah picked a table with black bench seats that had once been a part of someone's station wagon. We ordered exotic club sandwiches and pints of Mexican beer.

A small woman in hiking sandals and a green shirt sat at the lacquered bar. She languidly read the newspaper while sipping coffee from a white mug. The bartender turned off *One Life to Live* as I watched her underline a classified ad with her finger. "Free Pinto with purchase of a $300 black and white TV," she said. Her voice carried a quick and optimistic sheen.

"This place is unreal," Sarah announced, just as the sandwiches arrived. She picked off an avocado slice and put it on my plate. "I keep thinking they're filming a big Western, a musical somewhere around here — right where I can't find it."

"That's something to look forward to," I said.

She smiled. "Last night, when you two were outside talking, did Dad tell you how long he was going to stay?"

"September," I said. "Maybe October. It's supposed to be really something when the elk herd up to mate. That's what he wants to see."

"Even with these fires?"

"It's a part of the attraction," I said.

"Then what?"

"He said he wasn't going to worry about it and I shouldn't either. There was enough money to stay comfortable."

"How do we manage this?" Sarah asked. "How do we keep track of him without mutating into control freaks? Maybe we ought to get him a beeper."

"A radio collar?"

"That'd be good. We could fit him for a big one. Is this better or worse — knowing where he is?"

"Better," I said.

"Yeah, I guess," she said. She moved a second slice of avocado onto my plate. "Are you still surprised we're here?"

"A little," I said. "You know, he tells us all these facts only because he can. Like it's all new because his memory's back. I don't know how I'd be if my memory went away and returned like that."

My sister rubbed her forehead. "Don't you wish we could just graduate from some fucking twelve-step program and get this over with?" She laughed. "Maybe that's what this is."

A large man wearing an MVP T-shirt from a casino walked in and leaned theatrically against the bar. He took off his sunglasses, and Sarah said that just by the way he stood she could tell he was the relief bartender, and late. My sister shook her watch. When the second hand wouldn't move, she tapped the face and began talking about driving back to Boston.

"When?" I asked.

"A day or two," she said, and that surprised me. It sounded very finite.

"But what about all the stuff you said about never having to go back? This seems so sudden."

"When did I say I was never going back?" Sarah asked.

"In St. Louis, at that paddlewheeler where we were eating lunch. You were right, we don't have to."

Sarah drank some of her beer and seemed to be contemplating something around the corner. "Yeah," she said. "But I didn't really mean that when I said it. I was only trying to coax you into this. Now it feels like I want to get back, to one place, and get myself going. Like all of a sudden."

"You mean you want to go back to life as it was?" I asked.

"Nope," Sarah said. "See, finding him makes me want to go back and sort things out. It's weird. Like I'm restless and all freed up, together. I haven't felt like this in — I don't know. It's not that I want to go any place new. I only want to go back."

"That all seems way far away," I said. "The other side of the globe. Like, what time would it even be there?"

Sarah nodded toward the illuminated clock above the bar. "If it's 3:45 here —"

"Shit," I said. "I have to call in at work. I told them I'd let them know what was up on Friday."

"This is Tuesday." Sarah smiled. "Guess that pretty much makes you toast by now. Wouldn't you think?"

The phone was by the door, housed in a red booth that appeared to be imported from England. I stepped inside and started punching digits. It would be after five in Lawrence and Maris shouldn't still be there. I'd leave a message, I thought, something he'd find in his mailbox on a pink slip in the morning. The call that couldn't be returned. Then Connie, the night receptionist, recognized my voice.

"Yeah." Maris sounded annoyed, as if he'd been concentrating on untangling a lead and I'd interrupted just as he'd found a way out.

"This is Nate," I said.

"Oh Christ, hang on." He clicked off and the thousand and one strings, playing the end of a Chuck Berry song, filtered into the gap. "It's zooey," Maris said. "Where are you when I need you? Oh yeah. I got it, Wyoming. Did you find him?"

"Yeah," I said. I was surprised he'd remembered.

"Good, well hang on." Maris put me on hold and the strings slipped into "Staying Alive." He didn't return until the chorus.

"When did they start with the music?" I asked.

"I don't know. It's the new addition. When are you coming back? Shit, hang on." He clacked the receiver down on his desk. "No — don't," somebody shouted. The radio phone behind him made its annoying buzz. It sounded like a voice from another life.

"I'm trying to tell you something and you keep putting me off," I shouted.

"Tough," Maris said. "I've got most of a mill on fire and a television helicopter wrapped around Casey Bridge. All in the last ninety minutes." Then he sounded suddenly sleepy. "Other than that, it's only the normal measured chaos. Which is why I'm still here. When are you returning to simplify my life? I didn't hear you right the first time."

"I'm not," I said. I felt the syllables cross my tongue.

A blank space in the signal, a hole, bounced on through Wyoming, up against some satellite, and down across the plains before it rolled on into Massachusetts.

"What do you mean you're not?" Maris said.

"I'm in Jackson," I said, only just then realizing that this was not a full explanation. "I'm staying."

"What do you mean staying?" Maris said. "Forever?"

"I don't know. Maybe."

"Don't do this to me in the middle of the week. How about a leave? I can fix that."

"Nope," I said. "I'm quitting. I've got to be here for a while, I think. I mean, I know."

An odd string of squawks rose from the scanner. Maris exhaled loudly. "There was a betting pool out on you anyway," he said. "That should tell you something. Or it should have told me."

"How much did you lose?"

"Twelve bucks. Doris wanted to fire you. Just so you're aware. I had to fend her off with a pole. Is there a number for you there?"

"Nope." I said. "Not yet."

"They've always been happy to get so much out of you," Maris said. "Call me later."

I watched the phone's chrome and black digits for seven, maybe eight seconds after he hung up. I remember thinking that I might not have done it if Maris hadn't kept putting me on hold. I almost called back to say so, but my legs were tired. I stepped out of the booth, sat on a stool, and stared at the phone. I could almost see Maris in there, the pipe smoke swirling around his head, all boxed up like a tiny hologram.

The woman at the bar who was about to buy the $300 television smiled as I walked back to the table.

"What'd they say?" Sarah sounded puzzled.

"I quit," I told her. As if on cue, the waitress brought new beers. "I'm staying."

"Here?" Sarah looked around. "You mean here?"

"Yeah. That's what I just told them on the phone."

Sarah leaned back. She looked over as though I'd told a bad joke. "Why?" she said. "It's on fire. Is it because of him?"

"Maybe," I said. "I had this idea last night that it wasn't doing me any good to be mad at him for all time. It's the kind of feud thing Grant would start. I thought, this way, maybe I could break out of it." I was surprised to hear myself say this. "Did I ever tell you how, when I was little, I used to sneak downstairs and watch him set up breakfast. I used to listen to him talk, when no one else was there. Like a game."

Sarah shook her head. "You're not expecting that he's going to come around or something. That would be a significant mistake."

"No." I took a drink. "But I want to be here. I need to know him, and this seems like the time to do it. Last night I started to worry about what would happen if I didn't do it. Like if we all flew off again. Well, not you and me, because I don't think that'll happen, but with him, things could get lost."

My sister hummed in agreement and moved her pint of beer to the center of the table. "What are you going to do? Be this permanent tourist?"

"I don't know. Get some kind of job. Try other things. It's like I just figured that out on the phone. I've been looking at everything through the same lens for so long now. Maybe I'll join a fire crew. Work for the Forest Service. Whatever."

"That's not *too* romantic. You'll have to tell your housemates."

"True."

"You know, this place isn't real," Sarah said. "It's a wild West set, a fantasy with big breasts in the background. I was afraid you might do this."

"Maybe I won't stay here, exactly," I said. "But out here."

"You're going to have to call Claire. Will you do that?"

"I've left messages."

"This is such a Dad thing," Sarah announced. "You're not the type. You're more of a long-steady-progression person," she said. "You know we're not getting away with all this Grant stuff. With all this frantic activity to make it seem like it didn't matter. Like we're not affected? We're doing that modern thing — where you ignore it. But that only buys time, until it comes back to chew off your legs."

"Not necessarily," I said.

"Yeah? Think about Mom. You'll need a safe place when it gets here, and I don't know that this is it."

"I'll find out," I said. "This isn't convenient. This is difficult. The convenient move would be to drive back with you."

We watched as a guy with thick black hair arrived wearing a baseball jersey. He settled in next to the relief bartender. "Look, it's Sparky," the guy in the MVP shirt said. "When are you going to dry up and blow away?"

The new guy grinned. "Never," he said. "Besides, it's my presidential birthday. I'm thirty-five. I could be president, from now on. Buy me a drink?" They went on to talk with the woman in the green shirt, who had finished with the classifieds. She explained that until recently she'd worked at a classical radio station, but one night she got fed up and played the same symphony over and over. "Bartok?" said the baseball jersey guy. "Man, that's mean."

Sarah smiled quizzically. She looked at her watch and then at me, as if that little story could help make sense of my decision. "I guess," she said. "I mean, this could be OK. But you've got a lot to decide."

"I know. It's good."

We finished our beers and threw Grant's money down to pay the bill. Sarah followed me out past the red phone booth. When I stepped onto the boardwalk, I kept going, out of the shade and into the side street, to a spot where everything seemed unnaturally bright. I looked up and spun around. I wanted to find the most possible sky.

TWENTY-NINE

This is how to get the ash out. The eyelid must be pulled back and gently folded over. The exposed surfaces must be examined and checked for abrasions. Only then can you decide whether to irrigate. All of which will make a patient, such as myself, feel as though she's part of a great field of lettuce — a cabbage head, even.

Where was I? It was late the next morning and I was in the clinic, that burnt-umber building situated between the ranger station and the sea of stadium-size parking lots for the Old Faithful faithful. I was resting on a small examining table in an eggshell-white room. With the shades drawn, forgetting the alarming tinge of smoke, I might have been anywhere. In reality, I was awaiting the return of the nurse practitioner and holding a cold compress over my recently irrigated left eye.

My father was scheduled to work at the Upper Geyser Basin as a floater for the afternoon. Which was why we had come back that morning to examine more thermal sights — Splendid Geyser, Oblong Geyser, the Beauty Pool. As we drove down, I understood, probably for the first time, that the forest fires actually were closing in. They were closer than they'd been two days before. Unbelievable walls of pillared smoke waited on the ridges behind that Lincoln Log delusion of a building — the Old Faithful Lodge. I heard an older woman at the front desk demand to know what the management intended to do if those fires came any closer. The clerk smiled. "Each night we leave an extra glass of water beside every bed," she said. Two hours later, as Nate and I neared the end of our morning geyser tour, I walked — eyes open — into a tiny, suspended, earthbound piece of ash.

Ash stings. Don't let anyone tell you anything different. It feels like a telephone pole is suddenly sticking into your eye. The pretty nurse practitioner, Anne, told me this was an up-and-coming malady. July's new hazard. After that I did feel more on top of things.

I sat there, holding the cold compress in place, while my brother ran off with our father on a quest for postcard stamps. Nate wanted specific stamps — ones with buffaloes, as now he had many cards to send. I've mailed Nate's postcards before, all the way out here even. But not, of course, without reading them first. The early ones were a uniform jumble of apology and look-where-I-am-now sentiments. These next would be crammed with hasty plans for a more dubious future. One more western romantic boy dream after another. It looked so much like a quick escape. It worried me, as though he would be lopping off his tangled life at home instead of sorting through it. I was afraid he might be buying into the mythical math of reinvention — that life in a new place equals life as a new person. It seemed to be a thing my father would do in a minute. And that morning, when Nate had said he was staying, my father seemed quietly pleased.

What I liked about being out among the geysers were all the little steaming pools. I found them strangely fascinating. It all comes down to a question of scale, I decided. A small gushing mud pot could indeed look like an odd-colored lake, as if seen from a plane. From that distance, taking in the big picture, I suppose I could understand some of Nate's worry. The nagging part, telling him again and again that the men in our family sometimes die young. I suppose, for Nate, staying is taking a chance. Or maybe that was just the easy justification. A quick way of working yourself up to escape velocity.

Shouldn't my brother already know that tourists never really see the place they visit? That the very sights they take in cause a sort of blindness. That's the very thing people want again and again. That's why they keep on looking. But it's a false vision. The real place is always underneath and invisible.

The day before, in the van, as Nate and I were driving back from Jackson, I kept thinking of motion as a winnowing experience, the blowing away of a psychic skin. Everything from before had just spirited itself off, like ground smoke before a wind.

My mind, I saw, had begun to wander into scratchy new corners, all on its own. For instance, I'd unwittingly become an expert on thermal events — fumaroles, geysers, and roaring mud pots. Sportwise, geyser watching is like birding or competition art appreciation. Only here, the objects of desire explode and have much better names. Excelsior, Mustard Springs, Vixen.

Before I ran into this piece of ash, I was meandering along in the wake of the Old Faithful crowds when I saw a strawberry blond girl of not more than five yanking her father's pinky and jumping up and down on the boardwalk. "Daddy," she demanded. "What's nature? Is this nature?"

But the crowds — the crowds stared at these geysers with an open reverence. It was like science fiction. Is the geyser happy today? Must there be a sacrifice? True geyser watchers know every omen. They know that a little extra froth twenty minutes before the main event means a good eruption is on the way. They know that Old Faithful isn't the best, only one of the more dependable.

This, in the end, is what got to me. The crowd had already assembled for Old Faithful's 10:00 A.M. eruption. They'd taken their places a safe distance away on the semicircle of benches. But for some reason, the geyser took too long. And people begin to *clap*. As if. As if you could drag the thing out of its hole for one more encore. Was the geyser listening? Or were they only applauding themselves? Clapping for the dream of being able to influence events so far beyond their ken?

The applause grew and circled, and I watched it spiral around my father. In a curious way it clarified a few things. I watched the way he stood, a slight distance to the side, in his short-sleeve shirt covered with bright toucans. He held his elbows and listened with a faint smile, as he, too, seemed beyond influence.

At first I remember thinking, he hasn't changed. Not in the least. All this — his appearing here for no apparent reason. It's more of the same. My father had only moved one step further on. But as I watched him, a strange thing happened. I began to see that a lot of what he was, a lot of the way he acted, had to do with things that were absolutely beyond his grasp. Events he never could have avoided, and they still shaped everything.

Did he stay away because not seeing us might make certain aches smaller? I wondered. Did seeing us bring back my mother? The clapping continued, and it felt as though a blanket had softly settled down to earth. I knew where he was. He wasn't such a mystery. Besides — I'd gotten us there. I'd gone the distance and tracked him down, and that had tipped the balance. What could he ever say that would erase that?

When the push of steam got louder, I began to wonder if we were as connected as we ever would be. But I caught myself. Sarah, I thought, stop. I could make room for things as they were. This I would do. This was enough. It was such an unfamiliar feeling. Light and calm, all at once.

The thing I can't talk about any more is Grant. That sinkhole of deliberate misinformation. Maybe I never will talk about him. None of what's happened could change, except by an iota, the way I think of him. There are still moments when I dream of taking his van and driving that hulk off into the desert. Leaving it to die out there, alone. What was his point? What was his fucking point in keeping us all apart?

That morning I heard myself blocking out the days it might take to drive east. I even imagined calling Julie, at the bar, just to hear what was what. That seemed a sign. But afterward I began to feel really restless — frightened a little about going back to do the same things over and over. I had to stop working at the bar. I had to stop inventing silly ads for ridiculous products that people never needed anyway. There was something morally wrong there, truly. But I would take Grant's money and buy time, until I sorted through the things I really wanted to do. I had to think more about Doug. I should even call him before I leave. We should do things very slowly, and see.

The other night, when my father drove Grant's van up to Mammoth with me in the back, pretending to sleep, I was angry. Rightfully so, I think. Angry about his taking things for granted. Angry about his being so secure in the knowledge that we would one day show up. I was angry about his Copernicus crack, after we'd come all that way. Even so, I kept watching the outline of his shoulders, and the way his head never willfully swerved from the unraveling yellow lines.

Then my father said my name. But he said it quietly, the way you would if you came home late at night and thought everyone might be asleep. I wondered if I should answer, but I didn't. But as we got closer to Mammoth, he began to sing. He sang me a fight song. He sang, "On Wisconsin."

The next morning, when I woke up in the campground, I stared into the space my father had filled the night before, and I thought: OK. It's not as though I'm out of time. Yet.